# THE BOOTLEGGER'S BRIDE

A NOVEL

Also by Rick Skwiot

*Fail: A Carlo Gabriel Mystery*
*Key West Story*
*Christmas at Long Lake*
*Sleeping with Pancho Villa*
*Death In Mexico*
*San Miguel De Allende, Mexico*

# THE BOOTLEGGER'S BRIDE

## A NOVEL

# RICK SKWIOT

Blank Slate Press | Harrisonville, MO 64701

Blank Slate Press
Harrisonville, MO 64701

Copyright © 2025 Rick Skwiot
All rights reserved.

Publisher's Note: This book is a work of the imagination. Names, characters, places and incidents either are products of the author's imagination or are used fictitiously. While some of the characters and incidents portrayed here can be found in historical or contemporary accounts, they have been altered and rearranged by the author to suit the strict purposes of storytelling. The book should be read solely as a work of fiction.

For information, contact:
Blank Slate Press
www.amphoraepublishing.com
*Blank Slate Press is an imprint of
Amphorae Publishing Group, LLC*

Manufactured in the United States of America
Cover Design by Kristina Blank Makansi
Illustration: Shutterstock
Set in Adobe Caslon Pro, Quiche Sans

Library of Congress Control Number: 2024930888
ISBN: 9781943075935

*In memory of my parents, Edward Joseph Skwiot and Veta Lena Maulhardt Skwiot, whose stories linger in these pages.*

# PRAISE FOR RICK SKWIOT'S WORK

## *Fail*

"St. Louis noir... The slick prose readily entertains... Well-executed." —*Kirkus Reviews*

"The plot is intriguing – dirty dealings at City Hall, corruption in government and a super-smart cop who has gotten on the bad side of the bigwigs... An enjoyable read with such a St. Louis feel."—*St. Louis Post-Dispatch*

## *Key West Story*

"Key West is beautifully captured in all its shallow, hedonistic glory. Skwiot's ability to reveal it and its citizens in subtle, amusing ways eases the reader into this unique world." —*Kirkus Reviews*

## *Christmas at Long Lake*

"Rick Skwiot works his own magic...As usual, Skwiot's writing is sure...And his tale has a gritty, blue-collar cachet...This is good reading."—*Kansas City Star*

"Skwiot's vivid descriptions of the physical and emotional landscape...are poignant, entertaining, and instructional."
–*Library Journal*

## Sleeping With Pancho Villa

"A thoughtfully layered backdrop of Mexican culture...impressively crafted labyrinthine setting...Snappy and often funny dialogue." —*Publishers Weekly*

"Life in a Mexican town...laid out beautifully...A skillfully written portrait of an entire community. Highly recommended." —*Library Journal*

"This book alone heralds the arrival of a great new writer." —*The Colorado Springs Independent*

The bells have rung, the echoes sound.
The day is gone. Come back again…

*—Jacques Brel*

# 1 | A.J.'S DISCOVERY

Madison County, Illinois, February 22, 1953

Morning sunlight filtering through a frosted storm window woke A.J. Nowak where he slept on the narrow bed beneath two quilts, navy watch cap pulled down over his ears. Through clouds of breath, he studied filigreed ice patterns on the window. There he spied a white dog running across a snowfield etched on the glass. Beyond the glass he heard a blue jay squawk.

He found his heavy wool sweater and blue jeans on the frigid Masonite floor beside his bed where he had left them, slipped the sweater over his head, and pulled the jeans up over his long johns, then stretched wool socks tall on his calves and finally slipped his feet into combat boots, so-called, with laces and buckles. Next, he moved to the cold coal stove at the far end of the narrow room—the former fishing shack's screened back porch, where storm windows were affixed in winter.

He shook the grate, found a few embers still glowing, and fed in more coal from a tin bucket on the floor, the stale smell of the black dust rising to him. He straightened and moved to the window behind the stove, short coal shovel still in hand. With it he scraped a square in the ice so he could read the green metal Orange Crush thermometer nailed to the eave. Ten degrees Fahrenheit, where it had been holding for two days now. The lake would be good and solid again after weeks of warmer weather.

He opened the door to the main house and stepped into a coffee-scented kitchen forty degrees warmer than the room where he slept, thanks to an electric space heater on the counter and a stoked coal stove in the adjoining front room. His Aunt Helen, in a blue wool dress, high heels, and flowered apron, stood pouring a cup from a percolator that she then replaced on the front burner of the gas range.

Her dress and shoes reminded him it was Sunday. Which meant he'd have to make excuses so as not to go into Granite City with them and sit stone still in the First Presbyterian Church for an hour when he could be out skating on the lake or stealing across the fields of shorn corn stalks with Lonnie Sullivan and his dog Tippy, carrying their narrow-gauge shotguns in search of rabbit or bobwhite.

"Coffee?" she whispered.

He nodded at her back. "Yes, ma'am."

Now that he had turned twelve and thus considered a man he was allowed to drink coffee and hunt with the .410 his uncle had handed down to him on his birthday.

"Uncle Raymond still sleeping, huh?"

She turned, handed him a mug of black coffee and lifted her eyes to the clock above the sink, fashioned as a yellow plastic dog whose black eyes moved left or right with each second's tick.

"I'll wake him in a half hour… You wearing your boots and stocking cap to church?" she asked looking him up and down.

He scooped two teaspoons from the sugar bowl on the counter into his mug and reached for the Pet Evaporated Milk can beside it, holes punched in its top. Ever since he was a tot the label fascinated him, with the cow peeking from another Pet Milk can lying on its side whose label depicted yet a third can with another cow peeking from it and so forth, he imagined, to infinity. He poured a stream of ivory-colored liquid into his coffee, turning it muddy brown like the Mississippi.

"Well, I was thinking, since it's so cold and the lake is froze solid, and it might get warm tomorrow…"

"It's not going to melt overnight. No school tomorrow for Washington's Birthday. You can skate all day."

He looked up to his aunt who was struggling to suppress a smile, her dark eyes shining, reminding him of his mother. Both had the same dark-chocolate hair and high Cherokee cheekbones (his great-grandmother had been a full-blooded Indian, he'd been told) that made them both beautiful, especially his mom.

His aunt touched a warm hand to his chin. "I suspect you'd feel closer to God on the lake than you would in that old brick building. You go ahead before your uncle's up. I'll fix it with him."

A.J. beamed. "Thank you, Aunt Helen."

For the last year and a half, Uncle Raymond strove to be a strict disciplinarian, trying to be the father A.J. had lost in the war yet hardly knew. However, at heart he was a kind, inward-looking soul, more keen on hunting, fly fishing, and tending his vegetable garden than acting the stern patriarch. He would likely and gladly have foregone church for ice-skating with his nephew if given the opportunity by his wife.

"First sit down," she said, "take your hat off inside the house, and eat some Wheaties, champ."

"Yes, ma'am," A.J. said, doffing his stocking cap and sliding into a wooden chair at the oak table, on which sat an orange cereal box with a portrait of Stan Musial.

He did as he was told by his aunt and his uncle, most always, so they wouldn't have reason to send him back home. He loved his mother more than anything. Nonetheless he was afraid to go back to live with her nowadays, afraid of what could happen.

§

He fetched his ice skates from the cedar wardrobe beside his bed along with his pea coat, rabbit-fur gloves, and wool muffler. The skates had been his father's, though in the last year he had grown into them. He carried them laced over his shoulder as he pushed out the back door and made for the graying and rickety picket fence guarding the steep lake bank.

The cold stung his face and pinched his nose. The air lay calm. A whistling call made him look up into the denuded plum tree just beyond the fence to spy a female cardinal, beige and red, and, perched just beyond, her brilliant crimson mate.

Through the creaky gate and down wooden steps to the dock which he had helped Uncle Raymond rebuild last summer. The old slats had plunged into the lake one Sunday afternoon, leaving neighbor Homer Martin and his daughter Judy stranded at the dock's far end, where they had been fishing. Even frozen hard as it was this day the lake still smelled earthy like the flat fields surrounding it.

A.J. sat on the cold dock, undid his boots one at a time, laced on his skates then dropped down to the gray-white ice. He headed north toward Mitchell on the frozen lake, though it looked more like a river being only some hundred yards wide and seven miles long. Some said Long Lake was a dead branch of the Mississippi, which lay just a few miles west across the American Bottom, and nearby Horseshoe Lake a shallow remnant oxbow left behind when the river changed course eons earlier.

His long-bladed speed skates cut the ice, accelerating him, the feel of wind on his face growing. He veered around a dark patch of thin ice where one of the underground springs that fed the lake poured forth keeping the ice from freezing solid.

He was moving swift and easy now and didn't mind the cold. These skates carried him faster than the short-bladed kids hockey skates he had learned on. His father had used the speed skates on lakes in Forest Park, across the river in St. Louis where he had lived when courting his mother. A.J. harbored a keen memory of his father skating hand-in-hand with her over Long Lake ice, pulling him behind atop his steel-runner Flexible Flyer sled.

Now the speed and movement made him feel free, a lithe, graceful animal. Sliding faster, faster as he bent his knees and pushed to the side with lengthy strokes, tucking his head low and curving his back to lessen wind resistance, just like Uncle Raymond taught him. Though slender as he was, the wind didn't have much to grab onto, and his long legs, still growing, jetted him over the lake. Ahead he spied the railroad tracks and the bank that severed the lake just south of Mitchell and so began to slow and start a wide turn.

Now heading back toward home he flew across the smooth ice again gaining speed. Soon he passed the dock where his combat boots sat, crouching low, arms swinging at his sides, tall naked cottonwood trees flying by on his left where they guarded the Conyers farm. On his right he sped past humble homes like his aunt and uncle's, clubhouses, and fishing shacks, some with crude wooden docks, and Sis's Tavern, where the lake turned to the right.

Soon he approached his house, his mother's home, which was more than just a fishing shack. It was a modern cottage, with tall windows facing the lake and a white stone fireplace at the den's south wall. Staunch maples rose above the lake bank and in the front yard willows and sycamores shaded it from the hot afternoon summer sun. A.J. slowed as he passed the wide dock and boathouse and looked up the lake bank at the white clapboard home with green shutters. The back porch light was still on, the shades drawn, as if she was still in bed. Alone perhaps, for he spied only her Buick in the gravel driveway.

When he looked down again ahead he saw ice shards protruding from the frozen lake where he knew another subsurface spring to lie, and where earlier the ice had apparently broken then refroze. He lurched to skid around it. As he did a purplish flash beneath the ice caught his eye. He pointed his skates together and walked to a stop.

A.J. turned and stood erect, staring back at the jagged ice. He skated there. Dropping to his knees huffing, he brushed the ice aside.

Beneath it, suspended in the lake, hung a burgundy coat with brown fox-fur collar, his mother's good overcoat. And she wrapped inside it, her dark brown hair pulled to the side, eyes wide, lips parted, her last breath captured in ice as it bubbled toward the surface.

A.J. knelt staring, captivated by the fantastic tableau as if in a diorama box, a scene seemingly beyond reality yet one that would forever be etched in memory, like an ice pattern on frigid glass.

# 2 | A DAY AT THE RACES

Collinsville, Illinois, August 5, 1939

Hazel Robinson shielded her face from the sun with her racing program as she stood leaning on the white-painted paddock rail watching the snorting thoroughbreds, led by stable hands, circling over the sawdust and sand. Earthy aromas rose from the dirt and hung in the still afternoon air. From a loudspeaker on the nearby grandstand came a scratchy announcement, "Ten minutes till post time."

She loved the sleek muscled creatures with their somber eyes. And when they thundered down the stretch, the diminutive jockeys in colorful silks perched crouching in the stirrups, her heart raced. An apt contrast to the plodding that marked her life. Though she shouldn't complain. Count your blessings. Ditch the invidious metaphors.

Getting out of the house on a Saturday afternoon and away from her parents for the day was a breath of fresh air both literally and figuratively. She was glad Helen and Raymond had thought to include her. The hot arid summer seemed endless. She was keen to get back in her classroom despite its homeliness, but school's start was still a steamy month away.

"Got any ideas?"

She glanced left toward the resonant voice. A man in Panama hat leaned on the rail a few feet away studying the *Daily Racing Form*. Clearly his question had been directed at her as there was no one else standing nearby in the blazing afternoon sun. Hazel returned her gaze to the circling horses.

"The chestnut's a beauty," she said.

"'Beauty is as beauty does.'"

She flicked her eyes at him. *Imagine that. A racetrack tout quoting Chaucer.* This made her curious enough to look him up and down. Blonde hair beneath the hat. Roman profile, strong jaw albeit a bit pointy. Thirtyish. Despite the day's heat he wore a long-sleeved white shirt and blue silk tie beneath a seersucker sport coat.

"You have a better idea?"

"What about the filly?"

"Which one's the filly?"

He smiled for an instant and bit his tongue. "The roan, Grey Doll."

Hazel, dark hair fixed in a bun to cool her neck, turned to study the number four horse. Noticeably smaller than the others, her silver flanks glistened in the sunlight.

"What's to like about her? I thought the girls weren't as fast as the boys."

"This one is. Though no one knows that quite yet. She's an overlay."

"A what?"

"An overlay. Meaning she'll go off at good odds, better than she deserves. Likely six to one."

"So, you think she's going to win?"

He shrugged. "Who knows? They all got four legs."

She nodded. "Good observation."

He touched the brim of his hat. "Almost post time. I need to get my money down. Good luck."

With that he turned and strolled off, Hazel eyeing his departure. He moved like a thoroughbred, muscular, controlled, relaxed. Purposeful, not plodding.

Hazel found Helen and Raymond where she had left them, standing in the shade of the tall wooden grandstand. She took a twenty-dollar bill from her clutch purse, gave it to her brother-in-law, and looked at the racing program in her hand.

"Please bet number four for me, Raymond. Grey Doll. To win."

"There's a switch from the place-and-show girl. How much?"

"All of it."

Helen reached out to her sister. "Hazel! That's as much as you earn in week!"

She set her jaw. "All of it."

Raymond opened his mouth to protest, caught the look in her eye, and retreated in silence with the money, shaking his head.

Hazel had a feeling. An odd feeling for her. She'd done everything according to the book her whole life—all twenty-three years of it—always thoughtful and cautious. Worked hard in school and got good grades. Went to the University of Illinois and did the same, studying English literature and linguistics and getting certified to teach in the state's public schools.

Thanks to her father's Granite City connections she landed a job when so many were still out of work, teaching first grade at Nameoki School, where one of his childhood pals was principal.

Still, it was a disappointment. Literature was her love, not the ABCs. However her timing—rather, her parents' procreative phasing—was bad. Who knew that the Roaring Twenties would go out with a whimper—rather, a Crash and a whimper? The Great Depression led to severe budget cutbacks for most public schools. Some closed. Experienced English teachers got laid off. She was lucky to have a job at all, everyone told her. Though she didn't feel particularly lucky. Until now.

For once in her orderly life she decided to take a risk—a small one in the larger scheme of things, a mere two sawbucks. However, its impulsiveness—so out of character—made it loom large for her. She sensed something bubbling up inside that made her feel like a different person from the Hazel Robinson she'd always known—suddenly a daring woman, though certainly not on the scale of Cleopatra, Cordelia, or Scarlett O'Hara.

When Raymond returned with her pari-mutuel ticket the three of them moved down to the rail, which now lay in shade as the sun lowered behind the grandstand, and the scent of the rich earth again rose to her. The horses were being loaded into the gate a furlong to their left; the finish line lay just to their right. Hazel would get to see them and feel them pound past twice on the mile oval for the mile-and-an-eighth route.

The sound of a school bell's ring, the clang of the metal gates slamming open, and the raspy voice of the track announcer echoing from a loudspeaker on the grandstand behind them—"And they're off!"

Hazel crossed her fingers.

The animals flew past bunched together, hooves hammering the sandy Fairmount Park dirt, not far from Helen's Long Lake home on the American Bottom, where the Mississippi once flowed, leaving behind soft, rich soil. At the first turn the horses all moved toward the infield rail and strung out in a line.

The only roan in a field of chestnuts and bays, Grey Doll was easy to pick out as the thoroughbreds raced down the backstretch. Alas, she lagged at the back of the pack, and Hazel began to regret her rashness. Whatever made her risk a week's salary on the mere suggestion of a stranger? *This will teach the dreamy schoolmarm a lesson.*

Then as the horses entered the final turn the filly livened and began to move up. Hazel lost sight of her for a moment as the thoroughbreds fought into the stretch. Then she spied the roan farthest from the rail coming head on but couldn't tell how far back she was. Now she heard the announcer's call, "And that's Grey Doll gaining on the far outside..."

Hazel found herself screaming, "Come on, Grey Doll, come on!"

The ground shook as the horses hurled past, the roan now neck and neck with the chestnut for the lead.

"It's Brokers Tip and Grey Doll!" came the call. "... Grey Doll and Brokers Tip... Brokers Tip and Grey Doll... And Grey Doll takes it by a head bob!"

Hazel hugged her sister. "I won! I won!"

"We won!" said Raymond. "I put two bucks on her myself. Thanks for the tip, Sis."

"I'm not the one to thank…" She moved away from the rail and searched the crowd. Just beyond the finish line she spied the Panama hat and the handsome blond man. "There he is. Come with me."

He saw her approaching and seemed to study her walk, looking her up and down as if appraising a racehorse at auction. Out of breath, Hazel put a hand to her heart when she got to him.

"Gosh, what a race!"

"Did you bet her?"

"All I had. I thought I would die at the end!"

"Sorry for all the excitement. Closer than it should have been," he said, looking past her.

She turned. "This is my sister, Helen, and brother-in-law, Raymond. They won money, too. How can we thank you?"

His eyes were hazel, she now noticed as they fixed on her. A nice coincidence for Hazel Marie Robinson.

"You can let me buy you all a drink in the clubhouse."

"The drinks should be on us!"

He waved away her suggestion. "The quinella paid even better. Come."

Inside the clubhouse he doffed his Panama and said to the attendant at the high front desk, "These are my guests, Joe."

"Of course, Mr. Nowak."

Mr. Nowak—Jan, he had said when they exchanged names at the finish line—led them upstairs and outside to a table on the covered porch overlooking the track just past the finish line. When the waiter came everyone wanted beer on the hot afternoon. Jan ordered a pitcher of Hyde Park.

When the waiter returned with the beer and glasses Jan said, "I hope you'll excuse my hometown loyalty. I know Stag's the East Side favorite, but I'm from north St. Louis, born not too far from Hyde Park."

"Loyalty's a good thing," said Raymond, and the others agreed.

Hazel studied Jan, pursing her lips. "I'm a little surprised," she said.

"That I like Hyde Park Beer?"

"No, that you're from north St. Louis. You have no trace of the local dialect."

"There's good reason for that. English is my second language. We spoke Polish at home and in the Cass Avenue neighborhood where I grew up. So I didn't learn English from family or on the street, rather from schoolteachers who spoke grammatically and phonetically correct American and taught me the same."

"Hazel teaches school," Helen said. "In Granite City."

At the mention of her hometown Hazel noticed something in his eyes that made her think he had some history there, though something he didn't want to share.

Then he looked away, focusing on a tall, dapper, dark-haired man in a straw boater who had just stepped through the door to the balcony. Jan gestured him over. "Come, Bogdan! Join us."

Jan stood to shake hands and laid an arm across the man's shoulder.

"Friends, this is Bob Wade, the source of our good fortune. He alerted me to Grey Doll."

Bob Wade—or was it Bogdan?—stroked his chin, where an afternoon shadow of black stubble grew. "Happy you folks get in on it…" Here he turned to squint at Jan. "…Though I thought the odds would be a bit better."

Jan threw back his head with a laugh. "My fault entirely, my friend, for sharing it with this young lady, Hazel Robinson, who turns out to be a high-stakes gambler and odds-buster."

Bob shook her hand. "Good for you! You believe in long shots, Miss Robinson?"

She felt herself glowing, a happiness radiating throughout her.

"I think I could develop a taste for them… How did you know Grey Doll was going to win?"

Bob exchanged a glance with Jan and cleared his throat. "Got it straight from the horse's mouth."

The men sat. They all toasted to long shots and good luck. Helen unfolded a Kodak camera from her purse. Bob Wade insisted on playing the photographer and taking a picture of the smiling foursome. Then he turned the camera on Jan and Hazel.

"You two move closer… No smiling now."

They put their heads together, and she breathed in Jan's scent—tobacco, leather, and something that stirred her. Whatever it was she could not help but smile for the snapshot. He made her feel like Cinderella.

§

Motoring back to Granite City that afternoon Hazel asked Helen and Raymond to drop her off at a small downtown bookstore. Inside she found exactly what she was looking for: a leather-bound blank book with gold-edged pages of smooth, ivory-colored stock, subtly lined. On its shiny black cover a single word was embossed in a serif font: Journal.

Miss Pittman, the shop owner, raised her eyebrows when Hazel unfolded her racetrack winnings from her purse and peeled off two dollars to hand her.

Hazel caught the Madison Avenue bus, warm air wafting through the open windows. She debarked before reaching Nameoki Road and walked two blocks to her childhood home facing Wilson Park as the sun lowered behind the tall sycamores there—worlds away, aesthetically at least, from the steel mills at the far side of town.

After dinner she went to her room, sat at her desk, and made her first journal entry: "A Day at the Races." Hazel smiled recalling the Marx Brothers movie of the same name that she had seen the previous year at the Washington Theater. Then she wrote about the race, the racetrack tout Jan Nowak, and how lucky he made her feel.

# 3 | WHY A.J. WAS TAKEN FROM HIS MOTHER

Madison County, Illinois, June 15, 1951

Saturday morning Helen Robinson Lomax, wearing sky-blue pedal pushers and a white sleeveless blouse, moved barefooted with her basket of strawberries from the patch by the garage. Mid-morning sun warmed her bare arms and calves. By the end of summer, she'd be brown as a berry herself. That's what her mother always said, warning her against getting too dark. Mom's fault. That's from where the Cherokee blood sprung.

She crossed the gravel-and-grass driveway to the piebald backyard of the tar-papered house—a sandy, beige covering of fake brick. Grass didn't readily grow in the shady backyard thanks to the tall maple, willow, and fruit trees that surrounded it. A white cloud floated across the sun, and Helen looked up to the plum tree atop the lake bank and saw that the fruit was beginning to ripen. Same for the raspberry bushes that clung to the graying picket fence beneath it. The cherries were already finished. Later would come peaches, apples, and, in the garden, watermelon and cantaloupe. Also, vegetables: beans, peas, corn, okra, onions, and tomatoes. It would keep her busy picking and canning for months. A labor of love in the home she loved.

Before marrying Raymond she had known only city streets, living a short drive from the Granite City steel mill where her father—like her husband and his father—worked, but in the office, not in the plant. Though the lake home was small and cold in winter, the well water hard and unpalatable, and something always needed fixing, to her it was Eden. The fresh-smelling air enveloping her, the placid lake beckoning her, and the birdsong awakening her each morning year round came as daily revelations of nature's force and beauty. Their home was near perfect in her eyes. The only thing lacking was children, for which she continued to pray.

Raymond sat at the kitchen table sipping coffee and reading the *Press-Record*, his pecs and biceps bulging inside his white tee shirt. Like most men at the mill, he had started at the bottom, pulling hot bricks from cooling ovens and other taxing labor. That encouraged him to attend night school to learn to read blueprints and sharpen his math skills. Now he no longer worked with his muscles, though that hard history still showed on him, he worked with his mind and his eyes as an inspector of the steel castings, railroad supplies, and tank turrets that the mill produced.

"Good morning, sleepyhead," Helen said as she approached, and bent to kiss his forehead before moving towards the sink to rinse the berries.

Raymond said, "You'll be pleased to learn no more late nights for me. They're killing the second shift."

She turned back to him. "What happened?"

He nodded at the newspaper spread on the tabletop before him. "Looks like a stalemate brewing in Korea.

Folks in Washington finally losing their taste for war. Or maybe they just milked all they could from this one… New orders are way down. Laying off half my shift. Looks like I'm okay for now."

"Let's hope."

"If I lose this job I'll find another. Not like before The War."

"At least the defense work kept you out of that one and this one."

"The thought of leaving the lake and fields to go off and die in the dirt of Germany, Iwo Jima, or Inchon…" He moved his head side to side and ran a hand through his short-cropped red hair. "I guess you do what you got to do. Just glad I didn't have to go."

Helen looked out the window over the sink, staring across the adjacent vacant lot and past the tall cottonwood trees in the Sullivans' backyard, picturing her sister's home beyond the bend in the lake. Without turning she whispered: "Poor Hazel… I couldn't bear losing you…"

He turned to the sports page. "What'd you say?"

She bit her lip, realizing she had spoken her thoughts aloud. "Just talking to myself." Helen turned to him. "What would you say, handsome, to some strawberry shortcake?"

He looked up and spread his arms. "Beautiful!"

§

Raymond drove them in his black '41 Plymouth—a car that resembled the dented lunch pail that he carried to work each day—to the Tri-City Grocery in Granite

City. Now they traveled back toward the lake, turning away from Nameoki Road and the train tracks at The Blue Note nightclub as a steam locomotive with its long tail of hoppers heaped with coal from Southern Illinois mines roared past clanking, headed into town and the foul-smelling steel mills. Another reason Helen loved living on the lake, away from all the smoke and noise.

She wondered if Raymond had stopped in at The Blue Note for a drink on his way home from the mill last night. Helen was long asleep when he slid into bed beside her. She'd never question his whereabouts but was curious whether he had seen her sister there. Though it didn't really make much difference. If she wasn't there she was at Sis's Tavern or at clubs in East St. Louis or across the river.

Helen didn't like the idea of A.J., just ten, on his own like that. Which was why they'd been taking him in on weekends. Being around Raymond, whom he worshipped, was good for them both. He'd been teaching A.J. to ice skate, to box, and to handle a fly rod. Things his father would have done. It was a role Raymond took to heart. Having the boy in the house was good for her, too.

"What have you got planned for you guys today?" she asked as they passed the silver-green Mobil Oil tanks—announced by a tall sign with a flying red-winged horse—just the other side of the rails that ran north to Mitchell and gave their lake community its unofficial name: Tank Town.

"Thought we'd do some weeding in the garden this afternoon and then get out on the boat and catch some sunfish for dinner."

"He'd like that."

"Tomorrow afternoon the Cardinals are hosting the Phillies. Let's go sit in the bleachers and drink some beer."

"I have a better idea. Let's sit behind third base and sip in the shade."

He turned and gazed at her with pale blue eyes. "I can never say no to you, Helen."

"Likewise, as you've no doubt noticed."

They turned right and followed the lake south for a bit. Soon Raymond slowed the Plymouth and steered it onto a gravel drive shaded by sycamores and bounded by thick grass, past an engraved cedar sign hanging from a wooden post reading "Lazy Lane."

The house—a real clapboard dwelling with central heat and modern appliances, not just a gussied fishing shack like theirs—sat back a hundred yards from the road, facing the lake. Maple trees atop the lake bank shaded the backyard and boat dock. Somehow Jan had been able to pay cash for the home in 1941 despite having no real job.

"Car's not here," said Helen. "Maybe she went to town for something."

"Yeah, something," Raymond said, shaking his head as he braked to a stop.

He wasn't unsympathetic to her sister's plight. Losing your soul mate would be like losing an irreplaceable part of yourself. It could drive anyone to drink. Still, Hazel's behavior—her heavy boozing and carousing—grated on his sense of propriety, devotion to family, and affinity for orderliness in life.

They walked to the back of the house where windows running floor to ceiling allowed morning sun to warm the home in winter. Down the lake bank a rowboat bobbed tethered to the dock on which rested two Adirondack chairs beside a small boathouse.

Helen pushed through the home's back door into the bright den, the cold stone fireplace at the far end, crammed bookshelves running the length of the room floor to ceiling, a white baby-grand piano angled in the corner to the right.

"A.J., we're here!"

She moved into the adjoining kitchen, Raymond following. "Hello?" she called.

The house lay silent. Helen walked through the dining room to the living room, checked the bedrooms and bathrooms, and returned to the kitchen.

"No sign of him."

"Maybe she took him with her."

"I told her yesterday we'd be here around noon."

"Could be he's gone fishing. I'll check the lakeshore."

Helen sat at the kitchen table thinking about what she had just seen in Hazel's bedroom—rather, what she had not seen. Hazel used to keep Jan's picture on her dressing table. She wondered what that meant.

Then, startled, she turned to her right where she had heard a noise. A whimper. She frowned looking toward the kitchen sink. As she rose and moved toward it, Raymond returned.

"No sign of him at the lake. And the boat's there."

Helen held up a hand to silence him then knelt before the sink. She reached out and eased open the two cabinet doors hinged there. Inside crouched beneath the sink sat A.J., head resting against the wall, asleep, his late father's bone-handled hunting knife clutched to his chest with both hands.

She felt Raymond's hand on her shoulder and looked up to him, seeing his jaw clench.

"We'll take him home now, Helen. But I'm not bringing him back."

No, she saw in his eyes that he couldn't, that he never would, and nodded.

She turned back to A.J., brushed his cheek with the backs of her fingers, and lifted the knife from his grasp. God moved in mysterious ways. Seemingly her prayers had been answered after all.

# 4 | FIRST KISS

Madison County, Illinois, August 13, 1939

Jan Nowak worked not to stare at Hazel Robinson. She sat beside him in a folding chair at the card table that had been set under a maple tree atop the lake bank at her sister's home. She looked like a gypsy princess—dark eyes, full lips, square shoulders, and crossed bronze legs peeking from a flowered skirt. So instead he gazed across the table to her sister Helen, who was fine to look at as well and bright, like Hazel. A nurse, she had told him.

"That was a great meal, Helen. A treat for me to get away from the city, breathe fresh air, eat outdoors, and feel the breeze. I love the lake—so serene. Thanks for the invitation. You've got a beautiful home."

"It's humble for sure, but we love it. Should have seen it two years ago when we bought it. Ready to fall down. Only reason it's still standing is that Raymond, his dad, and his brothers worked day and night for months to make it habitable—a new roof, new wiring, floors, and windows. *And* indoor plumbing. We bought it 'as is,' meaning with an outhouse and a hand pump at the kitchen sink."

"What about, you, Jan? Are you handy around the house?"

This from Hazel. A throaty voice, but she didn't smoke, Jan noted as he held a match to another Lucky Strike. He turned to her, feeling a light wind off Long Lake tempering the hot afternoon. Yet she seemed perfectly cool.

He nodded. "Yes, I am. For example, if you had some Cognac and Cointreau, I could mix you a sidecar. Though when it comes to hammers, nails, saws, and pipe wrenches, I'm afraid I'm not much help."

She laughed. "I don't think we have the sidecar makings, but I could get you another beer."

"Perfect. Thank you."

He watched her walk to the house, the full skirt swaying and adding to the mystery of her movement. Subterfuge and concealment. Two formidable weapons in the female sexual arsenal and to which he always surrendered without much of a fight—though never remained a prisoner for long. He had fought too long and hard for his independence to relinquish it hastily. She disappeared through the screen door to the back porch, the door plap-plap-plapping shut on its long spring.

Birdsong drew his gaze upward to the tall maple. He saw a brilliant black-and-yellow bird wing away over the lake, undulating as if on an invisible roller coaster. Jan gazed out over the water, thinking how Jung in his memoir rhapsodized about *his* lake, calling it an "inconceivable pleasure…an incomparable splendor" and saying that he must live near a lake. "…Without water, I thought, nobody could live at all…" At the sound of Raymond's voice Jan turned back.

"You seem to be getting along fine in these tough times without using your hands," he said nodding at the green Buick sport coupe sitting in the driveway beyond a cluster of shrub roses.

"I've been lucky."

"At the racetrack?"

Jan laughed. "Not just there. I made some investments that paid off as well."

"In the stock market?"

Hazel returned with two damp, brown beer bottles and set them before the men. Jan raised his.

"No, in this," he pointed. "Beer and liquor…"

Jan felt Hazel's eyes on him as she again sat to his left. He never knew how people would react when he told how he had grown successful—if that was the right phrase for it—flouting federal law. Though he figured he might as well shoot craps with her. If you think a relationship might have some legs—he glanced down at hers again—you don't want to start off telling lies, at least not big ones. So, he went on.

"In Prohibition days I was an aimless kid. Had a school chum at Beaumont High, Stanley Goldberg, whose Uncle Leo was running liquor and wanted to break into the Cass Avenue Polish community. To do so he needed someone who spoke the lingo, since English wasn't that common there. That turned out to be me. I became his right-hand man. When Leo suddenly died I took over the operation. Then I cashed out before Congress repealed the Volstead Act and went into the banking business."

Hazel sat with hands folded under her chin, elbows resting on the table, red lips pursed. "Banking doesn't sound nearly as interesting as bootlegging."

"Agreed. But one is less likely to suddenly die." He took a sip from his beer glass. "Besides, I am the bank and make my own hours."

The only sounds were birdsong and leaves rustling in a gust as a cloud passed before the sun. Hazel, Helen, and Raymond sat silent, staring at him as if he might have been a Martian—maybe one that slipped away from New Jersey in Orson Welles' *The War of the Worlds* radio broadcast the previous fall, and somehow landed in Southern Illinois.

He smiled at Hazel, hoping he hadn't scared off the schoolmarm. She really was a looker.

§

The two men stood at the end of the dock, cane poles and beer bottles in hand, red-and-white cork bobbers floating on the blue-green lake. A cow lowed on the far bank where it stood in the shade of a tall cottonwood tree, drawing Jan's gaze. Flies buzzed, crickets creaked, frogs croaked. Willows on the near bank rustled in a puff of wind, carrying to him the mossy, green, fresh smell of the lake. An earthy aroma, but miles apart from St. Louis sewer gas. Behind him Hazel and Helen sat side-by-side on the dock murmuring, bare feet dangling toward the silvery still water.

"A little early in the afternoon for them to be biting," said Raymond nodding at the motionless bobbers. "I like to grab my fly rod and take the rowboat out just before sunset."

"You've got a fine life here, Raymond. Peaceful. I envy you."

Raymond nodded. "It's hard work at the mill. Particularly when you're pulling hot brick in the ovens and breaking your back. I'm not complaining though. Lots of guys got nothing."

"I know all about steelwork from my father."

Raymond looked at him. "There's a Josef Nowak who represents the Polish workers. Has a lot of clout."

"That's him."

"He came over on the boat, right? What's he think will happen with Hitler? Germans gonna invade Poland?"

"I don't know what he thinks. We don't speak." The two women fell silent behind him. He went on.

"The Poles will never give in to Hitler. It's not in their dreamy nature. They'd rather die fighting for a hopeless cause—they've demonstrated this before—than live under Prussians, Russians, Nazis, or what have you. Which means there will be war. Good for the steel mills."

Raymond lifted his line from the water and repositioned the bait a few feet further out in the lake. "I'd be happy to go on the breadline if it meant people wouldn't have to die… It's always the innocents and the little guy who pay with their lives and their livelihoods. Not the kings, generals, and tycoons who start it all… Sorry. I sound like some Bolshevik. I'm not. I just don't like being deceived, manipulated, and pushed around. You don't know what to believe. That European stuff's got nothing to do with us here."

"No need to apologize. I'm with you. That's why my people came here, to get away from being pushed around and all that ongoing strife an ocean away. Doesn't make much sense to go back and get involved in something that can't directly touch us."

"Let's pray it won't."

§

As dusk arrived, Jan—with everyone's seeming complicity—offered to drive Hazel home to her parents' house in Granite City.

She directed him along the lake road toward Pontoon Beach, the sun setting to their right, cooling evening air streaming through the Buick's windows. It enveloped them in a sweet, corn-scented atmosphere—along with the fecund aroma of the lake and the floral fragrance of her perfume.

"Nice car. What kind is it?"

"Buick. It's called an opera coupe. Not sure why."

"Looks brand new."

"It's a 1938… If one is in the banking racket it helps to look prosperous. Like you're not going to up and disappear with the deposits."

"Is it a racket?"

He glanced at Hazel. He'd have to watch himself with the schoolteacher—his connotations as well as his denotations.

"Wish it was more of one. The commercial side does okay. Consumer side's a bit sketchy right now. A lot of folks short on cash. They don't have jobs but still have rent to pay and mouths to feed. Who knows when or if they'll ever be able to pay it back."

He looked to the mossy lake, the palest green, sliding by on his left. "It's nice out here. Quiet. Restful. Clean. So different from what I'm used to in the city."

He slowed the Buick as a lighted beer sign came up on the left. There two cars sat in a gravel lot before a tavern on the lake.

"You know this place? How about a nightcap? Our first chance to talk without adult supervision."

Hazel smiled. "Sis is a little protective. Raymond's worse, like I'm still twelve."

"That means they value you," he said as the car slid to a stop on the gravel.

"Or they don't trust me around men."

He looked at her, wondering if she was suggesting there was a reason for that. Or maybe she was just being playful.

She gazed ahead at the dark, windowless saloon that sat on short stilts at the lakeshore. It looked more like a rambling fishing shack than nightspot.

"Don't expect too much," she said. "This is a homely hangout for local country folk."

"I'm becoming rather fond of country culture. Fascinating field study for a city slicker like me."

"You could get a graduate degree in this place on Saturday night."

They stepped through the heavy plank front door into an expansive room lit by beer signs, pinball machines, and a glittering jukebox. Jan found that it also smelled like a fishing shack. The aromas of beer, fried fish, and cigarette smoke thickened the air. In lieu of artwork, mounted fish adorned the slat walls. As Hazel slid into a wooden booth he went to the bar and got them two highballs from a smiling gray-haired woman.

"You're not from around here."

"My lady friend is. Recommends your tavern as a friendly place. I come in peace and goodwill."

"In that case, happy to have you, handsome."

He winked at her and left a tip. Jan sat across from Hazel. They touched glasses together and drank. He gestured with his toward the unvarnished floor.

"Sawdust. This a dance joint?"

"More of a hoe-down venue. On Saturday nights they have a fiddler and banjo picker who play cornball country music."

"Cornball's okay sometimes."

"Yes, it is. Everybody enjoys themselves. As little girls Helen and I came here with our parents and danced. Lovely times."

"Family's important to you."

That seemed to register with her, as she bit her lip. However, he had misjudged her thoughts.

"I overheard your conversation with Raymond... Sorry about your father, him not speaking to you."

Jan acknowledged her gesture with a nod. His youthful loathing of the old man had tempered over the years. Still, he had no desire to see him.

"A mixed blessing. Now I don't have to endure his lectures. And lectures in Polish are somehow more bellicose and discouraging than in English... He's like a lot of the Poles here. They come to get the aristocratic boot off their necks yet never really embrace America and all it has to offer them, all the opportunities.

"In my neighborhood all you hear is Polish—in the shops, the taverns, the church. My mother's been here thirty years yet still hardly speaks a word of English. An arranged marriage, working-class style. My father paid her passage over, and they married within a month even though they had never before met. She was eighteen, he over forty."

Hazel pursed her lips trying to imagine such a union. "Marrying without courtship, without love. They come from a different world and different time."

He nodded. "Which is why I've done my best to leave that all behind—particularly the working-class dread, self-abnegation, and resignation. Slogging away like a serf your whole life, forever doing the bidding of others, always looking fearfully over your shoulder… Not to mention mercantile marriage. You'd think that if two people planned to spend their lives together, might help if they knew each other a bit first. Perhaps shared some values. Maybe even liked each other, at least a little."

Hazel shrugged. "Guess it couldn't hurt."

Jan smiled. He already liked her—at least a little.

"I was fifteen when I first started working for Leo Gold supplying liquor to the Cass Avenue people and places. My old man soon heard about it. Told me he wouldn't have a criminal for a son or have him living under his roof. Said he could get me on at the steel mill, make a man out of me. When I refused he threw me out of our flat—literally. I've been on my own ever since.

"It's been ten or fifteen years since we've spoken. I sometimes visit my mother when he's at work. She's afraid to tell him, though I suspect he knows. He's got eyes everywhere."

Jan excused himself and again went to the bar, Hazel watching how he walked. Everything he did was easy, deliberate, and graceful yet manly. He got change from the woman there and moved to the jukebox. What a strange man. But his own man, seemingly. She'd never met anyone anything like him. After a minute, she heard the string introduction of the new Judy Garland hit—her favorite. How did he know? Jan returned and extended his hand to her.

"May I have this dance?" She smiled, stood, and moved into his arms. He led her over the saw-dusted slats, the music running through her, heart and soul.

*Somewhere over the rainbow*
*Way up high,*
*There's a land that I heard of*
*Once in a lullaby.*
*Somewhere over the rainbow*
*Skies are blue,*
*And the dreams that you dare to dream*
*Really do come true.*

Ah, thought Hazel. If only they would. She laid her head on his shoulder.

§

At Pontoon Beach Jan turned right as she directed him. It was dark now. The light from the dashboard gauges seemed to make her glow. Soon she told him to pull to the curb. Jan looked past her to a white clapboard bungalow.

"This where you live?"

She lifted her chin toward the other side of the street, where sat a two-story brown-brick building with tall windows, surrounded by stately trees. "This is where I work. Nameoki School."

He sat staring at it. Smaller than Webster School in St. Louis where he first studied and Beaumont High, where he didn't, at least not much. It brought back to him the smell of chalk dust, pencil shavings, and moldy textbooks.

"Great that you got to go to university. To get a real education and learn a profession. I'm envious."

"I thought you had. You're so well spoken."

"Never finished high school. When I dropped out I couldn't tell my father for fear he'd thrash me and kick me down the stairs—which he eventually did anyway. I got up every morning to walk to school then instead headed off to the Central Library downtown.

"After a while the librarians noticed me lurking about and took me under their wing, gave me books to read: Shakespeare, Whitman, Twain. Plato, Gibbons, Montaigne. Nothing all that useful, but I loved it. Even after I started bootlegging, I still spent long hours at the library reading."

"I think it was very useful. Helped make you into an interesting and sensitive man."

Jan wondered about her "sensitive" claim. Things he had done—and still had to do from time to time—might undermine it.

He stroked his chin. "Thanks, but that means I've been talking too much. Now tell me about your studies and your students."

She again pursed her lips. "I'm thinking maybe we've done enough talking for now."

He stared at her crimson lips, now parted, nodded agreement, and leaned toward her.

§

Hazel stayed up late writing it all down in her journal while it still sat fresh in memory, with pertinent dialogue and sensory details, like a real writer—the smell of the lake, the feel of sawdust beneath her soles as Judy Garland warbled, the press of Jan's lips against hers. "A magical day," she wrote.

Hazel finally fell asleep, believing that her life had been touched by beneficent spirits.

# 5 | FIGHTING WORDS

Mitchell, Illinois, September 7, 1951

He got off the school bus with Lonnie Sullivan at his side and followed Wayne Thurman through the chain-link gate into the dusty schoolyard of the brown-brick building.

"Hey, Thurman!"

The older boy stopped and turned with a smirk painted on his face. A.J. approached, heart thumping, and spat, "You got a big mouth."

Thurman looked down at him. "What are you going to do about it?"

"Gonna shut it once and for all."

"You and what army, little man," he said, smiling as he glanced at Lonnie standing beside A.J.

A.J. handed the book he carried to Lonnie. Then he turned back to Thurman with a left hook to his teeth and a right to his gut. When Thurman bent over he kicked him between the legs. The older boy fell to earth. A.J. jumped on his chest and began pounding his ears with either fist as the taste of rising dust and the smell of blood came to him.

Thurman, swinging wildly, managed to land punches on A.J.'s face and jaw that the latter did not feel. He sensed nothing but the black rage boiling inside. He continued to punch and kick even as Mr. Gage, the gym instructor, and Mrs. Bush, his teacher, pulled him off the other boy.

At last, he came back into himself. Gasping, he found his arms pinned behind him by Mr. Gage. A.J. looked down to Wayne Thurman lying on the schoolyard dirt, bright blood seeping from his ears and nose glistening in the warm morning sun. He wondered what exactly had happened. He remembered getting off the school bus and calling out Thurman, but after that it was a blur. Punches were thrown, he knew that much.

§

A.J. slouched in a polished wooden armchair clutching his book. Blood dripped from his nose to his new tee shirt and blue jeans. On the wide walnut desk before him rested a nameplate reading "Clyde Lee, Principal." Beyond it sat a scowling red-faced man, wavy brown hair parted down the middle. Leaning forward he rested his forearms on a green blotter as a ceiling fan limped squawking in circles above him.

"Not off to a very good start today, are we A.J.? Nor for the school year."

The boy stared down at the hardwood floor between his black P.F. Flyers. "No, sir," he agreed. But he didn't regret what he did to Thurman. He'd had no choice.

"Not the first time you've been in a fight on school property. I told you before: What occurs beyond the school grounds is beyond my jurisdiction. Why couldn't this wait?"

A.J. gazed out the tall, open, second-story window toward the schoolyard below. He felt the rumble and heard the roar of tractor-trailer trucks ambling through Mitchell, Illinois, on U.S. Route 66 By-Pass, where the school sat. The smell of their exhaust mingled with the grassy aroma of surrounding wheat fields and the school's perpetual scent of floor polish.

"Because."

Mr. Lee sat silent, waiting, still scowling. A.J. didn't take it personally. Lee scowled at everyone. Finally, A.J. went on, "Because Wayne was ripe for a whipping, so I gave him one."

"And why did he need a whipping so urgently?"

A.J. shrugged. "I dunno. Stuff he said on the bus."

The principal shook his head and harrumphed. "This is serious, A.J. You aren't a child anymore. We had to send Thurman to the nurse. I'm afraid I'll have to call your mother."

A.J. sat up straight. "She's got nothing to do with it!" He could feel the lie burning his face and looked away from Mr. Lee's steady gaze.

The principal leaned back and sat squinting at A.J. Then he rolled his chair away from the desk. "Wait."

The man rose and strode from his office, heels tapping the polished floor. Closing the door behind him he called to his secretary: "Mrs. Tate..."

A.J. rose and put an ear to the thick door. He could hear them whispering. He was able to make out a few of Mrs. Tate's words: "Blue Note...Richard Dupuis... with his aunt now..." Which was enough. The sound of footsteps approaching chased A.J. back to his chair.

# THE BOOTLEGGER'S BRIDE

The door clicked. Mr. Lee pushed through it and stood over him. He had stopped scowling for once, studying A.J. with pursed lips as if pondering a tricky math problem. At last, he said:

"Maybe you did what you felt you had to do, A.J. But you did it at the wrong time and wrong place. You understand what I'm telling you?"

A.J. continued to study the slat floor. "Yes, sir."

"I have to send you home for the day. Cool off over the weekend and put this incident behind you. Remember, if it happens again there will be serious consequences." Back came the scowl.

A.J. nodded. To first- and second-graders serious consequences meant being subjected to Mr. Lee's electric paddle, a myth the older boys helped spread. A more realistic consequence of continued violent behavior on A.J.'s part was likely permanent expulsion and maybe reform school. That he could not endure, to be taken away from the lake and locked up inside some dark institution. The thought of it made his stomach rise. It made him sick. The principal went on.

"Mrs. Tate is typing up a note for you to take home. I can drive you."

A.J. rose. "I'll hoof it."

"I don't think it's a good idea to walk on the highway, A.J."

"I'll go along the tracks. The shortcut. It ain't but a mile."

Mr. Lee grimaced and said, "Isn't." Then he laid a hand on the boy's shoulder. "Okay. But be careful. Watch out for hoboes."

A.J. promised that he would. But he'd never seen a hobo except in movies and wasn't sure he could tell one apart from other men who lived along the lake.

§

Book in hand he skirted the fresh-smelling wheat field behind the school and marched to the railroad track that intersected the lake. He walked between the gleaming steel rails, stepping from wooden tie to wooden tie over the white rock roadbed where wildflowers sprouted. The chemical aroma of creosote wafted up from the dark ties as the hot September sun rose toward midday.

Ahead he soon saw the lake on whose bank two low Indian mounds lay. These also were covered with yellow-green wheat standing dead still in the windless morning. He had been to Monks Mound, the tallest of the Cahokian structures, beyond the south end of Long Lake, where once sat the great Mississippian city that was home to tens of thousands. He wondered what it was like for them and wished he could have been among them hunting, fishing, and canoeing instead of sitting inside the old brick building doing reading, writing, and arithmetic—always stuff he already knew. A.J. figured they were people much like him, folks who cherished and worshipped the waters and woods, the fields and animals.

He didn't cotton much to church going and was no good memorizing Bible passages and such in Sunday school. And he wasn't afraid of God's hand or going to Hell like the other kids were. None of that stuck to him. But that didn't mean he dismissed spiritual existence.

He felt it springing from the earth, from every rock and blade of grass, in every firefly and fish he caught. From the bones of the Indians in the burial mounds along the lake and from the arrowheads he found there. The world vibrated with those presences, making it all sacred and meaningful to him, connecting him to the past and to the land. And he felt it as well in himself, kin to those beings dead and alive, animate and otherwise. This was his world and he felt it throbbing deep inside him. This was where he belonged. Which was why the threat of reform school scared and sickened him so.

He dropped down the steep bank to the lake and removed his tee shirt. With a branch he pushed aside a line of lime-green moss at the shore and squatted to wash the blood from the white shirt. Then he rose and used it to daub bloodstains from his jeans and rinsed it again in lake water.

When he was younger he and the other kids along the lake, boys and girls alike, played cowboys and Indians most every day. A.J. always angled to be an Indian Brave not a cowpoke, eager to scalp settlers and the Long Knives as if to honor his Cherokee heritage. Shirtless and barefooted, a red paisley handkerchief worn as an Indian headband where he tucked blue jay and cardinal feathers, a hunting knife sheathed on the belt of his faded jeans where also dangled a good-luck rabbit's foot on a short brass chain—this had been his summertime uniform. Even today he still listened to the stories of cowboys and Indians on the radio—*Tom Mix, Hopalong Cassidy,* and *The Cisco Kid, Fort Laramie, Red Ryder,* and *The Lone Ranger.*

He moved down the shore until he came to the boat dock behind the house where Uncle Raymond's parents lived, the last home at the lake road's dead end. There he wrung out the tee shirt and stretched it on the hot dock to dry. Then he moved into the shade of a willow on the lakeshore with his book to wait till school was out and he could go home as if nothing had happened.

As he lowered himself onto the sandy bank he heard the crinkle of the sealed envelope in his back pocket. He withdrew it, tore it open, and read the note inside, the one Mr. Lee had Mrs. Tate type. It stated simply that A.J. had gotten into a fight with another boy and as a result was expelled for the day. He would be welcomed back to class Monday, after he had promised to obey school rules and not fight on school property.

That wasn't quite true, as A.J. had made no such promise. To Mr. Lee's credit, however, he did not mention the cause of the fight, of which he was apparently aware. Still, A.J. tore the note into scraps and buried them in the sand beside him.

Then he opened the book he carried everywhere these days, a thick, fifty-year-old reference he had sneaked out of the school library. Everyone including his teachers thought he was dim or deranged and uninterested in learning because he seldom completed his homework or paid attention in class. No, he was just bored shitless. Miles ahead of the herd. While they were still reading comic books he was devouring real literature his mother had guided him to—Dickens and Kipling and Twain, books a boy would like—then more grown-up fiction and poetry. But what he liked most was history. Real stories about real people and places—the Oregon Trail and Lewis & Clark, explorers, presidents, and pioneers. But most of all Indian lore and stories.

Now from his pilfered book he read again of the Plains Indians and gazed at pen-and-ink drawings of the Kickapoo, Kaskaskia, Illiniwek, and Sioux roasting game at campfires, spearing fish from streams, canoeing reedy waters, and passing icy winter nights in caves and lean-tos.

Not knowing well his own father, he felt that these men who roamed the same fields and paddled the same waters as he were true kin as well. And he prayed that he might grow into that sort of man, a brave.

# 6 | A MODERN DAY FAGIN

St. Louis, Missouri, September 2, 1939

In the downtown Statler Hotel dining room, the waiter—in black dinner jacket and bow tie—approached their table. He took two conical glasses from his silver tray and placed the drinks before them. "Anything else, Mr. Nowak?"

"No, thank you, Hans."

The man bowed and retreated. He had spoken with a seeming German accent—not that unusual in St. Louis. However, it recalled to Hazel Robinson what she read in the newspaper that morning: The previous day Germany had invaded Poland. Though it was a surprise to no one, judging from what the newspaper said.

Jan raised his martini to hers. They touched rims of the etched crystal and drank, astringent yet clean tasting, with structure. Greek tragedy in a glass, she mused. Something she might have said aloud had she known him better. His voice brought her back into the moment.

"So you'll be back in the classroom next week."

She nodded. "Reading, writing, and 'rithmetic."

"No hickory stick?"

"Not part of the modern curriculum. However, Mrs. Thornhill, who has the classroom across the hall, keeps a paddle on her desk. Old school."

"And educators wonder why some of us drop out."

Hazel smiled then glanced toward the corner of the crowded dining room where she heard laughter. Their waiter—Hans—hovered over a party of four older men to whom he had apparently told a good joke. She turned back.

"Have you been following what's going on in Europe, Jan?"

He nodded. "A sovereign Poland—that won't last long the way things are going. Barely twenty years. Lots of worried talk in the neighborhood since so many still have family back there—Poles and Jews alike. Both of whom Hitler detests. Not to mention Gypsies, Communists, the infirm, et cetera. Not sure what he thinks of Slavic bootleggers, but I can guess… What's going on in Germany has people scared that the same will happen in Poland. The Jews likely the first to go though few will be spared."

"The Nazis seem so monstrous."

"Their Prussian predecessors weren't choirboys either, according to my father. He got out from under them soon as he could. Thank God."

"You're understandably worried for the Poles."

"And the Czechs and French and Dutch and everyone else in Europe. But yes: poor Poland. The end of their brief breath of freedom. When you lose that you lose everything."

As he said it he seemed to pull into himself, thoughtful, or reminiscing.

"Hard to imagine," she said, trying to picture it and failing. "We take it for granted, being able to live our daily lives without interference, without fear."

"Why my parents risked everything to get here. To a place where you can make something of yourself without someone slapping you down at every turn. My father disembarking in Baltimore forty years ago is more central to who I am than the blood in my veins. True for all of us, no matter how we got here and where our people came from."

Hazel nodded. "I see that in my students, the children and grandchildren of immigrants—Poles, Germans, Greeks, Italians, Macedonians, Irish. Now they're all American, through and through, and nothing else."

"If I ever have kids, Hazel, they'll learn no Polish from me. The sooner you throw off the Old World folkways and adopt American ways the sooner you can mix in and prosper."

Hazel again lifted her martini—a rare treat—and sipped. She also drank in the opulence of the hotel restaurant, the crystal chandeliers, crystal goblets on the white tablecloth, polished silverware, polished walnut on the floor, and wainscoting. At the center of the table sat a slim vase with a lone rose. A din of conversation from the packed room on a Saturday night despite the lingering economic depression. The clatter of silverware and china, the mingled aromas of grilled meat, cigarette smoke, and perfume. European strife, war, and death seemed so far way.

"This is quite an extravagance, Jan."

"A simple quid pro quo. Having beer and barbecue on the lake with birds singing was a rare treat for a city boy."

Another waiter passed nodding at Jan. "Good evening, Mr. Nowak."

Hazel pursed her lips. "You dine here often, Jan?"

"On occasion."

"You live nearby?"

He lifted his chin. "Upstairs."

She stared at him and raised an eyebrow. "Isn't that convenient."

"Room service is great for someone who doesn't know how to cook," he said, deflecting her insinuation.

"Don't tell me you have the penthouse."

"Just a small suite on the sixteenth floor. It's all I need. I like living above everything. I once lived in a cellar with rats and vowed I'd rise someday, literally as well as figuratively. Besides, living up there keeps disgruntled clients from banging on my door at night or coming through the window. The Statler bellhops are meaner than guard dogs."

"You have a lot of unhappy customers?"

He lifted a skewered olive from his martini and chewed. "Hard times are lasting far longer than most people thought they would. Optimists sometimes borrow money believing things will soon turn around for them. When things don't, they get scared and angry, realizing they made a costly mistake. Sometimes they direct that anger not at the cause, which often is beyond their reach, but at the nearby result."

Hans returned, again bowed, and handed them menus. Hazel scanned hers: Veal Cutlet Milanese, Columbia Shad Roe, Spring Lamb Chops a la Nelson, Steer Sirloin Steak, French Claret or Chardonnay, Roquefort Cheese, and Chocolate Éclair.

She looked up. "No prices listed."

"Not on the ladies' menu. Order whatever you like. We're still enjoying our racetrack winnings."

Hazel pursed her lips. *So you say.* But of course she had no idea how much he might have wagered and won.

She asked him to order for them both. He suggested the veal cutlet and chardonnay, the éclair for dessert.

He wore a beige linen suit, light blue shirt, and red tie with gold clasp. All of which went just fine with his tanned face, blond hair, and greenish-brown eyes. For the occasion—their first real date—she had splurged with her remaining pari-mutuel cash on a high-waisted and slinky zebra-print dress that draped to mid-calf. Nothing she would ever dare wear in the classroom.

"You always have good luck, Jan?"

He studied her for a moment and nodded. "At this moment I feel quite fortunate. Lady Luck has been good to me for some time. I pray she continues to blow on my dice."

He had an odd way with words at times. She ascribed it to English not being his mother tongue. Then, Hazel noticed him surreptitiously peel back a corner of the tablecloth to knock wood. The pagan supplement to his prayers brought a smile to her lips.

"Let's hope she's not too fickle... Tell me, Jan, did Lady Luck help you prosper in business."

He chewed his bottom lip and nodded. "Yes, she and Charles Dickens."

Hazel sat up straight. "Dickens! My favorite! You're not joking, are you?"

"Not at all. It's somewhat of a long story. First tell me who else you like besides Dickens."

She set off summarizing her lifelong love of fiction, drama, and poetry, beginning with playing make-believe, then listening to fairy tales, Mother Goose, and the Brothers Grimm stories. Next reading Hans Christian Andersen and *King Author and His Knights of the Round Table*. She told him of her childhood fascination with Lady Guinevere and other women, like Cinderella and Maid Marian, who were courted by knights, princes, and rogues. She graduated to Sir Walter Scott and Robert Louis Stevenson, then to Shakespeare, the Brontes, Jane Austen, and the Romantic poets and finally on to the Americans Twain, Dreiser, Cather, Fitzgerald, Whitman, and Porter, all of whom Jan said he too admired when she finally took a breath. Nonetheless she went on.

"Granite City's only a streetcar ride away from St. Louis, but it's a different world. A doughty steel town where virtually no one looks beyond its smokestacks. At least that's the way it seemed to me growing up there. No crystal goblets and chandeliers, no hotels serving roe and French wine. A place where most everyone was happy to settle for what was placed before them. But for me it felt like prison. Literature was my only escape. I'm afraid it still is. I have no one there to talk to—not about fiction and poetry and what I feel and what I want from life."

"Which is?"

Hazel gazed upward toward the crystal chandelier. "Something transcendent and beautiful. Something adventurous and meaningful. If that's not asking too much."

Jan appraised her, nodding. He himself could have spoken at length on the subject. But she had already said it in just a few words. "No, Hazel. It's not asking too much. But getting it ain't always easy."

Over dinner he told her his own tale. The Hogan Gang—after getting rid of Egan's Rats, its main rival—had been working with his boss Leo Gold to distribute liquor in North St. Louis.

"Then someone apparently got greedy, and Leo got shot. People say it might have been the work of Jellyroll Hogan or maybe some East Side gangsters, the Shelton brothers, who we'd been doing business with.

"Bad luck for Leo, certainly, though fortunate for me as it turned out. I was the only one who knew about some warehoused inventory that Leo had squirreled away. The real McCoy, genuine London gin, Canadian whiskey, and Jamaican rum. Not the bathtub stuff with phony labels that we pushed. And since he was a lifelong bachelor with no wife or kids, I decided to honor his memory by keeping his business running as best I could…"

He said it with a straight face. Hazel fought back a smile at his obvious appropriation—some might call it theft—and prevarication about it. But then what else could he have done? It was the smart move. He continued—

"Just a few weeks later the stock market crashed, changing everything. Lean times came fast and hard for lots of folks, and I saw an opportunity…

"Like I said, at the Central Library where I'd been hanging out," he tilted his head over his left shoulder toward the posh Andrew Carnegie-funded edifice just a few blocks away on Olive Street, "the librarians had been feeding me books, which I devoured. I happened to be reading *Oliver Twist*. St. Louis, I saw, was a lot like Dickens's London; folks out of work, lots of families with very little dough, things growing tougher every day. Oliver and the Artful Dodger reminded me of guys from my neighborhood that I grew up with and ran with, reliable rascals. All spoke Polish as their mother tongue and all having trouble pressing two dimes together.

"In *Oliver Twist* I saw how Fagin had organized London street urchins like Oliver and the Dodger to turn a tidy profit. I figured I could do the same here. I had this plan to use my neighborhood boys to bypass the speakeasies and retailers and sell direct to the Polish community door-to-door with secure delivery by an innocent looking kid..."

"Eliminating the middleman."

"Exactly! Just like Sears and Roebuck. I was only sixteen then myself and pulled together guys who were thirteen, fourteen, fifteen. Fellas whose families were suffering. They were eager and honest and hard workers.

"The real kicker came when I started extending credit. Until I came along no one did that. Maybe because no one wanted to owe money to the Hogan Gang, who played rough. People knew me and my team and trusted us, knew we weren't violent thugs, just kids helping out their families.

"In turn I trusted my customers, knew that they, too, were honest people who would pay me back eventually. So that got me into the banking business, which was a sideline at first. When I heard the chatter about Congress maybe repealing the Volstead Act, I knew I had to milk the liquor business while the sun still shone."

Hazel felt a little dizzy. The martini, the wine, and Jan's story—true or not—had her head spinning. She'd never met anyone like him, to be sure, or heard such tales except in storybooks.

"That's quite a yarn, Jan. Dickensian for sure."

"Worked like a charm. Best part was Jellyroll Hogan winked at it. His father was chief of police and he himself a Deputy Inspector for the Missouri State Beverage Department. He couldn't go around beating up or bumping off street kids.

"After two years when I had built up the customer list and depleted my special inventory, I walked up Cass Avenue to his bar on Jefferson and offered to sell him the whole liquor operation, keeping the credit business for myself. Jellyroll laughed. I guess my youthful impudence amused him, but he liked cutting deals. We ended up shaking hands on a buyout. As events passed, what with Prohibition soon ending, he didn't get much for his money. Though he never bothered to complain."

"And everyone lived happily ever after?"

"I know I did. As to Jellyroll…" Jan shrugged. "He's been in Jeff City now for five years."

"The Missouri State Prison?"

Jan shook his head. "Missouri State Legislature. We both went legit. I timed it just right. After FDR and his lot lifted Prohibition in '33, folks could get all the liquor they needed. What they didn't have was cash. But I did. Another commodity I could sell on credit."

Hands in her lap, Hazel sat staring at the decidedly handsome but dubious character sipping wine across the white tablecloth from her—shocked by the audacity of the thieving opportunist, stunned by his bravado, and amused by his over-cooked self-confidence.

As to his amoral, self-serving approach to life, she didn't know quite what to think. Never had she met someone so seemingly blasé about death and law breaking, about ignoring society's rules, and making up his own. Someone so materialistic, ruthless, and conniving.

She took another sip of wine and studied him. He was like a Shakespearian character—a self-possessed Petruchio, perhaps, or a discretely plotting Hamlet—or someone darker and more sinister, like Lady Macbeth.

On the other hand, he might have just stepped out of a fairy tale, a cunning Prince Charming, a man with real gumption. Someone who would likely use all his corner cutting and guile on behalf of his beloved—say, perhaps, on her behalf.

# 7 | A.J. VISITS HIS RECOVERING MOTHER

Madison County, Illinois, October 18, 1952

He stepped down into the gray wooden rowboat and released lines cleated to the dock fore and aft. He positioned himself on the center bench seat and pushed off. When the boat cleared the dock, A.J. fitted the oars into the oarlocks and lowered the blades into the water. He pulled on the oars and the boat slid south past the fallow field next door and the Sullivans' dingy home with its Gerry-rigged chicken coop and rabbit hutch. Two Sullivan boys stood on the sandy shore baiting a trotline. They looked up at A.J. as he passed and waved. The family ate carp and mudcat and whatever else the boys pulled from the lake.

Despite their humble existence he envied the Sullivans. Their house was just a repurposed tavern, the long back-bar mirror running the length of the living room. The five boys slept in a single room—previously the front porch—on straw-stuffed mattresses, the two girls on the living room sofa. Their soft-spoken, balding father worked in town as a machinist and the older boys did seasonal farm labor to help make ends meet. It was their youthful mother, Mabel, married and pregnant at fifteen, who solidified and brightened the home with her endless good cheer and high spirits. She'd organized her brood into a well-oiled domestic homemaking machine, with all the kids cleaning, cooking, washing, gardening, and keeping the rickety home standing. And it was Mabel who arranged softball games for the neighborhood kids on the adjacent vacant lot, wiener and marshmallow roasts on the lakeshore come fall evenings, and backyard watermelon feasts in summer. It was a real family, and she was its glue. Mabel even had A.J. pitch in on the chores whenever he was about, which made him feel part of the litter.

He rowed the flat-end boat on past the Sullivans' home under a sun high in a cloudless sky, barely a breath of wind swirling the aroma of burning leaves in the warming air. He hardly needed the sweater that he had pulled on over the flannel shirt Aunt Helen had sewn for him. Along the shore, maples had turned gold and crimson, cottonwoods and sycamores orange, weeping willows yellow, and oaks auburn, all reflecting on the glass-smooth water, which dripped cool on his hands when the oars tilted up.

A belted kingfisher's rattle drew his gaze east to the dirt lake bank of the Conyers farm, where the bird disappeared. Ahead a silver-green bass broke water, leaping into the air as if in pure joy. A.J. could not imagine living elsewhere—say, in the desert or a city—nowhere except on the water.

Soon the lake curved right and he rowed past Sis's Tavern. Then it bent left and right and continued south. He encountered no other boats despite it being a Saturday, but the serious fishermen would have been out at first light and back in before midday.

After a while he reached for a rusty coffee can under the boat seat and bailed out lake water that had seeped in and accumulated beneath the slats where his black high-top sneakers rested. Across the lake on his right lay a cow pasture with two heifers standing on a rise in the shade of a cottonwood. He wondered whether it was an Indian mound where they stood, like the ones behind Mitchell School.

Cahokians were the mound builders. He had read that their metropolis near Long Lake numbered 40,000 people by the year 1300 rivaling the populations of Paris and London then, though neither people knew the other existed. They disappeared before Europeans arrived yet left behind these testaments to their civilization, both here and across the river in St. Louis, once known as The Mound City. Most there had now been leveled. He thought of his father's grave somewhere in France and wondered if it were a small mound. He wiped wet hands on his jeans and again grasped the oars.

After a mile he let the rustic homemade vessel glide toward the west shore and dock at his mother's home. His home. His family's home once. He tethered the boat, crept up the lake bank, and peered over the top to find his mother's Buick sitting alone on the grassy gravel drive. Only then, figuring she too was alone, did he retreat and mount the stairs rising from the dock and boathouse.

Ever since A.J. had bloodied Wayne Thurman the previous year, he'd heard no more talk about his mother fucking other men. It didn't mean folks had suddenly stopped gossiping. But at least they knew to keep their mouths shut around A.J. None of their goddamn business. Maybe none of his business either. Nonetheless the thought of it and the images of it that he carried with him at all times saddened and sickened him and led him to keep to himself much as he could. He pretended like he was The Invisible Man. If he didn't talk to anyone it was like he wasn't there.

A.J. crossed the backyard. To his left near the sandbox where he used to play, the vegetable garden now yielded only a tangle of weeds. At the back door he knocked, pushed through it, and called, "It's me, Mom."

As usual library books piled everywhere—on the fireplace hearth, the coffee table, even the floor. The stacks were neat and the books dusted, which meant the cleaning lady had been in the day before. He found his mother at the kitchen table with a newspaper—the morning *St. Louis Globe-Democrat*—cigarette, and coffee cup, still in her pajamas and bathrobe. She held out her arms toward him.

"Come to your mother, my baby boy."

He went to her, embraced her, and pulled away from the scents of coffee, tobacco, and of whiskey, which seemed to seep from her pores. A.J. sat next to her across the corner of the oak table.

She took his hand. "How's my little fisherman this morning? Did you catch a nice sunfish?"

Even though he had turned twelve now and was nearly as tall as she, he was still a little boy to her. She lived in the past. Everything had stopped the day she learned his father had died, a day that A.J. recalled in vague images—the hot sun, family gathered on the lake shore to celebrate Independence Day, a man who came to the door. It was as if *her* life had ended that day too. A

Fourth of July without sparklers and fireworks.

He knew what his father looked like from photographs on his mother's dresser and in the family scrapbook, compiled before that day. A.J. wondered whether without the photos he could have pictured his father's face. Nothing like A.J.'s, who favored his mother, dark-haired and olive-skinned.

"Sure, Mom. The fish are biting today," he lied. "Thought I'd drop in to see how things were going."

He could plainly see. Dark circles under her eyes, chocolate hair matted and knotted. Gaunt, as if she were not eating; pasty, as if she never ventured outdoors in daylight.

"Fine, just fine. You doing well at school?"

He told her that his grades were good, that he had made some new friends this term, and that he was going to try out for the basketball team. All lies as well. What difference did it make? If he told her the truth about his insular life—his days as The Invisible Man—and the anger that surfaced with little warning, she might start crying, feeling guilty about abandoning him psychologically all these years. Though often she didn't need a reason to cry.

"How's your class, Mom?"

She reached for the Lucky Strike pack lying on the table and lit another cigarette with a gold lighter. Sometimes she inhaled deeply and other times just took a puff and blew it out, as if a ritual of some sort. Or maybe just creating a cloud of smoke to reassure herself of her existence, as if she was a lost soul walking the Earth without purpose.

"I'm not teaching this year, A.J. Changed my mind

last minute. I thought Helen might have told you. Felt I needed more rest. They gave me some more time off."

"You going back into the clinic?"

"No. I'm doing better everyday. Maybe you can come home again soon. Not just yet, but soon. Would you like that?"

"Yes, ma'am. I would," he again lied. As long as Dupuis or someone like him was hanging around, it hardly felt like home. It would lead to trouble. He knew he couldn't stop himself.

Oblivious to his further duplicity, she brushed back his hair, dark as hers though cropped short.

"You're what keeps me going, Son. The thought that we can be together again."

Why couldn't or wouldn't she keep going? He wasn't sure, but knew others worried about it. Last year when she was in real bad shape, when Aunt Helen and Uncle Raymond took him in, he overheard them talking about collecting his father's shotgun from her house.

"I love you, Mom," he said. As if that admission might help deter her from any such rash act.

Her eyes glistened. "Sure you do. You're my boy… How about I fix us some breakfast?"

He had had breakfast hours ago and just eaten lunch before taking the boat out. He nodded.

"Sure, Mom. That would be great."

A.J. watched her move about the kitchen—from the refrigerator to the range to the sink and back again—as if sleepwalking. She seemed to live every day not in the physical world around her but in the vacuum of his father's absence.

He remembered that after the first shock and grief she had been sort of okay. Then with time she got sadder and sadder as her solitude sunk in. Aunt Helen and Uncle Raymond and everyone else told her she should go back to her job teaching kids—to have purpose and something to fill her days. That lasted for a while.

By summertime, she started drinking wine during the day and crying. He didn't know what to do or who to tell. Then she started going out to taverns. Then she brought men home. He would hear them in the night. Sometimes he would sneak down to the lake and lie on the dock until the sun woke him.

He wished she didn't drink and go with men but tried not to judge her too much in that regard. Since he had not known his father well, he could not understand all that she had forgone with his death. A.J. couldn't know what it was like to lose the one person God had put on Earth for you.

All he knew for sure was that God had provided him a mother to love and care for him. He wished with all his heart that she would return to him from wherever she had gone and do what she was supposed to do.

# 8 | ASK FOR WHATEVER YOU WANT

St. Louis, Missouri, September 9, 1939

Jan Nowak surveyed the Ambassador Theatre: rococo proscenium with tall, gold-edged crimson curtains and red velvet seats that could accommodate three thousand patrons. Yet on this Saturday night, half the seats sat empty. Money was tight, prices high, and every sixth man still out of work. Going to the theatre was a luxury, but for those who could manage it, the movies provided a few hours of fantasy, a place where you could forget hard times and travel to gayer eras and venues. That's if you could scrape up two dimes for a ticket.

"I adore this place!" Hazel said. "Helen and Raymond brought me last year to see *The Adventures of Robin Hood*."

Jan turned to study her profile He snapped his fingers. "That's it! Whatshername."

"What are you talking about?"

"Maid Marian. That's who you look like."

"Olivia de Havilland? You can't be serious."

"Not exactly the same. Similar. Actually, you're better looking."

Frowning, she gazed at him askance as the lights dimmed. "Sounds like something Errol Flynn might have said."

Jan leaned toward her and whispered: "*I* always write my *own* lines."

Lowell Thomas narrated a MovieTone newsreel that showed Polish cavalry charging Russian panzers on horseback, causing Jan to shake his head. But he recognized the same hereditary propensity in himself, to risk everything on the wildest of hopes, with mindless bravado. Today's news on the radio hadn't been good either. The battle for Warsaw continued under a constant barrage of Luftwaffe bombs. God help them.

He felt Hazel's hand on his, sensed her eyes appraising him. Yes, he surely harbored a certain affinity for the Poles. His family, his neighbors, his friends—most all shared that heritage. Their lingo was his mother tongue. And there were those, like Bogdan, who embodied the mercurial, cynical, and romantic Polish soul, a man he understood without his speaking a word—English or Polish. But Poland was five thousand miles away, and what happened there didn't touch him. This was his home, where he belonged. Where his heart was.

The coming attractions followed, starting with *Gone With The Wind*.

"I have to see that," she murmured. "Loved the book."

The trailer cut from Clark Gable to Vivien Leigh to Olivia de Havilland. Jan lifted his chin toward the screen. "See? Your twin."

He savored her perfume as she leaned toward him. "That's the gin clouding your vision," she whispered while squeezing his hand. Her touch told him that her perceptions were blurring as well. Good. Few of us humans can stand much clear-eyed scrutiny.

§

They moved among the departing crowd down the curving marble staircase to the lobby with its glittering chandeliers, sconces, and gold-plated fixtures.

"I enjoyed that movie so much. Thank you, Jan."

"I've seen all three Thin Man movies. The characters remind me of guys I know. The heavy, Sheldon Leonard, sounded and shambled like Bogdan."

She wondered about his "guys"—bootleggers, hoodlums, street toughs—a far different milieu from a grade-school teacher's.

On the sidewalk warm night air—humid and fetid—greeted them. A southerly breeze carried a yeasty smell from the Anheuser-Busch Brewery, just a few blocks downriver, the aroma dominating the nearby Mississippi Valley atmosphere.

They strolled arm-in-arm up Washington Avenue, headed to his hotel for a nightcap. In the lobby when he turned toward the bar she put a hand on his suit coat sleeve.

"Can we have a drink upstairs, Jan? I'd love to see how you live."

"Pretty much like Nick Charles—room service martinis and such—but without the wife and dog."

The elevator operator, a slender redhead in a black uniform greeted him by name and carried them to the sixteenth floor. Down a carpeted hallway to its end, Jan keyed open the door and stepped aside to usher her into a softly lit sitting room with loveseat, wingchairs, cocktail table, desk, and chandelier. But she hardly noticed the elegant furnishings, instead moving to tall windows facing East where she gazed down on surrounding buildings and stared off in the distance toward the dark flowing river.

"What a view! Makes me dizzy. So beautiful. The city, the moonlight, the river…"

"'Distance lends enchantment to the view.'"

She turned to him. "Twain, right? Or maybe Thomas Campbell."

He shrugged. "Not sure… Whiskey okay?"

At a credenza where decanters sat Jan poured drinks. He carried one to her and they touched glasses. Jan drank and gestured toward the river with his bourbon.

"It's still pretty rough-and-tumble on the wharf, though nothing like it was back after the stock market crash. That's the site," he said pointing, "of the first Hooverville, as local people named it. By 1931 five thousand folks lived there. Largest in the country. Families with kids, old people, whites, and blacks, all mixed together in makeshift shacks.

"Some had nice clothes at first. That never lasted long with no running water or electricity. And no work. St. Louis got hit hard. A third of the men out of a job. Something was wrong yet no one knew how to fix it. People were hungry but farmers couldn't get their food to them."

The human suffering she'd heard about and witnessed since childhood contrasted vividly with his own surroundings—the elegant suite with maid service and room service, glistening crystal liquor decanters, and stunning vista. Hazel sipped her whisky. Smoother than she had expected.

## THE BOOTLEGGER'S BRIDE

"You seem to know a lot about Hooverville."

"A bit. Bogdan and I used to go talk to the people and hear their stories—lot of rags-to-riches-to-rags tales. Maybe take them a little food, spread some nickels among the kids. At Christmastime I'd carry over a few bottles for folks to share. None of it made a dent, of course. Though we weren't the only ones who brought something. Most everyone was living on handouts."

"A modern day Robin Hood."

He laughed. "You have an inflated opinion of me, Hazel. In those days it was hard to find someone rich to rob, if one was so inclined, since most everyone was suffering. Sure, you felt for the poor, but as usual I was looking out for number one, which was tough enough."

"Don't burst my balloon just yet."

"Truth is I was prospering, though modestly. But if things had gone differently, if I hadn't taken my shot"—he lifted his chin toward the wharf—"that could have been me in Hooverville. Seeing the down-and-out folks there gave me an incentive to keep pushing ahead. Fear of poverty and homelessness can either cripple a man or propel him forward. In some cases, it can make him take chances he wouldn't otherwise risk. And when fear is riding him hard, it can lead him to commit desperate acts."

Hazel saw him pull inside himself. Eyes unfocused, glimpsing something in the distant past, or maybe very close inside. After a moment he went on:

"My Polish forebears suffered much as well. Prussians pressing men into the army, Cossacks raiding villages, virtual slavery, real hunger; vicious regimes and indifferent aristocrats bleeding them. Desperation drove both my parents to take a chance. In my father's case, to cross the ocean penniless in hopes of finding work on blind faith. In my mother's case, venturing off to a strange land to marry a man twice her age whom she had never met. Though she may not have had much say in the matter.

"For all they suffered and whatever they dared, I thank them. As a result, here I am, their only living heir, happily ensconced in the land of opportunity without having to lift a finger to get here. To honor their courage and sacrifice I ought not squander my opportunity to make something of myself, the chance to be something other than a serf, a sheep, or someone's errand boy."

"You seem to have succeeded at that."

"I didn't have the advantages some enjoy but didn't suffer the high hurdles others face. Like everyone else I had to make the most of the cards I was dealt. And sometimes you have to take your best shot and bet it all."

"Even if you're just bluffing?"

He winked at her. "Especially then. If you see what you want and there's a chance for you to get it, you'd be a sucker not to make a grab for it."

Her dizziness seemed to intensify. She sat on the loveseat behind her, drank down her remaining whiskey, and looked up to Jan, who stood frowning at her.

"You okay? Whiskey go to your head?"

She closed her eyes and took a deep breath. Maybe the liquor was skewing her judgment—but what the hell! If she was going to be the odds-buster Jan had said she was and not just a cautious schoolteacher keeping within her own comfortable confines—that is, not just another sucker—she had to take *her* shot while she had the chance.

Hazel opened her eyes to find him still gazing at her.

"I think," she said, "this may be the time for me to be decisive and lay my cards on the table… Jan Nowak, I've decided you're the man for me."

"You've decided that all on your own?"

"Just me and the devil whispering in my ear."

"Well, that's a devilishly nice surprise."

"What's more, Mr. Nowak, I want to spend the night with you."

Jan studied her. *So much for the timid schoolmarm.* He spread his hands and shrugged. "Of course you're welcome. But what will your parents say?"

"Not sure about Dad. But I know what Mom will say—'What took you so long?'"

Jan laughed. "My fault really. My poker instincts told me to slow-play this hand."

She bit her bottom lip. "Slow is good sometimes."

She slid her hem up over her knees and beyond the top of her silk stockings where he could glimpse her thighs and garters. He held his breath, gazing at her transfixed. She felt her heart thumping in her chest as she saw him stiffening inside his trousers. She reached up to graze her fingertips there.

"Do whatever you'd like," she breathed. "Ask for whatever you want."

# 9 | THE KILLING OF LEO GOLD

St. Louis, Missouri, July 26, 1929

Jan Nowak was glad to be working in Leo Gold's cool North Side cellar that Monday morning boxing up orders for afternoon deliveries and not in the hot, airless warehouse on the wharf. Not yet noon and the metal thermometer nailed to the outhouse on the alley already read ninety-two.

Humid, windless air hung over the city like a warm invisible fog. It always did summers in St. Louis, sitting at the bottom of the Mississippi Valley. The muddy, earthy-smelling river swirled and surged downstream just a few blocks east of where Jan now stood. Downtown streets didn't smell so good either—a mix of outhouse, horse dung, rotting garbage, and distinctive St. Louis sewer gas. The last rose from storm drains with a sour, fecund, and moldy scent reminiscent of wet newspaper. When it's all you know you get used to it.

His pal Stosh lived in the shadow of the Krey Meat Packing Plant on North Florissant Boulevard, yet the slaughterhouse stench never bothered Stosh. Jan wondered what it might be like to live somewhere beautiful and sweet smelling, though he wasn't sure where that might be. Though the books and poems he had read gave him hints. Maybe Thoreau's Walden Pond or the Birks of Aberfeldy that Bobby Burns sang of.

Ever since his father learned of his son's bootlegging and physically chucked him out, Jan had been sleeping on an army-surplus cot in Leo Gold's dank, mousy cellar in his home on Mullanphy Street, with its coal dust and rat droppings and scent of decay leaching from the antebellum construction. Earlier that morning he had climbed the stone steps from the cellar to the redbrick backyard and hiked over to Tyler Street to fetch the Golden Bakery truck from Leo's brother. Then he had parked the truck in the alley, where soon he would load the deliveries.

Blocks of Poles here, a cluster of Jews there. Along with Germans, Irish, Italians, Czechs, Hungarians, and other immigrants and their heirs dotting the Near North Side, with the Negroes over in Mill Creek Valley. Everyone mixed (in varying degrees) and got along (more or less). They were all in the same boat, just trying to keep afloat and figure how to navigate the new land, its institutions, and a society where they were not always welcome. Yet no matter how tough it was at times—the work hard and tenuous, the rewards meager and erratic, the legal and extra-legal hurdles erected by the Anglo-French ruling class both socially and economically inhibiting— everyone knew it was even tougher back where they came from. Here at least you ate. Here you had hope.

Though these days things were booming and most everyone was thriving—at least by Central European standards. For the people he dealt with in the neighborhood the future looked rosy. If nothing else at least here you didn't have some aristocrat's boot on your neck or up your ass—so said the working-class customers in the speakeasies Jan serviced.

While he spent his nights and mornings in the dingy cellar amidst the coal dust and rodents, he passed afternoons and evenings delivering liquor with the truck and talking up his Polish customers. Most knew his father, Joseph Nowak, or knew of him. The elder Nowak served as spokesman for Polish steelworkers at the plant across the river in Granite City, Illinois. He had been best man at some thirty weddings held at St. Stanislaus Kostka Polish Catholic Church on North 20th Street. Though now sixty-years-old he still bore the strength of a young man—a fact to which Jan could attest thanks to recent hard personal experience. Yet Jan didn't mind spending so much time in the dreary basement of the hundred-year-old home despite its lack of household amenities and its dingy atmosphere. Here he was his *own* man, without his father's boot on *his* neck.

In the dim cellar he now read the order from Zofia Dudek, who ran a small speakeasy in the kitchen of her Hadley Street flat where you entered off the alley. She had penciled "four loaves of rye, eight loaves of white"—the former meaning four bottles of rye whiskey, the latter gin. She wasn't the only customer who had fun with the fact that their booze got delivered via a Chevrolet bakery truck. Bourbon was often "cornbread," vodka "potato bread," applejack "apple pie," and so forth. However, there was no need for subterfuge. Leo took care of the coppers, and half the neighborhood was making homebrew, bathtub gin, or plum wine. If nothing else, Prohibition brought out a can-do spirit in his neighbors along with their lurking disrespect for authority.

When he had all the orders boxed, Jan pulled on a canvas apron to protect his beige gabardine slacks, silk tie, and white dress shirt, sleeves rolled past his elbows. Up and down the short flight of stone steps by the cold furnace and coal chute, a dozen trips, taking his time. Still, as he hefted the final box and moved from the cellar into the hot day, his shirt stuck to his back and perspiration ran beneath his collar.

He decided that later he'd stroll to the Polish Falcon Nest on St. Louis Avenue, do some work on the rings, pommel horse, and high bar, then shower and shave—though the later hardly necessary or noticeable on the blonde sixteen-year-old. Yet he was a man doing a man's work, striving to make something of himself and rise, to transcend the working-class script that had been written for him. It paid to look the part he wanted to play.

Jan loaded on the final order, padlocked the truck's back doors, and lifted the apron off over his head. As he turned to retreat to the cellar for his suit coat he heard tires squealing on the street out front followed by a gunshot. It echoed off the dark bricks of the row houses, streets, and sidewalks of the quiet neighborhood. Then more tire squealing and a child screaming.

He sprinted across the brick backyard and down the narrow, shaded brick walkway between the tall row houses. Jan burst out onto Mullanphy Street where he froze at the curb. The eight-year-old neighbor boy was being pulled up their white marble stoop by his aproned mother, both gazing over their shoulders at Leo Gold. In white shirt, gray wool-worsted slacks, and oxblood oxfords, he lay face down on the herringboned brick sidewalk where a pool of blood spread bright red around his head like a ghastly aura, glowing magenta where sunlight penetrated the maple trees lining the street. Jan could see Gold's right eye staring at the bricks, like it was made of glass. He felt his stomach rise and his breath catch in his chest.

His gaze was drawn up from Gold's figure by Police Officer Oscar Pohlman turning the corner, running from North 13th Street. He stopped and stood over the body, nightstick grasped in both hands.

"Oh, my God. Leo Gold… You see who did it, Jan?"

He shook his head, ears ringing, heart racing. "No. I was out back loading the truck. Though I think the boy did… Leo liked to sit out on the stoop after lunch."

"I know. So did everyone…" He turned to Jan. "I'll go down to the corner to call this in," he rasped, breathing hard. "You better get the truck out of here just to be on the safe side. The place will be lousy with coppers and maybe even Feds, given Gold's livelihood. Come find me later, and I'll fill you in on what gives."

Jan again looked down at Leo Gold. He had not seen a dead man before except in a coffin. While the blood pooling on the bricks made his stomach swim, he felt nothing for Leo Gold. He knew he should feel something for the end of a human life, God's greatest gift. Yet all he could think about was what this meant for him, Jan Nowak. This would change things for him. But as of yet he had no idea how much.

# 10 | HOME ON THE LAKE

Madison County, Illinois, December 6, 1941

At the back door of her sister's home on Long Lake, Hazel took Alexander Jan—A.J. for short—wrapped in a chamois baby blanket, from Helen, who kissed them both. Hazel turned and stepped outside into the frigid dusk, Helen and Raymond following arm-in-arm. From the lake bank came the *chip-chip-chip* of a cardinal along with dank air rising from the fragrant lake as the temperature dropped. Though just after four p.m. the drive home to their St. Louis park-side apartment would be dark.

Jan rose from the Buick idling in the driveway to shake hands with Raymond. Helen kissed Jan's cheek as well.

"Don't stay away so long—and I don't mean just duck hunting with Raymond. I want to see my nephew again before he gets too big to hold."

"You'll be seeing more of us. Promise."

The car had warmed. Hazel cradled A.J. in her arms, his bonneted head resting on her overcoat collar. Jan moved the coupe down the drive, gravel crunching beneath its tires, headlights illuminating the denuded white trunks of sycamores to either side. He turned south onto the black-tar lake road.

Hazel had always found evenings rather melancholy as the days drew shorter and colder. She wasn't sure why. A feeling of things winding down, like a slowing clock. The weight of routine and stagnation. A sense of confinement. Though now, thanks to Jan and A.J., her former nighttime dread had vanished. Her life had turned on a dime—marriage, homemaking, motherhood. And time to read. Still, it seemed otherworldly and tenuous, as if it might disappear overnight and with it the sublime happiness and deep sense of well-being that now enfolded her night and day.

Soon they passed Sis's Tavern on the left and the Mobil Oil storage tanks on the right. But instead of turning west onto Morrison Road to head to Granite City and the McKinley Bridge that would carry them over the Mississippi to St. Louis, Jan turned left to continue following the twisting lake. Hazel looked at her husband, his gaunt face amber in the cream-colored light of dashboard gauges.

"Thought we'd take a sentimental journey," he said. "Maybe even stop and kiss like we did on our first drive along here."

She smiled. "You're such a romantic."

"Can't help it. I'm Polish."

"Don't apologize. It's a good thing."

He pursed his lips. "Sometimes. Sometimes not. Like when it compels you to charge German tanks on horseback."

She shook her head. "That war… I wish it would just go away."

"It won't until we do something about it. Yesterday the Brits declared war on Romania, Finland, and Hungary.

The Aussies are jumping in against the Japs, who have ramped up the anti-American rhetoric. It grows worse day by day. Who knows what tomorrow may bring. I have family there—cousins and such—though I don't know them. Still, you feel a connection."

Hazel nodded, though it was hard for her to imagine the emotions of families torn apart by war.

Before they got to Pontoon Beach he braked and turned onto a narrow tree-lined drive heading toward the lake.

"Where are you going, Jan? This is someone's house."

On the left the Buick's headlamps illuminated a carved cedar sign hanging from a wooden post and reading "Lazy Lane." He stopped the car beside a darkened home on the lake, a white clapboard ranch style house with forest green shutters and large stone fireplace chimney. The back of the home consisted of tall windows facing the water.

She turned to him. "Who lives here, Jan?"

"Nobody right now. Come take a look."

He opened her car door and took the infant from her. She followed him to the home's back door, which he opened with a key on his ring. Inside he turned on a green-shaded lamp on an end table. The white stone fireplace sat cold at the south end of the long den, furnished with cushioned bamboo sofa and chairs. Shelved books covered the knotty-pine wall ahead. To the right sat a white baby-grand piano positioned diagonally.

"Come see the rest."

In the kitchen he flipped a wall switch that lit a stained-glass lamp hanging over an oak table. He went to a thermostat on the wall and pressed a switch. "Central heat."

"What's this about, Jan? Who owns this?"

He turned away and gestured down the adjoining hallway. "Three bedrooms, two baths. Completely furnished." He opened the cabinets above the kitchen counter. "Even dishes and silverware."

She studied him. In his dark overcoat and black wool turtleneck he looked like a spy in a Hollywood thriller—except for the baby in his arms. Mysterious as always. At times super secretive. Like now. As much as she loved him, she sensed depths she would never plumb—and wasn't sure she wanted to. She approached and took A.J. from him.

"Jan, tell me what we're doing here."

He looked at her and let out a breath. "I've lived my whole life in the city. Redbrick flats with brick sidewalks and brick streets in front, brick alleys in back. Pre-Civil-War neighborhoods smelling of dung, decay, and factory smoke…" He reached across to brush his son's pink face with his knuckles. "No place for a kid to dig in the earth. No lake to swim in, no fish to catch, no fields to run in. No rabbits to chase and no birds except pigeons."

She felt lightheaded, ears humming. "Who owns this place?"

He whistled. "Well, we do if you want it."

"You're serious?"

He lowered his chin. "Dead serious."

"Can we afford it?"

He tilted his head from side to side as if deciding what to say then bit his lip.

"Already paid for. I got a good deal from a Cass Avenue friend who used it as a weekend getaway. He owed me money and needed some fast cash... If you don't like the joint I can always turn a profit."

She blew out a breath not knowing what to say and followed him down the hallway to a living room furnished in an art deco style that Nick and Nora Charles would have liked. He took A.J. from her again and lowered him onto the off-white carpet. The child began to crawl about, exploring.

Jan turned to her. "So what do you think?"

She stood shaking her head, not signaling "no" but disbelief. What a curious man she had married. She moved to him, laid a hand on his chest.

"It's wonderful, Jan. Still, I worry."

"About what?"

"The future. Money. Security."

"Everything's fine. I told you."

"You never show me."

He nodded and took a deep breath. "Sorry. You're right. Here's the whole story, Hazel... Sit and I'll explain."

She sat beside him on a curving turquoise sofa that could have come from FDR's yacht.

"Never been a husband before and didn't have a good role model at home, where my father imitated von Hindenburg. Always been my own boss since I was a teen and secretive thanks to the nature of my work.

"A lot of my assets—our assets—are markers I'm holding. Money that people owe me. It's the same for all banks. They loan money at interest and mark it up on the plus side of the ledger. I also have a cash reserve that can carry us forward for some time. Which is to say you have nothing to worry about. Trust me.

"But since you asked, I also want to show you. Next week we'll take a drive over to Cass Avenue Bank & Trust where you can rifle through stacks of sawbucks and c-notes in my safe-deposit box, just so you know we're not going to starve anytime soon."

She laughed and caressed his face. "All this talk of money puts me in an amorous mood."

"Hm. Always thought it was my animal magnetism."

"That too… I think it's time we kissed again."

"Past time."

He leaned toward her and pressed his lips to hers, inhaling the scent that made him mad for her. Then he straightened.

"Have I shown you the master bedroom?"

"Love to see it!"

Leaving A.J. to reconnoiter the living room on his own they moved to the boudoir. There on the bed they tore at each other's clothes as Jan figured what to do about the money. He'd simply get a second safe-deposit box and put a few gees in it for her to ogle instead of the whole lot. That should do it. Then she wouldn't worry about penury nor get too curious about how he had managed to stash away a king's ransom in circulated greenbacks so early in life.

With that issue resolved to his satisfaction, he gave her his full attention.

# 11 | SECRETS UNTOLD

Madison County, Illinois, January 10, 1942

When the song ended and The Blue Note customers applauded the band, Raymond Lomax raised his beer glass toward Hazel and Jan.

"Happy anniversary, Mr. and Mrs. Nowak!"

"Happy anniversary!" echoed his wife, Helen.

Jan lifted his highball from the café table, leaned to his left, and kissed his wife. "The fastest two years of my life. And the best."

He said it with conviction. His journey had always boasted intrigue, drama, great pleasures, fortifying camaraderie, and fantastical elements. But this was the most surprising and gratifying turn, one he never could have predicted. His life had somehow morphed from a gangster movie into a fairy tale.

Gazing at Jan, Hazel nodded. "True enough. But the best is yet to come." She noticed her sister staring at her. Helen reached across to touch her earlobe.

"Are these new?"

Hazel crooned:

*"On our second anniversary,*
*My true love gave to me,*
*Two pearl earrings…"*

Raymond shook his head. "Lovely gift, Jan, but you've set a costly precedent. Next year she'll be expecting three rubies, then four sapphires, et cetera, et cetera."

Jan spread his hands. "Now you tell me? Thanks a million. I'll be bankrupt by our fifth."

The five-piece combo—piano, drums, two horns, and clarinet—began a slow number, "Moonlight Serenade," and couples moved to the dance floor. Jan reached out his hand to Hazel.

She pressed herself to him as they glided to the music, breathing in the musky scent of his skin that mingled with his citrus aftershave, bourbon, and tobacco. She felt so safe in his manly arms, all sinew and muscle, enveloping her as if no harm could ever reach her. He still carried the physique of the young gymnast in photos taken when he competed for the North St. Louis Polish Falcons. A body she had come to crave in a way she never dreamed.

The visceral sexual attraction had been apparent and compelling for them both from the start. Yet over time their bond had grown far beyond the physical aesthetics and chemistry that first drove them together. Jan shared her love of books and film as well as a curiosity about the world and nature. As she deepened his appreciation of English literature he expanded hers for fine food and drink. Most of all their shared dreamy natures gave birth to a contemplative and deliberate rhythm that shaped and seasoned each day.

They spent winter evenings together on the couch before the fireplace in each other's arms silently reading—when A.J. allowed them—or listening to Jack Benny, Fred Allen, and Lux Radio Theater. Sometimes she read him poetry or played the piano. Jan taught her how to win at poker and make pierogi. They danced to big band music on the radio and ice-skated hand-in-hand on the lake. She led him to Shakespeare plays in St. Louis whenever possible. They went to the movies sometimes twice a week—Helen and her mother always eager to babysit A.J.

In summer, they passed hours at the lake. Jan showed her how to cast a fly and row the boat. Together they learned how to plant and nurture a vegetable garden. To her mind their life together seemed like a present-day Eden. God had sent her a soul mate, the one man for whom she was destined. And no serpent in sight.

As they moved to the music Hazel took in her surroundings. Dimly lit by small spotlights shining from a dark ceiling, The Blue Note, all navy and silver, resembled transatlantic steamship ballrooms as depicted by Hollywood. The décor, the music, and the two gin rickeys she'd drunk transported her.

"A nice nightclub," she said over the music. "Pretty classy for Long Lake. You been here before?"

Jan, too, seemed far away for a moment. Then he came back.

"Raymond brought me one Saturday afternoon for a beer and a bump after duck hunting. Nobody here then except us and the bartender. Nothing like tonight."

"Glad they planned this evening for us. So were Mom and Dad, so they could keep A.J. for the night."

"You didn't tell them he wakes up crying every hour?"

She smiled. "Not true! Though I suspect they've forgotten what it's like to have a one-year-old on their hands overnight."

Enveloped in the otherworldly atmosphere of the club Hazel imagined herself and Jan dancing on an ocean liner traveling to Europe and seeing the world. Someday. When the war was over. When the U-boats disappeared.

"Dear, that tall man standing at the end of the bar—I guess he's the manager. He keeps staring at me and frowning."

Without looking in that direction Jan replied: "He's staring at me."

"Why's he doing that?"

"Trying to remember where he knows me from."

"Who is he?"

"Richard Dupuis. We did some business years ago."

They danced to "Moonglow." Hazel pictured them moving arm-in-arm on their tenth anniversary and their twentieth and thirtieth. What adventures did Fate have in store for them? Only time would tell.

When the band began "Pennsylvania Six-Five-Thousand" they returned to their table. The two women soon excused themselves. Raymond ordered another round from the waitress.

"Did you see, Jan, that they raised the draft age to forty-four? I hear they'll start taking married men sooner or later, though not fathers."

"I'm not so sure. But I'm likely safe long as I stay sober. After Pearl Harbor, when Germany jumped in on the Japs' side, Bogdan and I went to a Cass Avenue bar to mull over the world situation. A half-dozen boilermakers later we decided to enlist in the Navy and liberate Europe and Poland—along with five other Poles we were buying drinks for.

"Next day when I told Hazel our plan she started crying. Begged me not to leave her and A.J. So, I finally relented and admitted I might not have been thinking straight the night before."

"A valid defense. Temporary insanity. Nothing you do when drunk should be held against you."

"Hard sometimes to remember I'm a married man."

"Always comes on after a few drinks, don't it?"

The waitress, a young blonde in a slinky, blue, off-the-shoulder cocktail dress that matched the décor, brought their drinks. Both men studied her retreat.

"Guys at the mill are talking about enlisting. They'll need some new people, Jan. Might be able to get you on if things change for you. Then you wouldn't have to go."

Jan pretended to think about it for a moment. "Thanks, Ray. I know it's good, honest work. Just not for me. I'd rather take my chances."

Raymond appraised Jan. After a moment he said, "I understand."

Jan nodded his thanks. Likely he did understand, at least in part. Going into the steel mill as his father had once urged him, belatedly succumbing to his wishes not to get beyond himself, would be a humiliating admission of failure on his part in the old man's eyes. Who would surely rub his face in it whenever he could, if they were ever to meet again. What Raymond didn't understand, however, was that Jan wasn't about to break his back for a few lousy bucks and a legal dodge. He'd handle it in his own way. He had connections.

"Don't mention your offer to Hazel if you can help it. She wouldn't get it. Let's hope I won't need a deferment."

Lomax nodded. "Lips sealed. Nothing to Helen, either. Just an idea."

The two Robinson sisters returned as the band broke into a swing number, "Tuxedo Junction," a Glenn Miller tune—or was it Benny Goodman, Hazel wondered.

She linked her arm in Jan's as she sat. "This music puts me in a gay mood. Or maybe it's the gin. Then it might just be my spouse of two years."

"Or maybe all three in a happy conspiracy… Same here."

Though in fact Jan felt less reassured by the jazzy music and the celebration. A wife, a child, and a war. Where would it all lead? He didn't control the future. Not his family's and not even his own. It bothered the hell out of him. Ever since his father threw him out at fifteen like so much trash, he'd been his own man. Called his own shots, for better or worse. Beholden to no one. Now he felt his independence slipping from his grasp, along with his own family's sovereignty, thanks to events far beyond his control. Other entities—the government, society, the economy, foreign dictators—were now setting the odds and laying bets that would determine his future and millions like him.

For the first time as an adult, he felt powerless. Either go to work for U.S. Steel and become a sheep or go into the U.S. Army and become ground lamb. Some choice. He prayed it wouldn't come to that.

§

Hazel lit candles on the dresser and strode to Jan the way he liked it—nylons, garter belt, and nothing more, as on their first night together. One crying baby deleted, a few drinks added, and it felt for her as it had at the start, fated and frantic. All of nature and God (and perhaps the Devil) conspiring to bring them together to advance the species, as if on a sacred mission. And perhaps they were, if one was inclined to believe in God and Fate as she did. Though Jan did not.

His scent made her crazy. And the taste of him. Maybe that's all it was, mere chemistry and aesthetic preference. But that didn't mean God didn't have a hand in it. With Jan she had come to understand what D.H. Lawrence had written about in *Lady Chatterley's Lover*. Hazel's English professor had once loaned her an unexpurgated copy of the banned novel in a clumsy attempt at seduction. While the graphic depictions of sex stirred her, she could not grasp the deep connection between Constance and Mellors on a primordial physical level, as woman and man. Now she did.

She stopped thinking about it all and tumbled into a sensual paradise—stepped outside herself and fell deeper into herself, morphing into a voracious creature that earlier she hadn't known existed. Demanding and submissive, rough and tender, debauched and divine. The essence of existence rippling through her as she felt their orgasms pulsing in unison within her, trembling with the unequalled pleasure of it.

She lay motionless as if semi-comatose in the arms of this enigmatic creature with whom she had merged, waiting for him to fall asleep and then follow him there. But when she glanced to Jan in the dying candlelight she saw him staring at the ceiling.

"Can't you sleep?"

"I will in a minute. Just savoring the moment."

But she sensed there was something on his mind.

"Everything okay?... Was it that bar manager who was staring at you? What's his name?"

"Dupuis. Most likely the owner... No, I'd forgotten about him."

"He stopped staring after awhile."

"I think he figured it out, where he knew me from."

"Yet didn't come over to say hello."

Jan smiled. "Maybe unsure what sort of greeting he'd get."

"Some tension between you?"

"He was working for people trying to muscle into our business in the neighborhood. He could have been the one who had my boss Leo Gold shot."

She gazed at the man to whom she was wed body and soul, wondering whether she knew him at all.

"You're serious? He killed your business partner?"

"Likely. Though it didn't help them. Leo had loyal customers, loyalty that I inherited and benefitted by. So, you might say Dupuis did me a favor."

# 12 | ANOTHER BODY SURFACES

Madison County, Illinois, February 12, 1963

Detective Kenneth LaRose moved his Madison County Sheriff's Department Ford police cruiser up and over the single pair of railroad tracks that intersected Morrison Road, past the greenish oil tanks, and along the lake road. A dim sun rose halfway up a gray sky to his right.

A half-hour earlier Sheriff Fraundorf himself had called him at home. A body had been found in Tank Town. LaRose's homicide expertise was needed "posthaste." He had arranged a day off for the school holiday—Lincoln's birthday—to take Ann and the kids to the Washington Theater in Granite City to see *The Music Man*.

"You all go ahead without me if I'm not back in time," he told her as he buttoned on his blue tunic.

She understood his having to work. Not every day a "prominent businessman" (Sheriff Fraundorf's description, not LaRose's) bobs up through the Long Lake ice.

He parked his black-and-white next to a row of some twenty tin mailboxes at the edge of a vacant lot facing the lake—Township property, he recalled. A similar car sat ahead by the roadside ditch, along with a red and white ambulance.

LaRose trudged across the lot dotted with waist-high brown weeds toward the lake, boots crunching through melting ice. Good to get out and move around. He was disciplined about staying in shape and could still fit into his Marine dress uniform a decade after demobilization. And still wore his blond hair in a military cut. But he was far happier and safer tromping through local ice fields than those of South Korea.

He paused at the top of the steep bank and looked down to the lakeshore. There, a brown canvas tarp covered a body. Two patrolmen—Bean, stocky, graying, and headed for retirement; and Shands, a dark-complexioned rookie—stood smoking cigarettes with the ambulance driver (he'd forgotten his name) at the water's edge, where a rowboat sat surrounded by sheets of cracked ice. The pungent, muddy scent of the lake rose to him.

It had turned bitter cold after New Year's and remained so until Groundhog Day. In the past week temperatures had climbed toward fifty, though it likely wouldn't get near that today.

LaRose made his way down the lake bank sideways, boots sliding in the loose dirt. He shook hands with the three men.

"Where's the doc?"

"On his way."

LaRose gestured toward the covered corpse. "Let's take a look." Shands bent to lift the tarp aside. LaRose nodded.

"Yep, right you are, Bean. Richard Dupuis."

Shands asked who he was.

"A thug that used to run with the Sheltons and Buster Wortman. Not a great résumé enhancer, that," said LaRose. "Former East St. Louis bootlegger and pimp. Still owns The Blue Note up the road. Or did."

"Think it was a gang hit?"

"Seems possible given his past."

"Who'd want him dead?"

"Present company excluded? Slick Dick was in the booze and broads business for decades. Bound to have made an enemy or two." Or a friend or two. Which made LaRose reflect on Sheriff Fraundorf's seeming eagerness about expediting the investigation.

He squatted next to the corpse. Black wool topcoat and sport coat, charcoal slacks, white shirt and red silk tie, cordovan wingtips—all now sodden, muddied, and ruined. Gold watch and diamond pinky ring in place. A couple broken fingernails and abrasions on his fingers and palms. Sand and lakeshore debris in his hair and mustache.

"No wallet?"

Bean shook his head. "Could be snatched or on the lake bottom."

Shands asked, "How long you figure he was in there, detective?"

"Maybe days, maybe weeks. Had only one other frozen corpse pulled from the lake and that was years ago. Doc Birkemeyer will know better... No signs of trauma other than the hands?"

"Check out his neck," said Bean.

LaRose pulled a ballpoint from his tunic, leaned closer, and used the pen to peel back the corpse's shirt collar. A thin red line cut deep into the throat.

The detective pursed his lips. His mind drifted back to 1950 and Parris Island Marine boot camp before he got shuffled off to Seoul. It had been a blistering hot and humid South Carolina afternoon when he learned how to fashion an effective garrote out of a length of wire and two sticks, and got to practice applying it to fellow grunts.

He rose and stared down at Dupuis. "Who found him?"

"Couple neighborhood kids off school today," said Bean. "You wanna talk to them? They live next door." He tilted his head over his right shoulder, toward a graying shingle home set back from the lake bank. A roadhouse in the old days, LaRose recalled.

He let out a breath whose cloud hung in the still winter air. "Yeah, after the doc comes and goes."

He would pursue this case with exacting due diligence, as homicide was rare in Madison County. And as Fraundorf had already suggested. Canvassing the neighborhood. Backtracking on Dupuis's movements from when he was last seen. Interviewing The Blue Note employees and customers and the deceased's known associates. Compiling a file with all the physical evidence. Dotting the I's and crossing the T's to see that justice would be done. But he sensed it already had.

# 13 | DOING BUSINESS ON THE SABBATH

St. Louis, Missouri, July 21, 1929

After Polish Mass at St. Stanislaus Kostka Catholic Church Jan Nowak jumped on the number 104 streetcar that ran down the middle of North Florissant Avenue toward downtown.

Just past noon and already sweltering. He stood on the platform by the back door, white straw boater shielding his face from the sun, seersucker sport coat folded over his arm. Humid air blew through the opened windows providing some relief. Yet the Sunday atmosphere always hung cleaner and clearer. No factory smoke. No one going to work, no trucks making deliveries. No stores open.

A day of rest, the Sabbath, when most everyone just stayed put.

At 12th Street the 104 deadheaded in the station beneath the *Post-Dispatch* Building. It felt better underground. Cool, damp air rose from limestone caves that undermined the city and now carried rail traffic. Before Prohibition, the caves had enabled St. Louis breweries to thrive, cooling and storing their beer and housing beer halls that remained comfortable whether it was baking or freezing on the streets above.

He climbed concrete stairs to street level, strolled south down 12th Street to Washington Boulevard, and headed east toward the Mississippi. Here at least there was shade. Tall brown-brick buildings lined the street: warehouses, hat factories, and shoe factories; then, as he moved closer to the river, department stores, office buildings, and hotels, though with few people on the streets today.

The local economy was roaring, the city growing. Some people making fortunes. He passed the twenty-story Statler Hotel as a well-dressed woman with shapely legs and silk stockings rose from the passenger seat of a yellow Packard Roadster at the curb, a bellhop holding open the car door. She glanced up at Jan as he sauntered past. He touched the brim of his boater and smiled. She smiled back. Now that's a woman. The sort of people who live here and not in dark cellars. Maybe someday…

At Broadway he cut over a block to Lucas Street, which soon dipped downhill toward the wharf and river.

Though just blocks from the elegant Statler, the riverfront was worlds away aesthetically—crumbling century-old warehouses and vacant tenements along with dingy whorehouses and speakeasies that catered to boatmen and bargemen. The air smelled of the muddy river, raw sewage, East St. Louis refineries, and coal dust.

In cold months the air there hung dark and smoky even at midday thanks to the soft coal burned to run factories, heat homes and businesses, and move riverboats. Someday—if he ever had the chance—he'd get as far away from the squalor of the wharf (where he often toiled at Leo Gold's warehouse) as Lady Luck would carry him. Though sometimes you had to make your own luck.

He looked up and to his right as a streetcar crossed from Illinois atop the Eads Bridge. On the bridge's lower deck a steam locomotive rambled east over the Mississippi, taking boxcars of shoes, garments, furs, electrical parts, paper, chemicals, meats, and more to market. It was a good time to be a retailer. Particularly when your popular consumable product-line could not legally be sold by department stores, grocery stores, restaurants, or bottle shops.

He found the address he was looking for just a block from the Mississippi, where another freight train lumbered north on a trestle that paralleled the river. He knocked at a warehouse door and waited. A gleaming black Chevrolet sedan with an Illinois license plate sat at the curb on the steep cobbled street.

After a minute the door slid open. A tall man twenty-five or thirty years old with wavy black hair and trimmed mustache, wearing a starched striped shirt and green silk tie with gold stickpin, squinted into the sunshine, studying Jan. Heavy-jawed and broad shouldered, he reeked of cologne. Likely fashioned himself a ladies' man. He motioned Jan inside with a head tilt and closed the door behind him. They reached out and shook hands.

"Jan Nowak."

"Richard Dupuis... Beer?"

"That would hit the spot."

He led Jan to the back of the vast, high-ceiled room, dimly lit by green-shaded electric lamps hanging from the ceiling. The warehouse smelled of wood—wooden ceiling beams, wooden crates stacked along the walls and lined in rows on the gray wooden floor. Behind a wall of crates sat a makeshift wooden bar.

"Have a seat."

Jan lowered himself onto a barstool as Dupuis moved behind the bar and pulled out two sweating brown bottles from a tin basin. He pried them open. The two men clinked the bottles together.

"You're younger than I expected. Buster says your boss Leo Gold is okay. Good to do business with."

"He's a good businessman."

"So, what's your problem?"

Jan swallowed. "Leo Gold."

Dupuis laughed. "Well, it's a dog-eat-dog world. If you don't mind my asking, what's your beef with him?"

Jan shrugged with one shoulder. "Nothing really. Not yet. I think he wants to get funny with me."

Dupuis studied Jan then finally nodded. "Okay. I understand. What's it worth to you?"

"Two-fifty."

"Let's say five hundred."

"For five minutes work? Some guys don't make that much in five months. This will be easy. He sits out on his stoop every day after lunch taking the fresh air. Such as it is in North St. Louis."

"You're not paying for my time, junior, but for my expertise, risk, and discretion."

Jan drank from his tepid beer, set it on the bar, and pursed his lips. "Okay. Three-twenty-five."

"Four. Up front."

Jan pulled a face, tilted his head from side to side as though considering whether he could afford it. He sighed and shrugged, defeated. From the six hundred dollars he had spread throughout his pockets that morning he collected forty sawbucks and handed them across to Dupuis, pleased to take the remainder back to his room in Leo Gold's cellar.

The men again shook hands. That's how you did business, with a handshake. Particularly in this kind of select business, where nothing gets written down and welching or double-crossing could cost you your reputation and likely lots more.

Jan climbed back up Lucas Street with the sun beating down on his straw boater and the stench of horse dung rising from the hot cobblestones. Yes, he had prevaricated a bit with Dupuis and was not as forthcoming about his situation as he could have been. That's the way you do business, keeping certain cards close to your vest.

His only outright lie was when he said that Leo Gold was a good businessman. What kind of businessman would allow himself to lose everything?

# 14 | FATHER MAREK BLESSES JAN AND THE WAR

Madison County, Illinois, December 18, 1943

The two men clad in canvas hunting jackets and carrying shotguns marched across the morning field of short beige and gray weeds, greased boots scrunching through the snow. A dull sun hung low behind a leaden blanket of clouds. The still air smelled good and clean to Raymond Lomax and stung his face. His bare hand carrying the gun ached from the cold and his legs numbed by it. But he hardly noticed. In fact, he gave nothing any thought, simply reveling in the moment, in the fundamental pleasure of being alive and doing what men had done for eons.

Jan Nowak stopped to tap a Lucky Strike from its pack and flicked open his Zippo to light it, his 12-gauge break-action Browning hanging in the crook of his arm. Though Raymond never got the cigarette habit he had always liked the smell of burning tobacco when out in the field or on the lake with his father. It was a comforting, manly aroma that accented the moment in a reassuring way.

Jan gazed down to the snowy ground. "Tracks everywhere around here. Must be a bunch of them nearby."

Raymond pursed his lips. "One rabbit can make a lot of tracks."

Jan smiled. "There's my epitaph."

After a silent minute—not a breath of wind to rasp the weeds, Jan staring out over the field as if searching for an answer to a tacit question—Raymond said:

"You heard anything?"

Jan nodded. "I report after Christmas."

"Hell."

"Yes it is."

"How's Hazel taking it?"

"Scared. Angry. Resigned… Me too."

"Not right taking married men away from their wives and children."

"Whoever, wherever, none of it's right. The war, the Axis, the Allies. Whole thing's a con. The bastards pulling the strings in Tokyo, Berlin, London, and Washington have peddled it, and the men in the mud have to pay for it. They try to make it sound like a turkey shoot or rabbit hunt. Difference is rabbits don't shoot back."

"It's a snow job alright. What's any of it to do with us, Jan? I can't see kamikazes dive bombing Granite City or panzers clanking down the lake road. Some diplomat sends a note that insults another diplomat and the next thing we got young men gunned down on beaches, trapped in sinking ships, and charging into machine-gun fire. Why can't they just leave us the fuck alone to live our lives?"

Jan nodded. "Another good epitaph: 'Just leave me the fuck alone.'"

"Bottom line is we don't need them; they need us."

"True enough… When I was a kid, the things that mattered were within reach and under our influence. The Church, the school, the beat cop, the committeeman.

People had a say in things… And what freedom we enjoyed. Running the streets sunup to sundown. Playing bottle caps in the alley and stickball in the schoolyard. Jumping into the Mullanphy Park fountain or the Mississippi. No one bothered us long as we didn't bother them…

"I moved to the lake to feel unfettered again. To hunt, to fish, to skate over the lake. To shape my days as I see fit. Now this. People thousands of miles away kicking us around like footballs…"

Jan stared off across the snow-covered flatlands. On the horizon a wisp of white smoke rose into the gray sky from a distant farmhouse.

"It's a good life here, Raymond. We're lucky. My luck has always held me in good stead. I've counted on it to get me through some tough spots. But with this I feel like I'm pushing it."

Jan threw his cigarette to the ground, hissing in the snow, and they moved on across the field.

§

Late that afternoon Jan drove across the river to St. Louis and St. Stanislaus Kostka Church on North 20th Street. Tomorrow morning he would attend Sunday service with Hazel and A.J. at the First Presbyterian Church of Granite City as usual. He hadn't been to Mass since long before he married, or to confession. Now seemed like a good time to correct the latter. Just to be on the safe side. You never know.

He had waited till late in the day when most parishioners (and his parents in particular) had already had their talk with Father Marek. Jan stepped into church, breathing in the aromas of candle wax and roses—the flowers likely left over from an afternoon requiem Mass. He wondered who had died. Yet the bright church interior worked to deter dark musings: pastel murals, white marble pillars, and colorful stained-glass windows now dimming as the sun lowered.

Outside the confessional just one other man waited. Jan sat studying the mural of Christ on Calvary. Although he continued to admire Christ's teachings and philosophy, he no longer bought into the Church mumbo jumbo—the Virgin birth, the Resurrection, the threat of Hell, the promise of Heaven, etc. Further, he had noticed that Homo sapiens needed no spiritual guidance in creating their own Hell on Earth. Still, he didn't want to live in a world without gods—merciful ones as opposed to just ones. Lady Luck, perhaps, among them.

Soon he moved into the shadowy cubicle and knelt. Its musty scent took him back to his youthful confessions when he was struggling to keep a clean conscience while committing unconscionable acts. Then he still believed in the Catholic version of God and in Heaven and Hell. Nonetheless, those beliefs had done little to temper his behavior.

He sensed the presence of Father Marek behind the wooden screen: a vague shadow, a shuffling of feet.

"Bless me, Father, for I have sinned. It's been four or five years since my last confession. Possibly longer." Already hedging his bets.

Silence. Once he had been close to the priest, who tried to guide him toward goodness albeit unsuccessfully.

Janusz Nowak surely had been a disappointment to Father Marek, as he was to his own father. He heard him sigh, likely recognizing Jan's voice.

"Too long. Any mortal sins in that time, son?"

Jan recited a few (wrath, lust, avarice), redacted others.

"There's something more I want to confess, Father, which perhaps falls outside sinfulness. I am afraid. Afraid I'm making a terrible error. I'm likely being sent to war. But my heart and my duty lie here, with my wife and child and our home. Not in some hellhole halfway around the world. I don't want to jeopardize the life I've created for us. I want to live straight with myself. Not die for something I don't believe in nor kill people I've got no quarrel with. It feels like a sin—against God, against human nature, against *my* nature. I'm betraying myself and my beliefs such as they are—no question. I don't want to be stupid but sense I am. I don't like the odds."

Another priestly sigh. Then,

"Terrible evil has been unleashed on the world. Opposing unjust aggressors is not a sin. It's a necessity in order to preserve goodness…"

"I'm no pacifist," Jan interrupted. "I know some people need to die. I just don't want to be played for a sucker. And I feel like I'm being set up for exactly that."

A momentary silence. The priest cleared his throat and went on.

"At times there are things larger than the individual, more important than our own selfish concerns. The people in Poland and elsewhere in Europe are suffering terribly under the scourge of Nazism. It must be stopped to avoid even more suffering."

# THE BOOTLEGGER'S BRIDE

"True enough. But what about the scourge of our Soviet ally? They're no better than Nazis. You've heard what they're doing in Poland. Virtual genocide since they stormed in from the east when Germany invaded from the west. Two million Poles dragged from their homes and loaded onto freight trains bound for Siberia and other Godforsaken regions. Thousands freezing to death in transit. The survivors landing in slave labor camps and collective farms, likely never to be heard from again. And the Katyn Forest execution of the Polish Army officer corps. Fifteen thousand shot in the back of the head and thrown into mass graves. And now I'm to march off and maybe die to help those bastards annex Poland? Makes me feel I'm being taken for a ride."

The priest had nothing to say to that. Jan took a breath and sought to redirect the conversation. "However, my concerns, Father, are not entirely selfish. I'm also thinking of my young wife and three-year-old son who depend on me both materially and emotionally. And what they would face if I were killed or crippled."

"Self-sacrifice can be noble. It is honorable to serve and die for one's nation, for one's family and countrymen…"

Jan rolled his eyes. Honorable? "Speaking of honor, Father Marek, how about the twenty bucks you still owe me," he wished to say, "for the case of brandy I delivered to the rectory at Christmastime 1930? You think that was a donation to St. Stanislaus?" Though maybe this wasn't the best time to bring it up. Besides, he had written it off years ago, moving it to the Religious Experience side of the ledger. Still, it stuck in his craw.

Instead, he said: "I know that's what Hollywood and D.C. are dishing out, Father, that this is a good fight and God is with us. But it's the same line Goebbels and Tojo are giving their folks. Hard to swallow when they're talking about *you* dying and not them, the ones who caused it all. I'm supposed to kill some Kraut who doesn't want to be there either? It's nonsense. That's what I get for playing it straight… I'm sorry, Father. This was a mistake. I should have never come."

"No, no. You speak from your heart, which is burdened… But understand, sometimes we are swept by things we cannot control. We then have to trust in God."

Jan nodded. "Yep, that's what's bothering me, Father. I'm being swept all right. Just hope not swept away or under the carpet. And frankly, I don't trust God. I don't believe He has any real interest in my wellbeing. I have no faith."

He heard the priest's cassock rustle.

"You used to have faith. You can regain it. It can comfort you through these perilous times. Read the gospels, pray the rosary, attend Mass, partake in the Eucharist."

Jan snorted then tried to cover it with a cough, hoping Father Marek hadn't grasped the derision it carried. Okay, do the ritual. Go through the motions. For what good end if no one's listening or watching, if there's no God? If we're all alone?

"Thanks for the advice, Father." That too sounded ironic and dismissive. He couldn't help it.

"I will pray for you, son, as I am sure others are. And as I am sure you will as well."

Prayer. Like confession, he guessed it couldn't hurt. Though he doubted that it would help.

He thanked Father Marek again, in Polish this time, trying to sound more sincere.

*"Dziękuję, ojcze, dziękuję."*

# 15 | A DEADLY MISTAKE

St. Louis, Missouri, July 12, 1929

Jan Nowak should have known better. He had heard stories about Leo Gold and his taste for young men. Now he had inadvertently roused the beast inside his boss.

July third had been a scorcher, and Jan had a lot of deliveries to organize, package, and load onto the truck for the coming holiday. He didn't want to soil his only clean shirt before going out to meet his customers in their speakeasies, so he took it off, hung it inside the dank cellar where he lived, and worked bare chested. A mistake. He now guessed that Gold had been watching from behind the curtains of the upstairs window. Focused on the job, Jan did not sense him admiring and coveting his body, damp with perspiration and shimmering in the sun.

So, he didn't figure anything wrong Friday evening the next week when Gold summoned him upstairs for a drink—a first.

"Business has been good, Jan. Let's take time to celebrate a bit."

They sat in tufted wing chairs in the upstairs front room before a cold fireplace with marble mantle. Red-and-gold brocade wallpaper lined the room. A Persian rug

# THE BOOTLEGGER'S BRIDE

covered the polished slat floor. Gold even had had indoor plumbing installed for the upstairs.

Gold's housekeeper, a thin woman, black hair streaked with gray, entered carrying a silver tray holding crystal wine glasses and a bottle of Champagne in a silver bucket. She placed the tray on the coffee table by the fireplace and stared at the bottle biting her lip, unsure how to open it.

"I'll take it from here, Mrs. Glazer," said Gold. "That will be all for today. You have a fine weekend."

"Thank you, Mr. Gold."

The tall windows facing the street stood wide open. An electric oscillating fan on the floor beside Gold helped move air about. Nonetheless the room felt stuffy and smelled of the mutton Mrs. Glazer had boiled for Gold's dinner. This time of year, Jan was glad to sleep in the cool cellar despite the rodent aromas and coal dust most everywhere.

Through the open windows he heard kids playing jump rope in the street below—the rope slapping the bricks, the girls calling in cadence with the rope and giggling. Gold popped the Champagne cork—it was the real French stuff, Jan noted—and poured.

"The take before Independence Day was very good. You are doing fine work, Jan," he said handing him a glass.

"Thank you, Mr. Gold."

"I think, Jan, that you should call me Leo. We're working hand-in-hand. Almost like partners."

Jan nodded. "Sure," he said, though the familiarity of the older man didn't sit right with him. Nor did the slippery way Gold had said it. Though most everything he said had that flavor, like he was always trying to sell you something.

They raised glasses toward each other and drank. First time he had tasted real Champagne, and its intensity surprised him. Sure better than beer. Something a guy with a few bucks could develop a taste for.

Gold looked fifty-years-old though was likely younger. A shiny baldhead with gray fringe. Portly, full-lipped, clean-shaven. His face glistened with a patina of perspiration. As most always, he wore a white shirt with striped tie, gray wool worsted slacks, and Stacy Adams cap-toe oxfords. It made him look more like a haberdasher than a bootlegger.

Gold went on:

"In fact, I was thinking we should have even more of a partnership. More responsibility, more in it for you..." He paused, lips parted, as he appraised Jan. "You work well with your people and have become invaluable to me. I think a reward is in order, a more secure future for you. I think we might even become good friends."

Jan shifted in his chair and became conscious again of the children laughing and yelling on the herringboned sidewalk below. He could not speak. He knew he should say something though nothing came. As if to encourage him Leo Gold smiled and reached across to pat Jan's knee.

"What do you say to that, Jan Nowak?"

Jan took a deep breath, heart thumping. "Gee, Leo. That sounds great," he said. But his thoughts were on what happened to Eddie Jankowski. Jan squirmed in his chair and Gold finally withdrew his hand.

"We can discuss details later. Maybe over dinner some night soon."

Jan sensed a ringing in his ears.

After two glasses of Champagne, he told his boss that he had to meet a friend and retreated downstairs. He stood on the darkened bricks of the backyard staring up at the lighted windows of Leo Gold's home above. Then Jan's gaze fell to the coal chute and worn marble steps that led down to the dark hovel where he lived.

§

Jan needed to get out of the house and get a real drink to clear his head and think straight. He strode across the brick backyard, past the outhouse on the alley, and over to Cass Avenue. Jan walked east toward 10th Street and the brick-bound passageway that led to Czeslaw Oswiecki's basement speakeasy. A clear night though with the usual humid July air that dimmed whatever starlight penetrated through city streetlights. A waxing crescent moon floated above tenement roofs.

He had to face facts. He was dependent on Leo Gold. For his job, his sustenance, and his home. For his rank as a young man of substance who knew his way around the Cass Avenue neighborhood and the larger city. If he lost Gold's patronage he'd be out on the street. Literally.

On the other hand, if he became Leo's "partner" he'd have everything—big bucks, Champagne, fine clothes, security, and an escape from the cellar, where winters he had to shovel coal into the furnace to heat Gold's home upstairs. All he likely had to do was let the guy French him once in a while. He pictured it—Gold's baldpate, fleshy face, and greedy lips. It made him sick.

How could he live with himself? How could he respect himself or expect anyone else to if he sold himself out in that way? Not to mention if folks conned onto the arrangement. People were not blind and stupid. And they always talked. Who knows, maybe there's already talk, given Gold's dubious reputation in the community. Vicious, jealous people fabricating lies about Janusz Nowak. My, how they liked to talk. Particularly when they could help bring somebody down. Like little Eddie Jankowski, who couldn't stand up to anybody. Certainly not to a rich bootlegger like Leo Gold. So maybe Gold used him. No reason to belittle, tar, and humiliate the kid. Human nature at its worst. The more he saw of it the more he questioned Father Marek's characterization of a benevolent and merciful Creator. Then Eddie—only twelve years old—disappeared. Maybe he hopped a freight. Maybe he got a job on a riverboat. Or maybe he took a swim downriver, all the way to New Orleans. Not that Leo Gold would give a fuck.

But without Leo, Jan saw he'd be homeless and penniless. No way he could go crawling back to kiss his father's butt for a two-bit backbreaker job at the steel mill. Yeah, there was other factory work. Henry Broz worked a ten-hour shift at Brown Shoe Company for four bucks a day until he lost his hand in a cutting machine. Safe, clean employment like department store work paid even less. Hardly enough to make rent somewhere, feed himself, and buy decent clothes. How will I eat, how will I survive? As a beggar who lives in the caves beneath the streets with the alkies and opium addicts?

# THE BOOTLEGGER'S BRIDE

Those were the practical, physical concerns. There were also intangibles of equal or even greater import if he lost Gold's support. No one wants anything to do with a bum or groveling errand boy.

The status and friendships he possessed as a bootlegger—someone with cash and swagger who lived outside the law—would disappear overnight. His life would spiral down and down. Janusz Nowak forever a nobody. Demonstrating to the Cass Avenue Polish community that his father had been right about his wayward son. He was trash that should be kicked down the stairs to the gutter. Someone to beat like an animal, like a mule, to make it move in the right direction. He felt his father's fists hammering his face. He tasted his own blood. He heard his father's Polish harangues—a dog, he had called him, a blood-eating dog. And now Leo Gold also sought to control Jan, to bend him to his will.

He moved down the dark alley toward Czeslaw's place, broken glass cracking under the soles of his brogues. Past the outhouse there and across another brick backyard, ducking under damp laundry dangling from clotheslines. Down hollowed marble steps to a solid wood door where he knocked once then twice then repeated it.

Soon he heard the bolt slide back. The door opened to reveal Czeslaw, round Slavic face, watery blue eyes, thinning blond hair combed down over his forehead. He wore a light blue workingman's shirt with sleeves rolled to the elbows. He smiled and took Jan's hand. Czeslaw pulled him into the smoky room smelling of stale beer, patted his back, and bolted the door behind him.

"Bogdan was just asking about you." This said in Polish.

He followed Czeslaw across the low, candlelit room to the homemade bar in the corner where sat a radio playing dance music and where eight men carried on in Polish all at the same time, arguing, laughing, bellowing, cursing. A ninth man, Bogdan Zawadski, occupied one of two barstools. Jan took the other one, and the two men lifted their chins at each other.

Jan ordered a round for them, specifying to Czeslaw a bottle he knew to be real Canadian whiskey (and not the "Canadian" whiskey distilled in East St. Louis that he himself had labeled) along with two bottles of a local lager he knew and trusted.

Bogdan, whom he had known his whole life and who looked after Jan like the big brother he never had, raised his shot glass. "May our children have wealthy parents," he said in English.

The men downed their whiskey and chased it with lager. The competing aromas (one pungent and sweet, the other yeasty and fecund) and tastes (the first sharp, the second bitter and cooling) mingled in a pleasing way. Jan ordered another shot and knocked it back.

Bogdan stared at him and said, "Where is Janusz Aleksander Nowak? You know, the smiling and sober gymnast who never lets his poisonous product pass his lovely lips. Who is this gloomy, drunken imposter?"

Jan and Bogdan always spoke English together, though the latter with a north St. Louis accent *à la polonaise* that made him sound sinister, matching his looks. English was part of their glue, both Americans heart and soul. Outside the neighborhood Bogdan Zawadski went by Bob Wade. Further, he didn't appear Slavic, more dark and wolfish, though who knew? The historic Polish genetic stew consisted of Slavs, Jews, Germans, Gypsies, Celts, and other tribes. Half a head taller than Jan, Bogdan boasted a strong nose, deep-set brown eyes, and curling black hair.

After Czeslaw poured them a third shot Jan stared into his on the bar and turned it round and round. In answer to Bogdan's question, he finally sighed and said: "This is a lost man, a man with a dilemma."

Bogdan raised his shot glass again and downed the liquor. "What's her name? She pregnant or married or in love with you or something?"

Jan smiled for an instant. "No, Bogdan. Not a woman. This is serious. A business problem."

Bogdan nodded. "I know that in your business, problems can be very serious."

Jan sat thinking how much to say and how to say it.

"Guys ever get funny with you?"

Bogdan reached across and pinched his cheek. "I'm not as pretty as you, *cukiereczku*."

"It's more than that…"

Much more than that. Tasting a year of freedom from his father's oppressive rule had opened his eyes to how life might be lived. He wanted his freewheeling independent existence to continue. Forever.

"…Everything I have is at stake. My home, my livelihood, my reputation. My future. I'm stuck."

Bogdan studied him at length, as if Jan had just made a big wager across a poker table. Finally, he said:

"This sounds like extortion."

Jan straightened. "Yes! Exactly. That's what it is: extortion."

Bogdan pressed an index finger to Jan's chest. "Once you give in and let them bully you, you are forever fucked, my friend. You must tell them to try their luck elsewhere and mean it."

"Wish it was that simple, Bogdan. They're not going away."

Bogdan pursed his lips and lowered his voice. "If that's so, if someone's trying to squeeze your balls and you can't escape, there's only one way to make the trouble disappear." He jerked his head over his shoulder, east, toward the Mississippi, which flowed dark and menacing but a few blocks away. "Maybe I can help."

Jan stared at Bogdan. Then he lifted his gaze above his friend's dark locks to the blackened ceiling beams. There in the dimness Jan Nowak glimpsed a curtain rising. Behind it he saw himself writhing in pain as a smirking Leo Gold crushed Jan's testicles in his fists. Gold had him by the balls—figuratively if not yet literally. Yet—and this was Jan's epiphany as the two men in his imaginative tableau abruptly exchanged roles—the opposite was also true.

Gold needed—and wanted—Jan. Without him or someone like him he had no ready access to the lucrative Polish-speaking market that Jan had cultivated for him. Conversely, Jan now saw he had no need of Leo Gold. He knew the operation, the suppliers, and where the special inventory was cached. He also had his own customer list. So, no Leo, no problem. It could all be his.

# THE BOOTLEGGER'S BRIDE

This, Jan realized, was a pivotal point in his young life—if not a life-or-death drama then damn near. As such, his cerebral approach—worrying how to somehow escape his dilemma through craft or compromise—had been too timorous and forgiving. Too New Testament. Whereas the Jew Leo Gold was Old Testament, a document that justified aggressive self-defense, Jan seemed to recall. And if this was not a case of self-defense, what was?

Bosses, teachers, cops, bullies—whoever gained power over people always stuck it to them good and hard. Which was why all the folks up and down Cass Avenue—Poles, Jews, Irish, Italians, whatever—were here and not back in the old country—to escape tyrants and tyranny. But they were deluded in part. You can't escape human nature. Even good people succumb to the urge to wield power once it falls into their hands. To bend others to their will. To lord it over them. To fuck them.

Still, Jan couldn't take Bogdan up on his offer of help. His friend had always guided and protected him, ever since they were kids. This would be no way to repay him for his love and loyalty, by pulling him into a scheme that could cost him everything if it didn't go just right. Also, if Bogdan got nicked it would then be too easy to trace it back to Jan.

He knew of others who might take on the job. Maybe someone from across the river, where no one knew Jan or the extent of their bootlegging operation. Where he might get a good price. And in the process even the score for Eddie Jankowski.

Jan rose to his feet, stared down at Bogdan on his barstool, and took his face in his hands. "You've shown me a way out. A road to freedom and success. Once again you have saved my life! Thank you, dear friend. *Dziękuję,*" he said, bending forward to kiss a startled Bogdan on the lips. And the speakeasy fell silent.

# 16 | FATHER & SON RECONCILE

St. Louis, Missouri, April 9, 1944

With A.J. and Hazel at his side Jan Nowak strolled over the herringboned redbrick sidewalk. A morning downpour had cleansed the near North Side's cobbled streets, and at midday they still lay damp, strewn with magnolia and dogwood petals. The moist air hung cool, crisp, and fragrant, smelling of spring. Low gray clouds skittered across a blue sky. The benign atmosphere took him back to his boyhood days, blissful times when he roamed these same streets with Bogdan and other pals, searching for…for something new, for any anomaly. For an adventure, even if it was make-believe. Though as they grew those adventures gained substance. Always doing whatever he could just to keep from going home to a mother who was distant and a father at times violent. Life effervesced on the streets among his comrades, not, certainly, within his dour and confining home, where he felt watched, fearful, and alone.

They rounded the corner onto Cass Avenue and soon turned down a narrow brick walkway between two tenements. It opened onto a large brick-paved backyard shaded by adjacent buildings. Jan ducked under cotton clotheslines strung there and paused at the bottom of gray-painted wooden stairs leading up to the second-floor porch of the old redbrick building. He took Hazel's hand and gazed up to the porch.

"Last time I saw my father I was coming down these stairs head over heels."

His wife stared at him askance. Just as well. Let her make up her own mind about the old man. Jan tilted his head toward the stairs and followed her up, hand-in-hand with A.J. At the top he took a deep breath. "He is risen!"

Hazel frowned at him and his dubious Easter jest, unsure what to make of his obvious nervousness and lurking family dynamics, about which he never spoke. Jan didn't know either. Fifteen years had passed. How much had changed, if anything?

To his right on the wooden porch beside a tall curtained window sat a door framed by red bricks (as was everything in the old neighborhood). He rapped a knuckle against one of its four panes.

Soon the door swung open to reveal a petite woman of fifty, Hazel judged, with curled silver hair. She wore a long-sleeved blue dress belted at the waist, and short-heeled black shoes with laces. The woman stood rigid, arms at her side, eyes darting from Jan and the child to Hazel and back.

"Happy Easter," she said somberly somehow, with a thick accent. "Welcome." She stepped aside, inviting them across the threshold into a kitchen smelling of boiled cabbage.

Jan spoke to the woman in his impenetrable mother tongue, nodding at A.J. then his wife. "Mama" was the only word Hazel could make out.

# THE BOOTLEGGER'S BRIDE

The woman responded in Polish, looked at Hazel with pursed lips, and led them from the tiled kitchen into a spotless high-ceilinged room with polished hardwood floors. It smelled of furniture wax and mothballs and contained a high bed and two towering wardrobes. Next she spread large, oak sliding doors to reveal the front room, where a man sat in a wingchair smoking a pipe and reading a newspaper by light pouring through tall windows overlooking the street.

The man—thick salt-and-pepper hair, brown wool suit, white shirt, and black tie—put aside the newspaper and the sweet-smelling pipe and rose. Though broad-shouldered and trim, he stood well under six-foot tall. Jan stepped toward him.

"*Tato*, this is my wife, Hazel," he said in English, "and this is your grandson, Alexander Jan."

The wizened man looked Hazel up and down with dark, penetrating eyes and nodded a greeting. Then he stooped and held out his arms toward A.J. "Come say hello to Grandpa!"

When the boy hesitated Jan put a hand to his back to urge him forward. The old man lay hands on the boy's shoulders, pressed palms to the child's cheeks, and bent to kiss his forehead. He straightened and said, "He is beautiful like his mother. You are lucky, Janusz, that he favors her."

Jan smiled. This was a good sign. The needling signaled all was forgiven—at least on the old man's part—though surely not forgotten by either of them.

"Very lucky." Jan turned to his mother, who stood aside with vacant eyes, and spoke to her in Polish, translating.

Eyes darting from Jan to his father, she managed a half smile.

Jan's father, Joseph, moved to Hazel and took her hand. "Yes, the boy has the same dark eyes. You are Gypsy, no?"

He spoke English well though with a heavy-tongued Slavic accent.

"No, not Gypsy. Part Cherokee."

"American Indian? Good! Now my family is a real American family. Right, Mama?" he said turning to his wife. When she made no response he spoke to her in Polish.

He told Hazel and Jan to sit on a tufted French loveseat by the front windows and followed his wife into the kitchen.

Hazel pulled A.J. up onto her lap. Jan took her hand and shook his head. "He seems to have shrunken. Always had such a commanding presence. An old man now but could still probably take me."

"I've never seen such intense eyes. I sense his charisma."

"A no-nonsense character if ever I met one. Why people trusted him."

She studied the fleur-de-lis wallpaper, sparse furniture—old but spotless—the varnished floor. Not what she expected, though she hadn't known what to expect. Hazel felt as if she'd stepped back into the 19th century.

"Is it always so clean and tidy?"

"Always. A matter of pride in their Americanization, such as it is. They both came from the same small Silesian town, then ruled by Prussia. Though he had immigrated

# THE BOOTLEGGER'S BRIDE

here before she was even born. Both families dirt poor—as with all peasant and working-class Poles then and there. Though they hardly ever talked about it...

"Mother did once tell me about Cossacks, as she called them, raiding her village on horseback when she was a little girl and one lifting her neighbor's infant from her arms on the tip of his sabre..."

"Here we are!" His father returned carrying three small tumblers of clear liquid. "Homemade lemon vodka," he announced and handed them each a glass. He lifted his. "He is risen!"

Jan smiled, pressing his knee against Hazel's. "He is risen!"

Hazel sipped at the burning liquor as the men downed theirs in a gulp. Joseph returned to the kitchen.

Jan shook his head. "First he throws me out for running booze and now he's distilling his own hooch. Lots to learn about being a parent."

The old man came back with a bottle and poured more for Jan and himself, its lemon scent perfuming the room.

"Did you attend Mass at St. Stanislaus this morning, Papa?"

"Of course."

"Father Marek still kicking?" Jan asked, even though he had visited him in the confessional just a few months earlier, before reporting to boot camp.

As they gossiped about other parishioners Jan's mother came from the kitchen with hors d'oeuvres: a plate of cold cuts and sliced Jewish rye bread from Lickhalter's Bakery, she announced, and placed it on the coffee table before them.

"*Kielbasa krakowska*, *szynka*, and *kishka*, my favorite," Jan told his wife. "A spicy mix of pork liver and snouts, beef blood, and buckwheat groats."

Despite the suspect ingredient list, she tried it and liked it. A.J. was less enthusiastic.

After a half hour chatting about neighbors and the neighborhood they moved to the dining table in the large kitchen, where ornate china and silverware had been laid on a white tablecloth.

The meal started with steaming cheese-and-onion *pierogi* topped with cold sour cream, moved on to *gołąbki*, that is, stuffed cabbage, and finished with *sernik*—Polish cheesecake—and coffee.

Throughout dinner Joseph focused on Hazel, quizzing her about her family and herself.

"…It is good to get an education…" Here he cast Janusz-the-Dropout a meaningful glance. "…and to be a teacher. What ages do you teach?"

"I was teaching first grade when I got pregnant with A.J. I hope to return when he starts school and teach literature at the high school… Did you attend school in Poland, Mr. Nowak?"

He nodded, fists on the white tablecloth, pensive. "Yes, a peasant school where the Prussians had banned Polish. So, I learned to read and write my language from Father Kreminski. Then they sent a German priest."

He went on about the Germanization of the Poles in Silesia, the exclusion of Polish culture and language, the expropriation of Poles' land, and mass deportations—a script being replayed in the 20th century by the Third Reich, Jan interjected.

The Prussian repression had encouraged Joseph to flee to America penniless when he was eighteen. A ship took him from Hamburg to Baltimore, he explained. He found work at a steel mill in Scranton, joined other Poles in Chicago, and eventually migrated to St. Louis.

Jan listened in silence as Hazel and Joseph chatted. It felt so surreal—wedged between his former life and his new. And now he was leaving both behind, not knowing what lay ahead. He felt as if standing on a precipice.

After dessert he turned to his father. "*Tato*, I am leaving this week. Overseas I suspect."

The old man frowned. Jan explained how he had been drafted in December and sent to training camp at Fort Leonard Wood, Missouri. Now, after a few days home, he was shipping out.

Joseph turned to Maria and spoke in Polish. She looked to her son then rose and fetched the vodka bottle from the front room. Joseph poured two tumblers, Hazel refusing more. The two men raised their glasses.

"*Powodzenia, synu!*" said the old man, which Hazel guessed meant "good luck" or such. Then in English: "Any idea where you might go, Son?"

"Camp scuttlebutt was all about the upcoming European invasion. I figure that's where I'm headed."

In a front-page story of that morning's *St. Louis Post-Dispatch* the House Military Committee chairman predicted that such an invasion would cost 150,000 American casualties in the first month. Jan had tried to calculate the odds that he might be among them. A long shot had he been a racehorse. Which suggested to him a morbid metaphor: Europe becoming a vast human glue factory.

"At least they let you say goodbye to your family before sending you off to war. When I was your son's age," Joseph said nodding at A.J., "the Prussians came and took my father right out of his field to fight the French. We didn't know until a neighbor ran to tell us. A year later he came home, walked back into the field, and went to work still wearing his Prussian uniform… Now my homeland is again swallowed by the Prussians. Once more it has disappeared."

"Maybe I'll get a chance to help drive them out," said Jan.

Hazel watched as father and son raised their drinks and made another opaque Polish toast. Joseph poured them more.

"Maybe you can work as translator."

"Me and fifty thousand guys from South Chicago."

"You will be the lucky one, Son, I know… To luck!" And they again touched glasses together.

§

The sun had set by the time they descended the back stairs, Jan again almost going head over heels after helping his father polish off a second bottle of bathtub vodka.

Hazel drove. A.J. slept curled on his father's lap. She aimed the coupe east on Cass Avenue then north on Broadway to Salisbury Street and the McKinley Bridge. It carried them over the dark, swirling Mississippi and down onto the American Bottom.

As they moved past the rail yards in Venice, Illinois, headlights of passing cars lighting their faces, Jan noticed

Hazel glancing at him from time to time and frowning.

"Sorry, Dear," he said, "for subjecting you to all that. Too much Polish. Polish immigrants, Polish language, Polish food. Not to mention mercurial Polish souls. Too much vodka. All too much."

She gazed at him then returned her eyes to the road ahead. "Jan, don't let them cut off all your beautiful hair again."

He laughed. "I'm afraid they might insist. But it'll grow back. Doubt they'll much care once the fighting starts. One way or another it's out of my hands. It's all out of my hands."

He stared at the dark road ahead. It might have been different had he been on his own. He could have put in a fix with the draft board or bought a doctor and a T.B. infection. Some angle. But being a respectable family man meant they had you. Now you had to worry what people might think, because it reflected on your wife and son and their reputations in the community, forever into the future. If it was just him it might have been different. In his milieu, people didn't much care if a guy cut corners to get what he wanted.

His father had faced a similar dilemma as a young man. Ruled by politics in faraway Berlin, he had no say in his own life or the life of his village. So, he did something about it. He fled Prussia and came to America to gain control over his fate. Ironic that Joseph's son now was being sent back there by distant, faceless powers. With no say in the matter.

As Hazel turned up their driveway toward Long Lake, Jan stirred from his reverie.

"Maybe I'll finally get to see Poland," he said. "Whatever might be left of it. Though Joseph Vissarionovich Stalin could have other ideas."

## 17 | MEN ARE FOOLS

Madison County, Illinois, January 23, 1953

Helen pushed through the back door at Lazy Lane calling, "Yoo-hoo!"

She had waited till noon before telephoning to tell Hazel she'd be dropping by for a visit. Helen didn't want to surprise her sister—or be surprised herself.

Hazel had a nice fire going in the fireplace on the cold, snowy day, warming and brightening the sunroom, filling it with a woodsy aroma. A plate of finger sandwiches sat on the end table beside the green leather couch. She came from the kitchen in brown wool slacks and beige sweater. Lipstick, hair pinned up nicely, her pearl earrings. Dark circles under her eyes, drink in hand. At least she was trying.

They moved together, embraced, brushed cheeks, Hazel fragrant with Chanel over Old Fitzgerald.

"How about something for you, big sis?"

Helen hesitated then thought, What the hell. She had come to keep her sister company. What better way to do that with a drinker than have one? She asked for a Tom Collins and sat on the sofa while Hazel went to fix it.

Stacks of library books lay on the mahogany butler-table before her: *War and Peace, The Iliad, All Quiet on* the *Western Front, A Farewell to Arms,* and other classic war literature, along with a few more recent World War II tomes. She picked up Tolstoy and saw it was weeks overdue. Ditto for Hemingway and Homer. Poor thing was wallowing in it.

Hazel returned with Helen's drink and sat in the easy chair by the fireplace.

"How's A.J. getting on? He's so sweet. Rowed all the way up here a few weeks back to visit. Acted like he was out fishing and just happened by."

Helen told her he was doing well in school, popular with other students, et cetera. At this point make-believe was easier for everyone to swallow. What good would it do to tell her that her son was an angry loner that no one could reach? That he needed his mother back? She had heard it dozens of times already, from friends, family, psychiatrists, and preachers. The message never breached the alcohol-filled moat she had dug around herself.

Hazel's life with Jan had been like a fairy tale, she a princess in her castle. Yet she couldn't count the blessings of their years together, only rue their end, looking at what she had lost rather than what she had been given. For a bright and educated woman it seemed a profoundly stupid choice. But of course, it wasn't a reasoned choice. She was stuck in a fable whose moral she was blind to or ignored.

They chatted about friends and innocuous local events. Then Hazel asked:

"How are Mom and Dad?"

Helen stared at her sister, who looked away to a pack of cigarettes beside her and lit one up. "Haven't you seen them?"

# THE BOOTLEGGER'S BRIDE

Hazel shrugged. "Not for months. Maybe longer. Dad won't talk to me. Rather listen to gossip." She took a deep drag on her Lucky Strike.

"What's wrong with men?" she went on, lifting her chin toward the stacks of books. "Fighting, hating, killing. Abandoning everything they claim to love: their mothers, their sweethearts, and their wives; their sons and daughters and their homes. For what? Abstractions for soldiers: patriotism, honor, glory—though it's money, power, and dominance for those calling the shots. But why go fight and maybe die? So, they can shine before other men? So, they can lay more women? In the process deceiving themselves and those they claim to hold dear. To protect us? From what exactly?... Maybe Lysistrata had the answer: Stop screwing them until they stop killing each other. Of course, Aristophanes was just joking. Ha ha."

Helen stared at her sister. Hazel had seemingly taken an even darker turn. Or maybe it was just a bad day. She hardly knew what to say.

"Hazel, you know that none of that applies to Jan. He went to war because he got drafted. He had no choice. Either that or go to prison and tar all of you. Not his doing, the government's."

Hazel took a drink of her highball and said: "Did I mention that Richard knew Jan back when he was bootlegging?"

Momentary confusion for Helen before realizing her sister was talking about Richard Dupuis.

"He told me stories about Jan that make me wonder if I ever really knew him. Whether he was ever honest with me about anything. Even whether he ever really loved me…"

"Hazel, you know he did. Jan worshipped you."

"He wasn't the angel he made out to be. Just another hoodlum who hurt people and ruined them. The whole time playing a public role of decent family man and benevolent Christian. What if A.J. has that same stain on his soul?" She took a long pull on her cigarette, exhaled, coughed. "What's wrong with a small life, a peaceful life? A life without strife?… Men are such fools."

"I can't do anything about that. Let me talk to Dad for you."

She stubbed out her cigarette. "You do that. While you're at it ask him what he would do if I had another child, a bastard child. Maybe a retard, pickled in alcohol. Could he love his grandchild? Could he love me? Could the foursquare Christian with perfect church attendance summon up a little New Testament forgiveness and compassion?" She lit another Lucky. "Let me know what he says. I'd love to hear."

Helen bit her bottom lip fighting back tears, rose, and crossed to her sister. She knelt and took her in her arms.

Tears poured down Hazel's powdered cheeks. "Prince Charming, a redoubt on the sleeping lake, a life of love and leisure. What a fantasy!" She sniffled. "Why, God, did it have to end?"

# 18 | A TOAST TO LONGEVITY

Cherbourg, France, June 24, 1944

Jan Nowak sat in a commandeered wooden chair on a side street—Rue de Normandie, the embedded blue oval wall plaque read—enjoying the sun and relative quiet. No grind and clank of tank treads, no gunfire or explosions near enough to make you jump or burrow into the ground. Nobody yelling, howling, or crying for his mother. Just the ever-present scents of wood smoke and gunpowder hanging in the air, or maybe wafting from his fatigues.

Inside the blown-out shop behind him he had found stationery and a fountain pen to write his wife, which he had not had the chance to do since they landed three weeks earlier, but he was having trouble knowing what exactly to say.

He could not very well tell Hazel what he had seen and done or how he felt about it. How truly harrowing, dangerous, and chaotic it was. Nor about the comrades he had already lost. Not without further worrying her. Or himself.

So, he wrote about Long Lake and the peace he found there with her, the freedom, and the joy. Then he crumpled that sheet and started over, writing in present perfect tense—"the peace I *have* found there with you"—instead of past tense.

He wrote of warm summer evenings rowing their boat over the still lake with her and their son. Fish leaping to snare insects, cows lowing on the eastern shore. Whippoorwills crooning, cicadas rasping, katydids scratching, and frogs croaking. The clean smell of the lake and fields rising as the air cooled. Jan told how he pined for her and their happy home. How he longed to shepherd their son into manhood, to make him into a better man than his flawed yet adoring father... "I hope to guide him and stand by him always, no matter what, to be the nurturing father I never had, embracing and comforting him when days turn dark." Jan tried but failed to recall any occasion when *his* father, Joseph Nowak, laid hands on him other than in anger.

A shadow passed over the page and lingered there. He looked up to find Jacob Wolfson, heavy black stubble on his gaunt face, standing over him. Realizing he was interfering with Jan's sunbathing, Wolfson stepped aside and leaned against the wall.

"Got a minute?"

"My time is your time, Lieutenant. Pull up a chair," he said, though none were in sight.

Wolfson smiled. Thoughtful and well spoken, he had been a stockbroker before the war and had given Jan some advice on how he might handle his capital when he returned home. Putting it where you get better earnings than in safety deposit boxes.

"Scuttlebutt has it you took a poke at Sergeant Rabee."

"I wouldn't call it a poke, Lieutenant. I'd call it a haymaker. He went down like a load of bricks."

"Didn't file a charge. Word is he had it coming. Good enough for me. Though I'd like to know if there's a problem here that needs solving."

"Thanks. I already solved it."

"I'd still like to know what the rub was."

"Sure…" Nowak capped the fountain pen, laid it across the pad of paper in his lap, and shooed away a fly that had landed there.

"We've got young guys here, Lieutenant, malleable college kids some of them, who have watched too many government propaganda films. You know, movies whooping 'kill the Krauts' and 'make the Japs into chop suey.' Personally, I thought that was what we were fighting against, killing others because they're different, like the Germans are doing to the Jews and Poles, and the Japanese to the Chinese and Filipinos, for starters…

"Putting that aside, these kids swallow that stuff whole, parroting abstractions like 'honor,' 'valor,' and 'justice.' They talk about dying for a righteous cause, going to heaven, and winning the regard of girlfriends and grateful Americans everywhere. In other words, they're asking for it. Rabee took advantage of their bravado, endangering them unnecessarily in my opinion.

"Then two nights ago after a bottle of Cognac I got in his face about it. Said that these were human beings. Real people. Not expendable markers in some patriotic table game. Things got heated—well, I was already pretty fired up—and he called me a 'pig-ignorant Polack.' At that point I had no choice. I decked him."

Wolfson fought back a grin then pulled a stern face and said, "I understand. 'Conniving Kike' moves me in the same way. But best to keep it under wraps. Particularly with witnesses around. Could cost you a court martial next time."

Jan brought an index finger to his lips and gazed up at Wolfson. "If I slugged you now, Lieutenant, could you fix me up with a discharge?"

"Won't do you any good, Nowak. We're all moving ahead together tomorrow."

"Damn."

The lieutenant patted Jan's shoulder and sauntered off. Wolfson was a good guy. Pity was that the good guys got it just as often as the assholes.

When he finished his letter to Hazel Jan thought to write Father Marek. Prayer and faith had recently re-entered his life—a topic they had discussed before he shipped out.

*On D-Day, Father, when we were headed to shore in the Higgins boat I noted a lot of praying going on around me. It made me think of the Mark Twain quote, 'I admire the serene assurance of those who have religious faith. It is wonderful to observe the calm confidence of a Christian with four aces.'*

*In this case, however, nobody knew whether they held a winning hand or not. And none were serene, calm, or confident. Including yours truly, who has once again taken to crossing himself and beseeching the Almighty—particularly when the shells start flying.*

*Which brings to mind Chaplin Cummings's field sermon at the Battle of Bataan, where he said, 'There are no atheists in foxholes.' True enough, perhaps. Still, I question the efficacy of prayer after seeing so many true believers blown to smithereens. God seems so far away or indifferent to human suffering and cruelty, to wrongheadedness and stupidity, to dark irony and senseless death. Nonetheless I continue to pray for a quick end to all this madness and my safe return home.*

*In all honesty I must confess that I also rub the rabbit's foot hanging with my dog tags and tap my cheek so Lady Luck might plant a kiss there. As you see, I am still not so much a good Catholic as a desperate pantheist who has just recently restored The Holy Trinity to prominence in his prayers...*

What he failed to tell Father Marek was that when praying in the name of the Father, Son, and Holy Ghost he also invited any other gods who might be listening in—Greek, Roman, Hindu, Toltec, whatever—to lend a helping hand if they had an inclination. Though no mischief, please. By way of expiating that omission Jan added:

*And when this is all over, Father, I promise to return to St. Stanislaus Kostka and take the Eucharist. First, though, you'll need to hear my confession if you can spare a few hours...*

Writing of Lady Luck summoned up a vision of the gambler and now navy gunner Bogdan Zawadski, alias Bob Wade. His best friend and guardian was somewhere in the Pacific. Jan had heard that the Yanks were giving the Japs hell at Iwo Jima and Saipan. American ships were being lost as well. So, he said a Christian prayer for his pal, the former altar boy and perpetual Catholic. He asked for his safe return home as well, in the hope that they would soon be reunited. That they would embrace and raise a glass together for old times' sake. He pictured them doing just that.

"*Na zdrowie, Bogdan!*" he said aloud. To health. "*Sto lat!*" One hundred years.

# 19 | A MESSENGER ARRIVES

Madison County, Illinois, July 4, 1944

Hot wind in his face, Tommy Freeman sped along the lake road thinking he needed to find a new job. He had come to hate this one.

He did get to wear the blue uniform and peaked cap and ride the motorbike, which was grand. But all in all, today he'd rather be out of the blazing sun and in the shady backyard listening to the Cardinals game with his dad instead of spreading bad news.

The Redbirds were running away with it, ten games up. They had Mort Cooper and Harry Breechen pitching a doubleheader against the Giants. And in the American League the Browns—of all people—were in first by a game. Already folks were talking about a St. Louis Streetcar World Series. But that was it for the good news.

The bad news telegrams had been coming fast over the last few weeks, ever since D-Day. Often you knew what it was when you saw the delivery address. No one out in the country hardly ever got a telegram unless it was something awful.

Lots of times, it was a woman they were addressed to, a wife or mother, who answered the door. He never even waited for a tip. Just handed them the envelope and jumped back on his motorbike before he could hear them howling and crying, see them fainting and such. Oh brother. What a fucking job.

He saved this one for last since it was out in the sticks. Had to stop twice to get directions to the right house. Now Tommy slowed the bike before a shaded lane on his right and peered down the gravel driveway with grass growing in the middle. This looked like it from what that last guy said.

He motored on down the drive and saw four cars parked by the house and on the lawn in back. Tommy smelled barbecue and saw people near the lakeshore drinking beer and playing horseshoes, laughing it up and having fun. At least for the time being. Jeez.

He braked on the gravel, slid to a stop, jumped off, and headed to the front door, avoiding the party out back. He rang the doorbell and waited. He rang it again. No way he was going to the backyard and join the party.

After a minute the green wooden door beyond the screen door opened wide and there stood a tall brunette in flowered dress, bright red lipstick, and pearl earrings. A real tomato. He swallowed.

"Mrs. Hazel R. Nowak?" he asked, hoping it wasn't her. And if it was, praying that this time he gauged wrong, and it was good news. Yeah, this time it was good news.

She stood transfixed, mouth agape, staring at the Western Union badge on his cap.

§

# THE BOOTLEGGER'S BRIDE

Raymond Lomax tended to the ribs on the brick barbecue pit. He called to the two men pitching horseshoes under the sycamores, his father Fred Lomax and father-in-law Roy Robinson.

"You guys gonna finish that game before nightfall? Everyone else will have eaten and gone home."

Fred turned to Roy. "I did a terrible job raising Raymond. Grew into a real smartass. Thinks he's Fred Allen."

"Well, he has some room to talk after whipping me in five minutes."

Their wives, along with Helen and Hazel, sat on folding chairs in the shade of a thick maple tree atop the lake bank sipping ice tea and beer. Raymond could hear the buzz of their conversation and occasional laughter. He took a drink from his beer bottle. Pale blue skies, puffy white clouds, a breath of wind when a cloud floated across the sun.

He hadn't been anywhere else, really, except St. Louis on occasion and Springfield once to see Abe Lincoln's house. He didn't want to go anywhere else. The lake, the fields where in summer errant sunflowers grew, and the clean, fresh air were all he needed. He even liked his job at the steel mill now that he could work with a pencil instead of his back. Raymond looked to his beautiful dark-haired wife, knowing his life was blessed.

A.J., who had been playing with toy soldiers in the sandbox at the far side of the house—a sandbox that Raymond had helped Jan build for the kid—came running to Hazel.

"Mommy! Somebody at the door."

She rose saying, "Who could that be?"

A minute later, over the clang of horseshoes, conversation, and green leaves rustling in a gust, a cry rang from the house. Helen jumped up and raced inside. Raymond set his beer on the smoking brick pit and followed.

He found Helen kneeling next to the turquoise living room sofa embracing her sister, who sat curled in her arms, shaking. On the coffee table before them lay a telegram. Raymond moved toward it and stared down. Then he bent and lifted it in his hand, tears welling in his eyes. He turned and moved back through the house.

In the backyard everyone stood rigid, staring at him. He bit his lips and shook his head. His mother-in-law gasped, pulled A.J. to her, and walked him back to the sandbox where his toy soldiers lay on the ground. Raymond moved forward and read aloud:

"The Secretary of War desires me to express his deepest regret that your husband Corporal Janusz Aleksander Nowak was killed in action on twenty seven June in France. Letter follows. Witsell Acting Adjutant General."

They stood silent encircling Raymond. At the sound of a raucous chirping, he looked to the bayberry bushes guarding the lake to spy a rust-colored wren hopping from branch to branch. He turned back to the others.

"I guess somebody should tell the boy what's going on. Hazel's in no shape…"

He looked to the telegram in his hand, picturing Jan at his side as they strode across a field of dry weeds on a gray winter day. Shotgun broken in the crook of his arm, cigarette hanging from his lips where also sat a soft smile, signaling his friend's unceasing pleasure in being alive:

savoring the smell of damp earth, the burn of cold air on his face, the joy in movement and in practicing what men had done since the beginning of time, connecting himself to them.

"God damn this war."

Raymond folded the telegram and slid it into the back pocket of his khakis. He turned toward the sandbox and took a deep breath. "Guess I should tell the boy something."

§

Though after eight in the evening the sun still sat on the horizon across the wheat field as Helen and Raymond Lomax returned to their lake home. He rose from the black Plymouth, beer bottle in hand and strode to the back fence and down the steps to the dock. She led A.J. inside the house.

Raymond lowered himself onto the dock, sitting cross-legged Indian style, listening to the cicadas sing and breathing in the dank, aromatic air.

Long Lake lay flat, darkening and shimmering. Near the opposite bank a bass leapt from the water, startling Raymond and sending across waves that eventually lapped at the shoreline behind him.

As the sky turned indigo Helen appeared, handed him another beer, and knelt beside him.

"The boy's asleep."

"Will Hazel sleep? Will she be okay?"

"Doctor Markopolus gave her a shot. Mom will be there with her tonight."

The wavering din of the cicadas echoed across the water.

"Those bugs drive city people crazy with their racket. Always sing me right to sleep in summertime," said Raymond. "Have all my life. Not so sure about tonight."

"Don't worry about it, Dear. No need to go to work tomorrow. Your boss will understand."

"I'm part of the war effort… Steel armor, steel tank hulls, and turrets. That's what we're producing. Wonder what got Jan. Maybe a tank…"

"Don't, Raymond."

"I work in a factory making weapons that kill other factory workers and their brothers in Germany and Japan. Others get rich off it. Others smoke cigars and move us around like chess pieces. What do we get from it? They say they're looking out for us. Know what's best for us, better than we know for ourselves. It's a racket, Helen. They're just taking care of themselves, that's what I think. Plotting to win the game. If a few pawns and knights get removed from the board, well, that's just how you play it."

He drank from the beer bottle. Helen laid her hand on his. The cicadas quieted for a moment. He went on.

"The world's a fucking mess. I feel for the poor people being bombed out of their homes or forced into uniform and shot, whatever their ilk. I know we have to do business with the Germans, Brits, Russians, French, and whoever. But do we really need to destroy and kill each other to do that effectively? I truly don't get it. I have lots more in common with a German steelworker or a French fisherman than with the conmen in Washington and New York. Can't we all just live with each other in peace?"

He shook his head, lips pressed together. "The First World War was bad enough with all the slaughter of men in the trenches fighting over a few yards of dirt. But as stupid as that was at least then you had soldiers killing soldiers. Now you have planes dropping bombs on cities from a mile high not knowing if they'll land on a factory or a schoolhouse. It's a crime, Helen, whether it's London or Stalingrad or Berlin. Innocents die just to spread terror. Destroy everything and anybody until they give up."

He took another drink and stared off over the water. "Jan loved it here. Loved the lake, loved to hunt and fish. To drink beer and enjoy life."

"You're right, Raymond. It's wrong. So wrong."

"What will become of A.J. without a father? How will Hazel go on?"

Helen patted his hand. "We can help. They'll be fine. We'll pray for them and trust in God."

Raymond started to speak, to blaspheme, then bit his lip. Tough enough for all involved to swallow that Jan was dead. Trying to digest that maybe God was also dead was too much to handle just now.

# 20 | A LETTER FROM FRANCE

Frenouville, France, July 12, 1944

Rays from the setting sun split two poplar trees, passed through the broken window of the chateau's kitchen, and lit dust motes floating over the table where sat a dark-haired man pen in hand, scribbling out a letter and muttering to himself. Another soldier came through the open back door, stopped before him, and saluted.

"Captain Cira. You wanted to see me?"

Phillip Cira glanced up to the lieutenant standing rigid before him. "Relax, Jake. Pull up a chair and pour yourself some Calvados," he said, nodding toward an amber bottle and three thick glasses on the table before him. "Wash the road dust from your throat."

Lieutenant Jacob Wolfson did as he was told. He sat, poured, sipped, and held the glass up to the lowering sun, turning the amber liquor golden. Even though the day had been hot as hell and made him long for a cold Schlitz, the strong liquor hit the spot. "Nice stuff." If nothing else its applejack aroma masked the smell of his own stale sweat migrating up from his fatigues.

Cira shuffled through a short stack of papers to his left and pulled out a typed document.

"Who was this Nowak? I don't remember him."

## THE BOOTLEGGER'S BRIDE

"Older blond guy. The sarcastic bastard who slugged Sergeant Rabee."

"Can't very well tell his wife that. Why didn't I ever hear about this?"

Wolfson scratched his unshaven chin. "A morale issue, sir. The guys wanted me to pin a medal on Nowak, not court martial him."

"Well, too late now. What else?"

Wolfson took another sip and licked his lips. "Say he was a good soldier. Tell her that."

"Was he?"

"Not really. Terrible at following orders. Didn't respect the chain of command. Always pushing back, like this wasn't the fucking army but a damn debating society. I think he had been on his own since he was a kid, always his own man. This was the last place he wanted to be."

"Ditto on that."

"His wife was a knockout judging by her photo. They had a little kid."

"Hell."

"Scuttlebutt was he'd made a killing during Prohibition running liquor in St. Louis. You'd never guess it. Talked more like a college professor than a bootlegger. Going on about books he'd read—Dickens, Dostoyevsky, Aristotle, ancient history..."

Cira lifted his glass of Calvados and inhaled the scent of aged apples and butterscotch. "I'm liking this guy more and more. How'd he die?"

"Got blown to bits by an incoming Flak 88. Couldn't even find his tags. Just bad luck: wrong place, wrong time. Likely didn't know what hit him."

"Well, I can't tell her that either."

"Ironic, that," Wolfson said, staring down into his drink and shaking his head.

"How so?"

"Whenever I asked whether the men understood their objective, he'd pipe up: 'I understand *your* objective, lieutenant. *My* objective is the get my ass home in one piece.'"

"Nowak sounds like a piece of work."

"He was a mensch. The men liked him. I did too. Pity."

"It's all a goddamn pity. A hundred lives lost to gain a meaningless village… This helps, Jake. Thanks."

Wolfson, rose, saluted and left.

Cira went back to writing letters, sipping apple brandy, and muttering to himself about the fucking army, the fucking Germans, the fucking war…

## 21 | HIS MOTHER'S SECRET

Madison County, Illinois, March 29, 1953

He sensed they were hiding something from him. Something important.

Friday, A.J. fetched the mail from the row of tin mailboxes where the lake road and the cutoff intersected. He found four or five business envelopes, some with cellophane windows that looked like bills. He didn't bother checking to see where they came from. None of his business. When he delivered them to Aunt Helen in the kitchen, where she was fixing their supper, she froze.

She dropped what she was doing and took them into the bedroom. When she returned she looked worried and sad, on the verge of tears. But she'd been that way a lot over the past month, ever since his mom died. Same for him, unsure what he felt from moment to moment. Numb, like he had been frozen inside.

Then Saturday mid-morning as the sun began warming the spring air a bit he came up from the lake where he'd been raking the moss for crawfish. As he moved onto the back porch where he slept, A.J. heard through the open kitchen door his aunt talking to Uncle Raymond, who had worked late and slept in.

"She never mentioned it to me. Such a shock when I read the report…"

"I'll be damned."

"Though she did say something curious around Christmastime…"

She looked up to find A.J. standing in the doorway and stopped mid-sentence. She reached across to touch Raymond's hand. Then they both sat quiet staring into their coffee mugs.

So, this morning when it was time for church A.J. clutched his stomach and said he wasn't feeling well. Though in truth he felt fine and was itching to get out of the house and into the spring day after he did what he needed to do.

Aunt Helen squinted and raised an eyebrow like she didn't believe him. But all she said was, "You know it's Palm Sunday."

Now that he was orphaned they didn't discipline or question him so much. But he didn't take advantage as he could have except when he really needed to. Like when he couldn't eat dinner and had to be alone. Or when he yearned to be with Lonnie Sullivan out combing the fields, shotguns in hand, just to get away from everything and get his mind off what had happened. Or like today, when what they were hiding was eating at him. In their absence he would search for the piece of mail that had upset Aunt Helen so. Then he would make his sudden recovery, and they would find him fishing off the dock when they returned from church.

Once the black Plymouth sedan had backed down the drive under the greening willows and headed up the cutoff toward Granite City, A.J. moved to their bedroom.

The bed's dark mock-walnut headboard had ornate designs cut into the wood that echoed those above the dresser's large mirror. A reddish-brown fake-mahogany desk sat to the left by the window facing the lake road. Atop it stood two hand-carved owl bookends, Uncle Raymond's handiwork, clutching a dozen envelopes that had been slit open. A.J. moved to the desk and retrieved the envelopes.

Bills from the electric company and Dressel's Dairy, a letter from Commonwealth Steel, another from the First Presbyterian Church of Granite City. A brochure for a fishing lodge at The Lake of the Ozarks, and an envelope whose return address read "Madison County, Illinois, Coroner's Office."

From it he unfolded an autopsy report for "Decedent: Hazel Marie Robinson Nowak." Clutching the three sheets of paper with both hands A.J. lowered himself onto the padded desk chair.

First the report listed her age, race, sex, length, and weight. Brown eyes, dark brown hair. "Body identified by Helen Robinson Lomax, sister of the deceased," it read.

Next it described her clothing—her topcoat with fox-fur collar, black cocktail dress, silk undergarments and stockings. He scanned the external examination and toxicology report—blood alcohol level .28. A.J. didn't know what that meant exactly but could guess.

Then under "Gross Description" he read: "approx. 16-week fetus, .27 lbs."

A.J. looked out through the window whose wood-slat blinds had been raised to the sun-dappled front yard. The willows swayed in a light wind. An orange-breasted robin strutted across the emerald grass.

He knew what that meant. Growing up he had seen cattle and dogs mating without understanding why. That is, until the older boys on the school bus—the same ones who had revealed that Santa was a fraud—filled him in, suggesting that their parents did it too. Then one hot Friday night two summers ago when he still lived with his mom A.J. was awakened by anxious muffled voices. He padded barefoot over the carpeted hallway. The door of his mother's bedroom stood ajar. A.J. peered through the opening and in ochre candlelight saw Richard Dupuis kneeling naked behind his mother, mounting her much the same as he had seen animals doing. Now that image resurfaced and lingered until he shoved it aside.

Further down he read: "Immediate Cause of Death: Acute drowning, hypoxemia and cerebral anoxia," and "Manner of Death: Accident."

Again, he looked up out the window to the willow trees. He traveled back to wintertime as a child, which came to him vaguely. He pictured the frozen lake as if in a fog. He saw himself standing on the cold dock at their home and his mother and father ice-skating back and forth, up and down the lake hand-in-hand, looping around the thin ice of the nearby spring where later he discovered her body.

# 22 | A NIGHT OF FORGETFULNESS

Madison County, Illinois, November 18, 1950

He had just signaled Karl for a nightcap when he saw Jesse, who was putting his horn away, look up toward the front door and pause for an instant. Richard Dupuis followed his gaze past the tables where customers were still drinking, smoking, and laughing. There a slim brunette in high heels and slinky black dress beneath a burgundy topcoat stepped toward the far end of the bar. She walked real straight and tall and composed as if she had had a few. She deposited the coat on the last barstool and slid onto the next.

He had seen her before in The Blue Note though not alone. He couldn't remember when or with whom. Could have been years ago. But hers was not a face you'd forget: a looker. And her figure just right. He'd always liked slender. Hedy Lamarr? That's it: A real Hedy Lamarr. Wasn't often someone with real class came into the joint.

Karl served her a highball. When she slid a pack of Luckies from her clutch purse lying on the bar, Dupuis sauntered down the row of padded chrome barstools, left hand grasping his drink and his right the cigarette lighter in his sport coat pocket. As she lifted a cigarette toward her lips he caught Karl's eye, and the bartender turned away.

"Let me," he intoned over her shoulder.

He clicked the lighter and held the flame before her. The faintest lines at the corners of her eyes told him she was closer to thirty-five than twenty-five. That is, perfect. An age when a woman knows the score. The paper crinkled and burned. Only after drawing deeply on her cigarette and exhaling did she turn to see who held the lighter.

"Thanks."

"You just missed some good dance music. Jesse used to play trumpet for Woody Herman."

"I'm sure. However, I did hear some pretty good music tonight across the river at the Casa Loma. The Harry James band."

"We can't compete with the likes of that."

"We?"

"I'm the proprietor here. Richard Dupuis."

"Hazel Robinson," she said, extending a cool hand to him, diamonds set in white gold wrapping her wrist. Her perfume wasn't cheap either. The kind that said she was an animal not a flower.

"You look familiar to me, Hazel Robinson," he said, leaning an elbow on the bar. "Like I might have seen you in here once. Or maybe in the movies."

"I was here a few times years ago with my husband before he died."

"Sorry to hear about that, Hazel."

"In fact, he recognized you. Said you had once done some business together."

Alarm bells started clanging in Dupuis's head. She looked like the sort of dame who could have been with some big-time hood, guys who sometimes buy it

## THE BOOTLEGGER'S BRIDE

prematurely. Likely still rationed by someone post-hubby. Best to tiptoe.

"I've done business with a lot of good people over the years. What was your husband's name?"

She stubbed out her cigarette in the blue glass ashtray on the bar, staring at it.

"Jan Nowak."

He bit his lip and frowned at the smoke rising from the ashtray as if trying to recall. Recall he did: fucking devious Polack punk. Guys seldom got the better of Richard Dupuis when doing business. If certain people found out it could ruin you. But in this case it wasn't the sort of job the Slavic shit would have been bragging about. Good to hear the prick was dead.

"Nowak... Nowak... Sounds familiar. Did he tell you what kind of business?"

"No. Just that you probably wouldn't want to talk about it."

Dupuis shrugged. "Maybe it'll come to me... How about another drink on the house, Hazel?"

She raised an eyebrow, pursed crimson lips, and looked him up and down. He lifted his chin at Karl and held up two fingers.

§

Hazel woke parched to a bright day, raw throat, and throbbing headache. Typical Sunday morning though a bit more oozy woozy than usual. It was the damn cigarettes. If she could quit the smokes she'd feel a whole lot better mornings. Not likely. She loved them.

Hazel remembered feeling good the night before. The music, the dancing, the drive back across the bridge from St. Louis—she recalled all that. Getting home was another story. After crossing the Mississippi, she drew a blank. Maybe it would come back to her later. Odd the way that worked. Hours of her life often irretrievably lost. But she didn't much care.

She heard a noise in the kitchen—a coffee cup hitting the counter—sat up straight and found herself naked. She put her palms to her temples and stared at her silk stockings lying on the carpet beside her ivory tap pants. What the hell had happened? The previous night hung distorted, dark, and, for now, incomplete, like an expressionist jigsaw puzzle with pieces missing. She found her robe and ventured toward the kitchen.

The electric percolator sat warm on the counter. She crossed the kitchen to the den, where logs crackled in the fireplace. A tall black-haired, mustachioed man in a navy blazer, coffee cup in hand, stood at the windows overlooking the lake. He turned as she padded barefooted across the floor and plopped in the leather armchair by the fire.

"Good morning, Hazel."

"Good God," she said, shaking her head but finding that just made things worse. Slowly it was coming back to her. "Fetch me a cup, black."

He smiled and moved off.

A few of the missing puzzle pieces floated into place. Drinks at The Blue Note. How many? What difference did that make? No recollection of driving home from there. She looked up to see her car in the drive and a cream-colored Cadillac convertible behind it. No memory of anything else, though she could imagine.

The man returned with her coffee. Richard Dupuis. That she knew from before. From years before. She could even remember the exact date: January 10, 1942. Their second anniversary.

"You have a lovely home here, Hazel. I think I know the guy who built it. One of Jellyroll Hogan's gang."

"That name sounds familiar. Memorable enough... You have a cigarette?"

He pulled a pack of Pall Malls from his sport coat pocket. She took one from it, and he lit it with a gold lighter. Then he lifted his chin toward the bookcase behind her.

"Who's the kid?"

She turned and reached for A.J.'s gold-framed school photo. With her sleeve she smoothed dust from it. "My son. He's nine. Fourth grade at Mitchell."

Dupuis frowned. "He here?"

"No, no. Stays with my sister and her husband weekends to give me a little breathing room."

A.J. was likely in church now with Helen and Raymond. She couldn't remember the last time she went. The pastor did stop by one afternoon to see how she was doing. She was in her cups early that day, that's how she was doing. He didn't stay long and left disgusted.

"Nice looking boy. Takes after you. What's he gonna be when he grows up?"

"Rich."

"So, he likes the moolah?"

Hazel took a deep drag on her cigarette and studied A.J.'s photo, trying to see Jan there. "Not so much. He likes books, and he likes the lake. His father set up a trust fund for him before he went off to war. It'll kick in when A.J. turns twenty-one."

Dupuis made a mental note of that.

"Trust fund, eh?" he said. "Must be nice. Always wanted one of those. Unfortunately, my ancestors were not very industrious."

"His father was, at least when he was young."

"And this is him, Jan Nowak?" he said, pointing to another framed photo on a bookcase shelf.

She nodded. "Yes. That's Jan."

"I think I do remember him now," said Dupuis. "Nice fella."

## 23 | A.J. RECRUITED

August 26, 1955, Granite City, Illinois

Head Coach Erik Nordstrom and defensive coach Monk Monihan stood atop a rise with the sun lowering behind them, looking down on a rising cloud of hot dust. From it came the camphor smell of liniments, the sound of shoulder pads slapping against helmets, and the grunts of young men colliding.

Some thought it barbaric competition that glorified violence and aggression. Nordstrom, who'd witnessed deadly violence and aggression on his march up Italy, thought football an intriguing entertainment that safely siphoned off teenage testosterone.

Monihan shook his head. "That Nowak kid's a freak, Coach. Most guys hate the box drill. Everyone pounding you one after another. He loves it. Him against the world."

Nordstrom nodded. "Freakish in a good way. Balance like a cat and quick as a jackrabbit. Gets lower and outhits bigger guys."

"Sure does."

"But it's his ferocity that makes him. Never seen anything like it in a fifteen-year-old." Though he thought he understood why. "Let's work him at safety, Monk. When he fills out, maybe next year as a junior, he'll make a great middle linebacker. For now, he'll be our secret weapon."

"Where'd you find him? He just walk on?"

"Recruited him from gym class. Had to twist his arm."

The previous February in freshman P.E. he had separated Nowak from two other guys in a dustup on the basketball floor. Afterward when he called him into his locker-room office the kid stood before Nordstrom's desk shifting his weight from one leg to the other as if preparing to spring.

"What was that about, Nowak? Eckman said you were throwing elbows. In theory basketball is a non-contact sport."

"Then tell them. They're always pushing and putting hands on me."

"What did you say to Eckman?"

"All I said was to leave me alone. In so many words. Then he poked my shoulder. I told him, 'Touch me again and I'll deck you.' He didn't think I could do it."

Odd kid. Often didn't show for class and kept to himself when he did. But not a slouch or couch potato. Agile, keen on gymnastics, always first in wind sprints. Nordstrom had heard the other guys call him Chief Nowak, though not to his face. He now noticed that the kid carried a thick book on Cherokee history and the Trail of Tears.

"Who taught you to fight?"

"My Uncle Raymond. He learned to box in the C.C.C.s."

Nordstrom knew about the family arrangement. Everyone did. Lots of kids lost dads during the war, one way or another. Then he lost his mom too.

Most students at Granite City High were open-faced Midwesterners, particularly the country kids. Accessible, guileless, smiling. Not A.J. Locked down, humorless, suspicious, and cold—a countenance that encouraged others to keep their distance. Though Nordstrom had seen worse in the army: vicious, fucked up characters you wouldn't turn your back on. Sometimes they made good soldiers, though generally not for long. Nowak wasn't bad or mean just incognito. Whoever he was.

"You ever play football, A.J.?"

He shook his head. "No, sir. We live out in the sticks on Long Lake. Not enough guys around for that. Besides, no one's got a football. Just fishing poles and shotguns."

Nordstrom smiled briefly. "Some say it's a contact sport, A.J. They're wrong. It's a collision sport. A team sport with well-defined individual responsibilities. Where you can be yourself and also part of something bigger. I think you'd like it. A chance to knock people down without getting kicked out of school for it."

"You gonna kick me out for fighting?"

"Wasn't much of a fight—one punch."

That almost made Nowak smile.

"Football's for big lummoxes," he said. "I weigh one-thirty."

"That didn't stop you from slugging Eckman who goes one-eighty. But maybe you just don't have what it takes."

Nowak stared at him for a moment. "What's it take?"

"Physical courage, self-discipline, and teamwork. Most of all toughness. Grit."

Nowak stopped squirming. Finally, Nordstrom had hit on something that got his attention.

Now, after two weeks of summer practice he saw something in the kid that pleased him deeply—something even more than the natural athleticism and raw potential of A. J. Nowak as a football player. Nordstrom saw him becoming a teammate.

# 24 | THE ORPHAN STRIVES TO HEAL HIMSELF

Madison County, Illinois, March 17, 1956

On a sunny Saturday afternoon with the temperature rising toward sixty A.J. guided the rowboat south on Long Lake, rowing easily. He hadn't been at the oars since late summer when football season started. Over the intervening months he had grown another two inches, putting him near six foot tall, and added thirty pounds of bone, sinew, and muscle. He could feel the difference through the oars as they sliced into the greenish water and propelled him effortlessly over the windless lake.

Soon he glided toward the dock at what had been his mother's home and his father's home and his home. Now it was his alone. Or would soon be, when he came of age. Though he didn't know what to do with it. Or how he felt about it. Mixed memories, mixed emotions, for sure.

Nor was he certain how he felt about himself, who he had become as a result of losing both his parents. He'd been thinking about it more lately, wondering whether he was on the right path. A.J. recognized that he was all jammed up. He was lonely a lot but didn't much like being with other kids. Most didn't seem to take things seriously. Did a lot of silly shit that he had no interest in. He liked playing football. Nothing childish about it.

Willows along the shore were leafing out and catkins showing on the larger trees atop the lake bank. Sunfish stirred beneath the dock. High above, a red-tailed hawk circled searching for food. Spring was coming early this year. The air smelled fresh and expectant.

He lifted himself from the boat seat, climbed up on the dock, and stood feet spread gazing at the wooden stairs that led up the bank. Three years ago now that his mother had died. He'd not returned home since, nor shed a tear.

A.J. felt for the key in his jeans pocket, slid it out, and grasped it in his fist. Still, he could not move. Then he kicked himself mentally—What? You afraid of ghosts? He heard Coach Nordstrom growling, "Get up off the ground, you pantywaist!" A.J. climbed the stairs.

At the back door he turned the key and pushed into the den. Was it the lingering spirits he'd have to face that had scared him off those three years? Or something he'd have to confront inside himself, his conflicting notions of his mother and what she had done to herself and to him. And then there was his father, who had also deserted him, though perhaps under duress. He wasn't sure about any of it. It was all a jumble.

He lit the green-shaded lamp on the end table by the divan. The room lay cold as a crypt. He recalled the placid look on his mother's face as she lay in her casket amid the sweet-smelling flowers surrounding her. Hands folded together as if she were merely resting for a while, like she had decided to nap in a flowerbed. He remembered too the next, cold morning when they lowered her into her grave. He had yet to return there either.

# THE BOOTLEGGER'S BRIDE

Now he reprised the image of her encased in the ice of the frozen lake, as he had hundreds of times, even in sleep. A.J. knew that someday, somehow, he had to melt the ice that held him and inhibited him. He just didn't know how. But recently he came upon a quote from Franz Kafka in his literature class anthology that gave him a clue: "A book must be the axe for the frozen sea within us." Those words had clung to him and now had compelled him to return home.

Though musty smelling, the room remained much as it was the last time he visited his mother just weeks before she died. He guessed Aunt Helen had cleared out the library books that had been stacked throughout the den. She likely returned them and insisted on paying the overdue fines. But the books he sought today were from his mother's lifelong collection dating back to her childhood and school days, to her college literature classes and beyond. Those would still be on her shelves.

He first went to her Charles Dickens collection, which numbered a dozen books. There A.J. pulled out *Great Expectations*, *David Copperfield*, and *Oliver Twist*. He moved left then, back down the chronologically arranged English fiction to locate *Tom Jones* and back right to *Jane Eyre*.

Next he ventured into the American lit section and withdrew Mark Twain's *Adventures of Huckleberry Finn* and Edgar Rice Burroughs's *Tarzan of the Apes*. That should do for now. A good start.

He reckoned that if he were ever to hack through whatever held him or affect a thaw, if he were ever to overcome the twin childhood traumas of his parents' deaths and deal with that burden effectively, it might help to see how other orphans managed similar abandonment. And what they might all have in common. He hoped that Pip, Oliver, Tarzan, Jane, Huck, and the others might point the way home.

He had seen that his mother had been attempting something similar: to come to grips with her husband's death via literature. However, she had taken off in the wrong direction. Instead of looking inside herself to where she might find her strength and regain her bearings, she foundered in books cataloguing the chaos, stupidity, and futility of war. That is, things she could do nothing about. It was not self-healing she had engaged in but self-flagellation.

Similarly, being orphaned was nothing A.J. could do anything about. That die had been cast. He could continue to be frozen by it emotionally and spend—or, rather, misspend—his life posing as an angry victim of parental abandonment. Or he could respond to it in a way to free and actuate himself. Perhaps with altruistic works like Superman, another orphan. Or with guile and goodness like Huckleberry Finn. Or with the resourcefulness and courage of Tarzan. He would learn more from his close reading of their stories and others.

One thing he had already figured out was that despite the love of his aunt and uncle and the financial legacy of his father, he needed to be able to rely on himself, to love himself, if he was ever to be the hero of his own life. Something he craved heart and soul. He searched for tools that might enable him to do just that.

Next A.J. moved to the bookshelves at the northern end of the room, to his father's books. Not as extensive as his mother's lifelong collection and more a mixed bag, both topically and spatially. History, philosophy, and mysteries; essays, poetry, and memoirs; American literature, varied nonfiction, and more, all shelved without any rhyme or reason that A.J. could perceive. He knelt before the moldy-smelling shelves gazing up and down, left and right, to see what might further his quest.

Books by Montaigne, Mencken, Melville, Henry Miller, and Hemingway. Others on English grammar, Australian aborigines, and songbirds; on economics and Siberian travel. Then, tucked away on the bottom shelf, he discovered a title that struck him, describing himself to a T: *Modern Man in Search of a Soul*.

He pried the worn hardcover book from among the others and rifled through it—a discarded library book—finding many of the thick, yellowed pages dog-eared, with passages underscored in blue ink.

A.J. was not familiar with the author, C.G. Jung. In the front matter he read that the man was a preeminent Swiss psychologist. On the title page, again in blue ink, he found a quote inscribed in his late father's emphatic hand:

*"Until you make the unconscious conscious it will direct your life and you will call it fate."—C.G. Jung*

The words seemed to speak personally to A.J., even though he wasn't quite sure what they exactly meant. He would find out.

A.J. rose, added that book to his stack, and retreated with his take through the back door. He had done what he came to do. Enough for one day. He could return later to wrestle with the ghosts in the rest of the house that he needed to subdue and dispel. Or, it occurred to him, embrace.

# 25 | SHOCKING WORDS

September 28, 1956, Granite City, Illinois

A cool Friday night. Hometown fans cheered the Warriors as they migrated from the lighted field toward the locker room after dispatching their upriver rival Alton Redbirds 19-14.

The players slapped each other's shoulder pads, roared, waved, and smiled. All except for one, cheerleader Lana Markopolus noted: A.J. Nowak. He retained his usual stoic demeanor despite having good reason to celebrate. The junior linebacker had made numerous tackles—the field announcer calling out his name a dozen times—and snared a late interception that sealed the victory.

Lana wondered about him. He had a hard, chiseled look and a reputation for edginess. A fighter. Though he was no fool. In her American history class spring semester he brought the same intensity he displayed on the gridiron. He asked good questions out of honest curiosity as opposed to brown-nosing and added background about American Indian participation in various wars—interesting info not found in the textbook. Though infrequently in either case, never showing off or acting clever. She got the impression he didn't care what anyone else thought of him, including the teacher. Or her.

Though she had never spoken to him she knew about him. Everyone did. His father had died in The War. Then his mother had drowned after falling through the Long Lake ice, a tragic story recounted on page one of the *Granite City Press-Record* just a few years earlier. So maybe he had good reason to be distant, to avoid attachments that might end in loss and suffering.

Though dark and mysterious he seemed like someone who needed help. Her parents, physicians who had immigrated from Greece at World War II's onset, taught her that helping other people was the noblest effort one could offer God and humanity. She wished she could break through his cold façade to help A.J. Nowak in some way. While others thought him a tough and self-possessed outsider, she saw him as a fragile and lost loner. Seemingly shy around girls, he never dated anyone, at least no one from Granite City. Stigmatized as an orphan, he likely felt insecure, wondering whether he really belonged.

The last player to leave the field as if striving not to draw attention to himself or engage with others, he moved through the cordon of cheerleaders lining the team's exit. As he passed Lana she waved her red and white pom-poms and called to him:

"Hey, 44! What can I do to make you smile?"

He paused and turned to her, looking her up and down with a glint of recognition in his eyes. Then he stepped to her, leaned forward, and whispered in her ear—six simple words—before following his teammates to the locker room.

Lana stood frozen, eyes wide, while the other cheerleaders zeroed in on her. Then—she couldn't help it—a smile rose from deep inside her, spread across her face, and would not abate.

The Warrior cheerleaders gathered round imploring her:

"What did he say?"

"Something dirty?"

"What'd he tell you?"

She just shook her head and remained mute, realizing that she had totally misjudged him. Hardly shy. Hardly fragile or self-conscious. And certainly not lacking in self-confidence.

Lana, still smiling, turned away from the other girls, A.J. Nowak's six words echoing within her: "Marry me and have my baby."

# 26 | A SENTIMENTAL JOURNEY

Granite City, Illinois, October 17, 1957

First day back after his suspension everyone stared at A.J. and his fading black eye as he moved down the aisle toward the back of the school bus. No one said a word, which meant they knew what happened or at least a version or two of it. Lonnie Sullivan winked at him as he approached, and A.J. patted his shoulder.

They rode alongside the railroad tracks toward town in relative silence, passing a slow-moving line of coal hoppers pulled by a chugging steam locomotive. The rattletrap bus, however, was anything but quiet, engine clamoring, gears grinding, seats and windows squeaking and clanking. Wind buffeted through the lowered panes on an Indian Summer morning that smelled of engine exhaust and coal dust.

The bus pulled to a stop in front of the massive brown-brick high-school building. When A.J. stepped off Lana Markopolus stood awaiting him—straight black hair, bangs, red-and-white Warrior cheerleading uniform. God, she was pretty. She squinted at him and said: "Shiner's looking better."

"How's Gibson's nose look?"

She smiled. "Hard to tell what with all the bandages."

"When your dad set it I hoped he gave him a big hooked schnoz to remember me always."

Lana laughed. "The mark of Nowak."

"His own damn fault."

"Melissa said Tom told her it had to do with what Gibson said about me."

A.J. frowned. "Just something he muttered after I rocked him with a clean tackle. Told him, 'Say that again and I'll kick your ass to Collinsville.' That's when he got in my face and pushed me, acting the All-American Golden Boy quarterback. Stupid of him to yank his helmet off, grandstanding for the guys. Cost him the broken nose."

Lana looked up to him eyes smiling. "I can sort of guess what he said… I ever tell you how much I admire your tackling technique?"

A.J. pictured it, feeling his stomach flutter. "You phrased it different."

"Will I see you tonight after practice?" She bit her bottom lip. "I can give you a ride home."

Her resemblance to his mother was not lost on him. However, his feelings for Lana were of a much different character. He now fought against those urges, telling himself to stick to the plan despite the visceral allure of the "ride home." He needed to do this now rather than later since he didn't know about later.

"No, go on home, Lana. Got some things I need to take care of. I'll see you tomorrow, okay?"

Her eyes told him she knew something was up. They were always straight with each other, and he hated keeping her in the dark. Still it would be better to wait till it was more settled.

"You okay?" she asked.

"I'm good. And everything's fine with us, Lana. You know that."

Once inside the building he went to his locker and retrieved his brown suede jacket and a library book he wanted to keep. He doubted they would miss it or that anyone else would ever want it. When the class bell rang he moved back out the building's front door and down the sidewalk.

On Madison Avenue he caught a county bus that carried him southwest across the city, up a bridge over railroad tracks, and down into Venice, Illinois, which was nothing like the Venice, Italy, he'd read about in Edith Wharton and Henry James. The American Bottom flatland that bordered the Mississippi across from St. Louis was marked by steel mills, slaughterhouses, rail yards, oil refineries, munitions factories, and chemical plants. No floating gondolas or gondoliers that he knew of.

Near the river at the end of the bus line he changed to a waiting green East Side Railway streetcar, faded and rusty, with worn brocade seats, dating from another era. Maybe the same streetcar his grandfather rode from St. Louis to the Granite City steel mill every day for decades. It soon carried him up and over the Mississippi via the McKinley Bridge, tracks running down the middle of the automobile lanes.

Once on the Missouri side the car curved left on a wooden trestle, steel wheels squealing as it leaned over scrapyards fifty feet below, the electric line crackling above. Next the tracks bent west and dropped into a subway tunnel that led to the 12th Street terminal.

There A.J. detrained and climbed concrete stairs from the underground station to street level and walked north through the crisp autumn day.

He crossed Cass Avenue and turned onto Howard Street, lined with redbrick tenements. Despite the sunny day and brilliant autumn leaves the neighborhood struck him as somber. It smelled old, not fresh like Long Lake, and looked unkempt, with old tenements, abandoned storefronts, and litter in the gutters. The city lay decaying and neglected, particularly the older inner city, where much of the housing dated from long before the Civil War.

He paused and pulled a yellowed envelope from the back pocket of his chinos. Once more he studied the return address before jamming it back into his trousers.

A.J. found the home, climbed the worn marble stoop and, heart pounding, knocked on a door where dark green paint peeled.

Beyond the door he soon heard heavy footsteps approaching. It swung open to reveal a tall, bearded man in a green corduroy shirt and black slacks, dark hair flecked with white strands. He gazed at A.J. in bewilderment.

A.J. cleared his throat and said, "Godfather, I am Alexander Jan Nowak."

Bogdan Zawadski spread his arms and stepped forward to embrace A.J., pressing him to his chest and crying like a child.

§

They sat at a mahogany kitchen table, china coffee cups before them. In the adjoining dining room in lieu of a dinner table a green baize poker table rested beneath a brass chandelier. Six high-backed armchairs surrounded it. Post-impressionist prints in gilt frames hung on the walls, papered in dark green and red stripes as if from another era. The front room they had passed through from the street also claimed an anachronistic elegance, as if harkening back to when the city served as an anchor of New France.

"How many years, A.J.? I am so ashamed I too abandoned you. I should have done more."

"No, please…"

"There were such troubles. Let me explain…" He drew a breath and gazed off over A.J., remembering. "I found out about Jan aboard ship six months after he died. My sister Magdalena wrote me. When I get back and go to see you and your mother she's not the same woman. Two years since your father was killed. I figured time heals. In her case I was wrong.

"Whenever I visited I felt unwelcome, that I made her uncomfortable. Maybe made her feel guilty. You see, after Pearl Harbor Jan and I got drunk and vowed to enlist in the Navy together. Next day he tells your mother, and she talks him out of it. They weren't drafting guys with kids yet, and she tells him maybe he wouldn't have to go at all.

"When he says has to break his vow that we'll go in the Navy together, I see it ripping him up. So, I let him off the hook, say it's no big deal. We were drinking! I shrug it off and tell myself, What do I know about being married? What do I know about women, really?

"But here was the payoff for her. If he had gone in the Navy with me he'd still be alive. That's what she thought.

She said so once on the phone when I called to see how you all are doing. 'If I'd only let him go…' She was in her cups, of course. Wouldn't listen when I tried to talk sense. She wanted to wallow in her guilty feelings, to punish herself.

"Too bad she was Protestant. She could have a used a priest and some absolution. She needed to confess, get God's forgiveness, and get on with life. To forgive herself and stop cursing Fate. Which ain't real anyway. That's what I tell her. But she wouldn't listen. She had written a tragic script for herself and could not stop playing her role. I saw the direction she was headed—spiraling down. I felt powerless to help.

"Next year the Christmas card I sent came back. I tried to call but the phone was disconnected. So, I ask around and find out that your mother died the winter before, but I don't know what happened to you. No one knew anything. I prayed you were being well cared for."

"I was, and I am. My Aunt Helen and Uncle Raymond took me in."

"Good folks. I first met them on the day your father saw your mother at the racetrack…"

Bogdan stirred his coffee and again gazed off.

"…Jan and I went to the paddock between races to check out the horse we were playing. There was a dark-haired woman, so fresh looking, standing alone at the rail watching the ponies. Jan couldn't take his eyes off her. I never seen him like that. Women were always like interchangeable parts moving past him down an assembly line. He lifted his chin at her and said, 'There she is, Bogdan.'

"'Who?'

"'The woman I'm going to marry.'

"Of course, I think he's joking… He goes over to her and talks her up awhile. Then he comes back and says, 'I owe you one, my friend.'

"'Why?' I ask.

"He says, 'I gave her the winner in the next. But didn't tell her about the quinella or the fix.'"

A.J. sat mesmerized, seeing it in his mind—flying to the racetrack and time traveling, just as he had done as a child when listening to The Lone Ranger or Captain Midnight on the radio. Bogdan went on to recount Jan and him growing up together and life on the streets. Then Prohibition, The Great Depression, Hooverville, and the flavor of the neighborhood in distant days.

This was not what A.J. had come for. He had yet to ask Bogdan for the favor he wanted—the whole point of his trip across the river. Yet now, sitting with his godfather, he was getting something even better. In his stories Bogdan brought A.J.'s father back to life.

At last Bogdan paused and studied A.J.

"You walk into a wall or something?"

A.J. frowned then realized what he meant, reaching up to touch his black eye. "Yeah, but the wall got the worst of it."

Bogdan laughed. "Your father was a fighter too. Built like you. Not an ounce of fat."

Then he gestured toward the book on the table. "What are you reading?"

"World War II history. I read a lot of it, along with other things. This one's about Navajo code talkers in the Pacific theater."

"I was there on a tin can—a destroyer. Could have been among the destroyed. Those Indians maybe helped bring me back alive."

"Their culture's interesting. Emphasizes strength—physical, mental, and spiritual—along with wisdom and courage."

"Good words to live by if you can pull it off… Your father he was a book man too. Always hanging out at the library. History, like you. Philosophy, psychology…"

"I love books—Mom's influence. Problem is I hate school. Don't like being cooped up inside all day, just sitting around… I was thinking about joining the Marines."

Bogdan nodded. "Now's a good time. No shooting war, just Cold War."

"A good time on a personal level too. There's a girl I'm crazy about. But I need to leave town before I knock her up and ruin both our lives."

Bogdan laughed. "There's wisdom and courage! If she's the one for you she'll still be there in four years. If not, you've dodged a bullet."

A.J. smiled then got serious.

"There's something I want to ask… Before I go away I need to see my grandmother. It's been a year or more. My aunt and uncle drove me over once, but it was awkward. We could barely communicate… I was wondering if maybe you could go with me sometime and translate."

Bogdan spread his hands. "Let's go!"

"Now?"

The older man rose. "Both your father and grandfather were men of action. Decisive men. You have the same blood. Let's march!"

# THE BOOTLEGGER'S BRIDE

§

Bogdan led him down Hadley Street to Cass Avenue and headed west. A.J. looked around as they strolled and tilted his head right. "She lives on Warren Street now. Up that way, isn't it?"

"I know. We're taking a sentimental journey."

After a minute they approached a vast area of high-rise apartments on the south side of the street, eleven-story buildings, more than thirty of them.

"This is where your grandparents lived, where your father grew up, in a two-story flat right about there," Bogdan said, pointing across the street to a parking lot. "Now new public housing for the Colored."

A sign there read: "Wendell O. Pruitt Homes and William Igoe Apartments." A.J. gaped at the massive structures and shook his head.

"I've always lived on the lake with my feet on the ground. Wouldn't want to be up in the air in a box. It's like a prison cell."

Bogdan shrugged. "Depends on the box. When Jan met your mother he lived in a swank downtown hotel with room service and a nice bar where we used to hang out. You're right though. Hanging out on the lake was even better."

Bogdan gazed across the street at the high-rises. "I guess they're trying to help people. But you gotta help yourself, A.J. You gotta fight for what you want in life—fight the gods, the other guy, and yourself. Not sucking up but muscling up. That's how you make a home for yourself. And no one else can do it for you because no one else knows what's in your heart."

They moved on past boarded-up storefronts and old brick homes with sagging roofs, picking their way over a herringboned sidewalk with missing bricks, like a mouth with rotting teeth.

"I always loved the neighborhood," said Bogdan. "It's still home to me but who knows how long it'll last? The old people like your grandfather and grandmother, the ones who came over on the boat, are dying off. The young ones are moving away. Who can blame them? It's crazy," he said, stopping, spreading his arms, and gesturing palms up toward a dilapidated tenement. "Two thousand years ago the Romans had indoor plumbing and these places still have outhouses."

They moved on and he continued:

"No glue to keep young people here. Used to be the language and Polish culture. The food, the Falcons, and St. Stanislaus; the families and traditions. Now hardly no one speaks Polish. So that's the end. So be it.

"Now we're Americans not Poles. Not even Polish-Americans, which makes no sense once the language and culture curl up and die. Same with the Irish, Italians, Germans, and Jews who came here. Now we all embrace the new land. It's all for the good…"

He shook his head and laid a hand on A.J.'s shoulder as they walked. "So why can't I stand the thought of leaving? You're planning your future. I live in the past."

They headed north on 19th Street. Cars lined the curbs of the cobbled thoroughfare though little traffic passed to disturb the neighborhood. The leaves had turned from green to gold, ochre, red, and brown. A.J. noticed that the fall colors came later here than on the lake.

"Your grandfather took it hard when he lost Jan. I saw him first thing when I come back home after the war. How much he'd aged in four years! How weakened. He thought Jan tried to prove something to him by going to war. To show his manhood and win back his father's respect. Joseph scolded himself for being so tough on his only son. For sending a fifteen-year-old away from home to live on his own. Forcing Jan to do whatever to survive… Finally, the old man gave up and died. Nothing left to live for."

After a few minutes they turned right on Warren Street and soon moved through a narrow passageway between buildings to a brick patio defined by tenements on either side and a cobblestone alley in back. They climbed wooden stairs to the second floor where Bogdan knocked on a curtained door. Soon through it came the clack of heels on linoleum. The curtain moved; the door swung open.

Maria Nowak stood rigid and unsmiling in a belted gray dress and black laced shoes with low heels, looking much the same as always: fearful. In their few encounters over the years A.J. never remembered her laughing or even smiling honestly. Never recalled her touching him, much less hugging and kissing him like his other grandmother did.

Bogdan said something in Polish. She responded by nodding at A.J. and stepped aside. A.J. followed his godfather into the kitchen, through the bedroom, and to the front room, which overlooked Warren Street. There the leaves of tall sycamores had turned light brown and floated to the redbrick sidewalk and street below.

The apartment looked and smelled like her flat he remembered from early childhood—the same furniture arranged identically, the same aroma of floor wax and mothballs.

Bogdan and A.J. sat on the sofa by the front window as his grandmother disappeared into the kitchen. She returned a minute later with two cans of beer that she set on coasters atop the coffee table before them. She sat on a chair facing the windows behind them, a third beer can cradled between both hands on her lap. His grandmother remained rail thin, as if she never learned to eat well or never embraced the pleasure of it.

Bogdan exchanged words with her and turned to A.J.

"I told her you were going into the army and might be gone for awhile. She wishes you safe travels and a safe return home."

A.J. thanked her then said to Bogdan: "See if I can ask her some questions about her family."

She responded to Bogdan's query by nodding and sipping from her beer can.

"Ask about how she grew up, what her home was like."

When Bogdan translated the request, she pursed her lips and stared off over their heads to the sycamores. Then she began to speak, and went on and on, Bogdan nodding to encourage her and translating on the fly sotto voce so as not to interrupt her.

"Their home sat outside the town where her father worked. She can't remember what kind of work. Maybe a carpenter at times, maybe a carter... Her mother had a vegetable garden and pigeons... Two older brothers left home. One, Szymon, came to America."

She told of her neighbor who had a daughter her age and how they taught Maria to read and write. They became her second family. She described how cold it was in winter and how they strove to keep warm. How frugal life was. How little they had to eat. When she was twelve-years-old men on horseback rode through the village with sabers drawn, cutting people down.

When she was seventeen or eighteen—she couldn't remember exactly—she was sent to America to be married. After she arrived she wrote letters home. She got no reply for years. Finally, her father wrote telling her that her brother Piotr had been killed in The Great War. She also exchanged annual letters with the neighbor who had taught her to write. Communication from her ceased in 1939 and never resumed.

At last, she fell silent and looked to A.J. as if ready for his next question. He held her gaze and said:

"How did you meet my grandfather?"

She raised her chin indicating she understood and began again to speak.

"She met him when she got off the train at St. Louis Union Station," Bogdan translated. "He was with her brother Szymon, whom she had not seen since she was a child. Within a month she and Joseph married, as had been arranged. After a year she had a child, Stanislaw. He died before he reached age two. Then she gave birth to your father, Janusz, who was a healthy baby, a strong boy."

A.J. sat leaning forward studying this strange bird of a grandmother as she went on about her son, her days in America, Jan's death, and her husband's. Within a half hour she had summed up her life. Afterward the two men descended the stairs and moved across the brick backyard. Bogdan laid an arm across A.J.'s shoulders.

"There you have it, my boy. The All-American immigrant tale. Remember it well when you get to boot camp and want to bitch about the food or cry about how rough they treat you. Remember it always."

§

The silver-haired woman behind the polished bar placed two bottles of Falstaff on felt coasters alongside two short beer glasses.

"Sandwiches for you and your pal, Bogdan?"

"Sure, Anne. Whatever you got."

When she moved to the back room to fix their lunch, A.J. asked, "Do I look twenty-one?"

"You look seventeen but you're with me… I used to come in here before Prohibition when I was this high…" He slid his hand off the bar top to indicate how small he had been. "My father would send me down with two tin beer buckets for him and his pals. We lived upstairs next door. Your father lived across the street.

"He was five years younger than me and had no big brother to watch out for him. So, I kept an eye on Jan, kept him out of trouble. Later helped get him in trouble. He helped me with my English."

A.J. poured beer into his glass, sniffed the yeasty aroma, and drank. The tavern itself smelled of stale beer and cigar smoke. Its high tin ceiling had been painted white once upon a time. Tall windows facing the sidewalk had had their lower half blackened for privacy.

The tavern's front door stood open. Two wooden-bladed ceiling fans turned lazily. Flies buzzed above spittoons that sat on the unvarnished floor beneath the brass foot rail. Three tables with cane chairs lined the wall behind them, where lighted beer signs hung, as they did above the mirrored back bar. There were no other customers.

"It was good hearing your stories about my father. I don't remember him much. Most of what I know I learned from Mom."

"As I said, love at first sight. Though it came to be more. Soul mates. He worshipped her and vice versa. Despite his past—or maybe because of it—she saw him as a knight on a white charger."

Anne brought sandwiches of Polish ham on Jewish rye, kosher dills on the side, and two more beers. Bogdan sat chewing, thoughtful, as if he were time traveling.

A.J. was also pensive. "The knight's armor," he said, "got tarnished for her after awhile."

Bogdan turned to him. "What do you mean?"

"Mom got it into her head that Dad was a murderer who took advantage of people. That he had hidden his true nature from her."

Bogdan frowned. "Why'd she think that?"

"A guy who owns the nightclub up the road used to know my dad. Some old-time thug, Richard Dupuis. He told her."

Bogdan took a drink. "Richard Dupuis." Then he sat silent, jaw moving laterally.

A.J. studied him. "You know something."

Bogdan stroked his mustache. "Nothing for sure... There was talk. When Jan's boss Leo Gold got shot your father benefitted. Took over the business though he wasn't even your age. None of the other bootleggers muscled in because it looked like just some Polack kids running a lemonade stand, though with a more potent product.

"And the neighborhood people liked Jan. He was one of them. They protected him and maybe were a little afraid of him, too, because of the rumors. Talk that he had Leo Gold bumped off. And he had his runners, tough street kids, to take care of him, and he took care of them…

"I do know this much to be true. His boss, Leo Gold, came onto Jan. Not sure how or how much. He asked my advice…" Bogdan sighed and shook his head. "Your father depended on Gold for everything. Without him, Jan would have been living on the streets because your grandfather had beaten him and turned him out."

Bogdan fixed A.J. with a gaze. "Whatever your father did he did because he had to. To protect himself, his name, his future. When a man is boxed in, he has to free himself. Sometimes that means doing things others don't understand. Sometimes a man has to act."

# 27 | POISON

Pontoon Beach, Illinois, September 19, 1952

The place was a dump, in Richard Dupuis's professional opinion. A no-class hayseed dump. Pinball machine, bowling machine, ten-point buck head over the front door. Smelling of fish grease and stale beer. A half-dozen stuffed largemouth bass turning yellow with age on varnished wooden wall plaques. Lighted beer signs—Stag, Black Label, Griesedieck Brothers. Tables and chairs from the last century and hard-ass wooden booths, like the one where he and Hazel sat sipping Presbyterians.

Country music twanged from the jukebox. And the cliental. Families with yelping kids who pointlessly and endlessly slid the puck back and forth on the darkened shuffleboard machine. Geezers with their gray-haired old ladies. A couple sodbusters in bib overalls at the bar. Dupuis felt like he was trapped in the Grand Ole Opry.

She had dragged him there for the Friday fish fry even though it was nothing special. And her jabber. Nostalgic crap. Stuff she had told him a dozen times before and couldn't shut up about. After a few snorts she always got real talky and couldn't remember that she said the same thing ten minutes ago.

"…It was the first time we had a chance to talk alone. We'd been at Helen and Raymond's for a barbecue. Jan offered to drive me home. Well, Helen and I conspired to arrange it. Stopped in here for a nightcap. Place hasn't changed at all…"

"I bet."

She stared off glassy-eyed, maybe feeling sentimental about the dead fish on the wall. Even with all the booze and smokes, she still didn't look near thirty-five. Still had it. And a terrific lay—at least when soused enough to pretend she was with the Polack. Afterward sometimes she'd start crying. Always moping about *him*. Despite the Class-A tail, Dupuis was getting sick of it. Funny how often that happened. You have a few laughs with a broad, but soon she starts showing her true colors, wanting this or that and getting on your nerves. Can never leave well enough alone.

Now the kids moved from the shuffleboard machine to the jukebox by the door, dropped in a nickel, and played "Aba Daba Honeymoon." Jesus F. Christ. He lit a Pall Mall and sipped his drink.

"Why do you miss him all that much? Just another guy."

She huffed and took another hit on her pres. "If you'd known him you'd understand. A real gentleman. So romantic. A thinking man who appreciated good books. Kind, considerate, and generous. People respected him."

"Ha! So he said. But you never did business with him, did you? Bet he never told you how he did business." Dupuis snickered. "Hardly 'kind, considerate, and generous.'"

# THE BOOTLEGGER'S BRIDE

"Says who?"

He dismissed her question with a flick of his hand. "Everybody... A slick operator, that Jan Nowak. Acted like he was still some altar boy, but you couldn't trust him. Pulled the wool over Jellyroll Hogan's eyes and even duped me."

"You told me you met only once."

"Once was enough." Dupuis took a deep drag on his cigarette. "He pitched me what he made out to be a nickel-and-dime deal. Turned out it was the move that made him, and I helped him do it." He shook his head and crushed out his smoke in a tin ashtray. "I should have gotten a piece of the action instead of just chump change."

"What deal was that?"

"You really want to know the truth about Saint Nowak?"

"I know the truth. He was a good man."

"Well, Mrs. Nowak, good guys don't go around hiring hit men to whack their boss."

"That's a lie. What do you know about it?" she spat. Though something Jan had once said about Dupuis being involved in Leo Gold's death floated back to her. She couldn't remember exactly what. So much of the past came to her in a haze these days. She feared it was all drifting away from her. Then all she'd have left was the present.

Dupuis leaned forward over the drink cradled between his hands on the tabletop and whispered. "I know that in July of 1929 Jan Nowak paid me four hundred dollars to put an end to Leo Gold."

"Jan paid you to murder a man? Absurd."

185

He held up his palm then put a forefinger to his lips, signaling her to lower her voice.

"No, no, no. I never did any rough stuff. I was just the middleman. I knew a guy who knew a guy. I got only a buck and half out of the deal and Nowak got a fortune."

"Jan could never do that!"

"Worse, he low-balled me. Said it was personal. That the guy was getting handsy with him. Didn't bother to tell me he was gonna steal a warehouse of Canadian whiskey from the dead man and set himself up in business. This I learned later from Jellyroll's boys."

Hazel took a cigarette from her purse and lit it, her hand shaking. She blew out a stream of smoke.

"You're making it all up."

Dupuis shrugged. "Then tell me how a teenage kid got the scratch to start a first-class bootlegging operation? To pay suppliers, grease the cops, and build a network what with all the competition around? Just hard work and good business practices? Right. Then when they repealed Prohibition he used those ill-gotten liquor proceeds to expand his loansharking operation."

"What loansharking operation? He was a banker."

Dupuis guffawed. "Banker! That's a good one. Some bank, charging fifty percent interest each month. Ha! He was a shylock, pure and simple. Had a gang of tough young Polacks who did his enforcing, slapping people around, breaking bones, chopping off fingers, what have you. Meanwhile Saint Nowak sat above it all, playing the role of community benefactor. Dishing out cash to the church, the Polish Falcons, and widows while his punks put the screws to his debtors. The whole time he's over here at his lake house acting the country gentleman, hunting and fishing, being the good family man."

Hazel gazed down at the sawdust on the floor. An image appeared of Jan holding her close as they danced their first dance, Judy Garland's voice echoing…

"Why are you trying to hurt me with these lies, Richard? Why are you trying to take him from me? You're just jealous because you're not half the man he was."

Dupuis snorted and lifted his highball. "I'm sure he'd be proud of the way you're honoring his memory."

She stiffened. Dupuis smiled. That one hit home.

"Let me tell you one last thing, sister. You never knew the guy. It was all an act. He was feeding you a line." He shook his head. "You never knew him."

# 28 | A.J. PLEADS HIS CASE

Madison County, Illinois, October 19, 1957

He spied Raymond's two-tone Dodge in the high school parking lot. Most other cars had already left. A.J. carried his gym bag to it, tossed it in the back seat and slid in beside his uncle. Lomax depressed the clutch pedal and ground the starter.

"Tough loss," he said, steering the sedan left onto Madison Avenue. "Always stings to lose to Collinsville. You played a good game. Got another tricky one next week at East St. Louis."

A.J. rolled down the window. The sun was dropping low to his left, the autumn air cooling. He took in a deep breath and blew it out. Now was as good a time as any to tell him. Aunt Helen would be home from work soon. Better to do it man-to-man without the two of them ganging up on him. Besides, Uncle Raymond was a softer touch. Maybe he could win him over and have him carry the ball with his aunt.

"Not me."

His uncle glanced at him. "What gives? You get hurt?"

"I'm finished with it."

"What? You're quitting the team?

"Quitting school."

Raymond Lomax turned left onto Nameoki Road then looked to A.J.

"You having more trouble with that Gibson kid and his pals?"

A.J. snorted. "They turn tail whenever they see me coming… No, it's not that, Uncle. I'm joining the Marines. Talked to a recruiter last week."

Raymond's hands tightened on the steering wheel and his eyes went to the rearview mirror. They drove in silence until they reached Morrison Road and turned toward home.

"What is it, son? What's the problem?"

"Not just one thing. Just fed up. You know I always hated school."

"You love reading and books. We figured you'd be headed to college next year. Been putting money aside."

"I'm just not ready. Maybe in four years I'll feel different. And I'd have the G.I. Bill and my inheritance. Can call my own shots then."

"You know how I feel about the military."

"Given family history you'd think I'd feel the same. But I don't. Besides, there's no war going on. I like the idea of doing something physical and learning how to handle myself. Being part of a team."

"You sound like a recruiting poster. Besides, Jim Gibson might argue that you already handle yourself just fine."

A.J. smiled as the Dodge moved up their driveway toward the lake and rolled to a stop beside the garage. Raymond killed the engine and turned to him.

"This all seems so abrupt and rash. What's the hurry?"

A.J. looked at his uncle. "There are things I haven't told you. Things I've been reading up on and trying to understand… You've been like a father to me, and Aunt Helen like a mother. But I'm still an orphan to the world and to myself. It does something to you. Even though I was never alone, part of me felt like it. A door had shut behind me and the bolt slid. My parents are on the other side."

Lomax let out a breath and nodded. A.J. went on.

"Instead of beating on that door and crying I need to turn my back to it and face the future on my own, and on my own terms… I've been reading about orphans and studying the orphan archetype in history and myth and literature. Orphans have things in common. A lot of our heroes both real and fictional were orphans—Moses, Aristotle, Huck Finn, Madame Curie, Superman. Without family obligations they had a certain liberty. And because they were on their own they had to be self-reliant and self-confident. That's what enabled them to be heroic. I don't expect to be a Superman. I just want to live my own life and not some pre-ordained cookie-cutter existence."

Raymond studied the Dodge's 8-ball steering wheel knob, thinking. "Of course you have to live your own life, A.J. I'm glad you're studying up on things that matter, taking your life seriously. Nonetheless, I think that the smart thing would be to hold tight for a few more months, finish out the school year, and go on to the future fully loaded instead of half-cocked."

"I don't want to do the smart thing, I want to do the right thing. I want to make my life an adventure. I'm not looking for a secure life—already got that handed to me.

# THE BOOTLEGGER'S BRIDE

And I don't want to be a sheep doing somebody else's bidding. I want to fight villains and slay demons—the ones inside me to start with."

Raymond smiled and shook his head. "You sound like your father. I can't say you're wrong to follow your heart, A.J. Though your aunt will feel like it's her fault, like we haven't made a good enough home for you that you want to run away from it. Maybe I feel the same."

A.J. swallowed. "It's a wonderful home. You're my family. You're all I got."

The sky was darkening. He felt the damp from the lake rising and turned his head toward it, sensing his uncle's eyes on him.

Raymond sighed. "I know what your aunt will say. Finish out the school year and get your diploma."

"I can always get a G.E.D., no sweat."

"You'd be letting down your teammates. You'd be a quitter. That's what Coach Nordstrom will say."

A.J. sat silent, thinking. Then, "Coach has been terrific. He's helped me a lot and always backed me."

"Maybe you should talk to him first. At least finish out the semester and the football season. It's only another month or two. And then see how you feel about the last semester."

"Maybe you're right, but there's another problem—Lana."

"Lana? Thought you were hooked on her. I know she worships you."

"She's a big reason why I need to go now."

"Why? What's happened?"

He turned back to face his uncle. "Nothing yet. I just don't want to get her in trouble."

"Oh, Jesus, A.J."

"We're real careful and everything. But we're pretty crazy about each other and sometimes get carried away. Besides, nothing's foolproof. We had a scare last month. I don't want to get stuck here and screw up her plans for med school, too."

His uncle sat pursing his lips and nodding at A.J. "Good to see you're trying to be responsible and do the right thing by her. But I'm not sure that's something I want to mention to Helen."

"Wish you wouldn't."

"Though maybe she could talk to Lana woman-to-woman, give her a few pointers."

"Forget it. She's already talked with her mom."

"Okay, okay. I won't say anything to Helen. But maybe the three of us should sit down together and talk this over. It affects us all, you know. We're a family."

A.J. realized he'd been holding his breath and exhaled.

"Sure, Uncle Raymond, sure. I don't want to leave the lake and you all and my home. It's just that I have to."

"I know. Sooner or later you have to. Just wish it was a little later. I know you've made up your mind, and we can't stop you. But understand that no matter what you do and where you go you'll always have a home here."

A.J. felt his chest tighten and bit his bottom lip. "Most people only have one family. I've had two. So I guess I'm really lucky after all."

§

That night A.J. lay abed unable to sleep, thinking and imagining what might have been. A fruitless exercise, perhaps even damaging, yet maybe all orphans did it. Maybe all people did it. What if? What if Fate would have wobbled in a more benign direction? What if his father had dodged a bullet in France. What if his parents were still alive? He pictured big game hunting in Africa with his dad. Fishing for char with him and Eskimo guides above the Arctic Circle. Benefitting from his mother's literary guidance and tender hand. Perhaps he would have had a younger brother or sister. He imagined family vacations in Florida and France. Family outings, family dinners, festive Christmas mornings, and holiday parties with relatives and friends gathered round the fireplace. Having a dad to play catch with. Having a sober mother to help him with his homework. What would it be like not to be angry, defensive, and hostile toward the world? To have friends instead of pushing people away and scaring everyone off? What would it be like to be happy? What would it be like to be someone else?

But he was a young man with his life ahead of him. Still time to be that other person. By force of will to remake himself into the man he could have been and might still be. Or someone he could never imagine. But to achieve that metamorphosis he would have to kill off who he now was, a prospect that chilled him. As much as he would like to shed the belligerent persona enveloping and confining him, that protective cocoon was all he had. The thought of not being himself and being someone entirely different and new and not knowing who that stranger was going to be—it made him feel like being abandoned all over again, being thrown out into the world naked and defenseless. Further, he had to do it all on his own…

Or did he? Aunt Helen and Uncle Raymond were there to guide and comfort him. And so was his worldly godfather Bogdan. Then there was Lana, Lonnie Sullivan, Coach Nordstrom, his teachers, teammates, and classmates, all ready to help shape him if he would just let them. Yes, he was an orphan. No, he was not alone.

With that final thought he finally drifted off, sailing away on a mystery ship across a dark sea…

## 29 | A FAREWELL

Madison County, Illinois, February 20, 1953

A frigid, dead-still night with temperatures dropping into the teens. Hazel Marie Robinson Nowak, attired in her black cocktail dress, sat on the divan before the fireplace gazing into its flames. On the coffee table before her rested a stack of library books, her lap desk, dried flowers in a porcelain vase, and a fifth of Four Roses bourbon. She raised the cocktail glass grasped in her right hand to her lips and drank down more liquor as if by habit, not savoring it.

The fire mesmerized her, her mind a blank. Then a log popped, and she snapped out of it. Released from the flames, her dark reality returned full force, a bleakness that painted everything a monotone gray and stretched as far into the future as she could see.

She set down her drink and reached for the lap desk. She slid it open to retrieve stationery and a fountain pen. She squared the cream-colored pages before her and wrote:

*My dearest Helen,*
*Never could we imagine how life might play out given its serendipity. Now, however, I've realized that the seeming randomness is but a myth, cloaking*

*mischievous Fate. In my case after my day in the sun a pre-ordained rank of double-blank dominoes falling one after another like black tombstones, revealing God's dark sense of humor. Another dead Indian as they say when the bottle empties, another vacant vessel. But no burial mound for this Cherokee princess. Better a Viking funeral (a first for Long Lake, surely), to be consumed by flames (ashes to ashes, eh?) and leave no trace.*

*Alas, not likely.*

*I apologize for the somber tone this letter is taking. I cannot help it. The bleakness speaks through me; I am its slave. I cannot stem the futility and flatness of endeavors on my part and on my behalf to cure my malaise. The psychiatrists, therapists, counselors, preachers, well-meaning friends, and even my own dear sister stand impotent against the dark wave in which I flounder.*

*You are a good soul, Sis, the finest. A.J. too is a good boy, a brave lad, who will fare better with your care and love than mine. My life has lost its bloom and atrophied into a desiccated and gnarled vine that strangles everyone it touches. All of you will more likely flourish without my presence, without the pain and shame I spread, darkening the lives of my son, my sister, my silent parents. And it now grows even darker. Can you picture my bringing another child into the world, the dubious spawn of yet another killer? Would Cain (read A.J.) then slay his sibling, this unwanted and star-crossed second son? The ironic hand of Fate again squaring things, settling scores, fostering satanic justice. No, it is just too much. I must nip it in the bud (since I seem to be cultivating agricultural metaphors tonight).*

*Although I have been sliding downhill for some nine years now, my most precipitous and ultimate decline came when I began frequenting The Blue Note. I thought it safer than drinking in St. Louis and having to decide each night which of the two bridges looming before me was the one I was driving on. Conversely, at The Blue Note whenever I really got loaded Richard or Karl or one of the band (or an obliging customer) would drive me home.*

*And there were plenty of guys to dance with. Richard didn't care. Though I didn't advertise it he knew I sometimes slept with one or another. Nonetheless he never said anything about it. I didn't care that he didn't care. A dark and cynical relationship all around. (Don't ask what I got out of it. Not sure I could answer. "Convenience" doesn't quite justify it.)*

*And keeping with the blackness theme, there looms the threat of blackmail. Of course, I admit to profound ignorance when it comes to the ways of the world, particularly the criminal world where my dear departed husband traveled. What do I know of bootleggers, stolen whiskey, hit men, loan sharks, and leg-breakers? Nothing. Yet now I must answer threats germinated in that world poised to undermine the financial wellbeing of my son. However, they are threats that I seemingly have the power to quell by the simple expedient of ceasing to exist.*

*As did my dear Janusz—cease to exist, that is—thanks in part to my naïve interference. When he wished to go to sea with Bogdan I couldn't bear the thought of our separation, fragile little thing that I was (and have since proven to be). So in effect— given the vagaries of the draft board and the long arm of Providence reaching across to slap my petulant little face—I sent my soul mate off to die in the mud of France while Bogdan sailed home hearty and healthy, all thanks to my shortsighted selfishness and hubris. I just could not leave things well enough alone. If there is a just God (I've already divined there is not a merciful One) I suspect, I will get it good and hard when we meet.*

*As to that meeting… Nothing so sinful as despair and suicide, I am told. Or so criminal either, at least in Illinois, where by statute it is considered murder. (I've checked.)*

*However, one desires that nothing would call into question A.J.'s windfall as my beneficiary nor stain his psyche further by his mother's willful abandonment of him. So something seemingly unintentional to end my soul's tenure hereabouts (meaning lush Planet Earth).*

*For example, a Buick colliding with a thick tree, a sturdy old maple perhaps. (And another drunk driving charge, although this one posthumous and unpunishable, at least by the legal system.) Or, say, an inebriated stumble down the lake bank in the cold dark night, resulting in concussion, unconsciousness, and fatal hypothermia. Or something similar.*

*Since I long for a purportedly accidental exit I can hardly let you read these incriminating musings on my self-destruction, Sis, without your promise to burn the letter immediately upon reading. And though I trust you implicitly in such matters of honor, I sense I should let you off the hook. I can't see my letter lightening your load in any way. So I will destroy this missive first and myself second. In the interim I shall fly these words to you telepathically.*

Somewhere over the rainbow

Skies are blue…

*But not here. I leave you for now and forever, dearest Helen. I doubt that you will see me in heaven.*

*Love,*

*Hazel*

She drank down more bourbon, stood with effort in stockinged feet, and carried the three-page letter to the fireplace. There she fed the pages to the fire one by one, watching each flame, curl, shrivel, and blacken.

She found her black high heels beside the couch and slipped her feet into them. Next she moved to the hat tree by the back door and donned her burgundy overcoat with fox-fur collar. Then she poured herself another and stepped out into the cold, which she barely felt, moving toward the frozen lake.

# 30 | FATHER & DAUGHTER ESTRANGED

Granite City, Illinois, April 5, 1953

The congregation filed from the First Presbyterian Church. Despite the chill gray day many lingered on the concrete steps and sidewalk chatting and shaking hands. A number of women wore flat sailor hats—the latest fashion, Helen had read—for Easter bonnets.

Day of joy! He is risen! Yet Hazel remained in the grave, lying in perpetuity within her pricey maple coffin (thanks to their dear father, who had spared no expense in putting on a good show, though with Hazel's insurance money). And there he stood in his pinstriped suit, white carnation pinned to its lapel, glad-handing and smiling.

She walked down the block between Raymond and A.J. to their car parked at the curb beneath a towering sycamore. Raymond opened the door for her as A.J. jumped into the back seat. Purse in her lap Helen sat staring straight ahead, not seeing the leafing trees that lined Delmar Avenue. When Raymond got in and started the engine she blurted:

"I can't."

He looked at her. "You can't do what?"

"Wait here." She threw open the door.

Helen strode down the street and crossed over to the

church where her parents were conversing with an elderly couple, the Popovskys. When they moved off, she stepped forward. Without preamble she said:

"We're not coming to brunch."

Her mother's jaw dropped. "Why not, sweetie? What's wrong?"

"What's wrong? What's wrong is that my only sister is fresh in her grave and I don't feel like celebrating anyone else's resurrection. Your daughter's dead," she spat, turning to her father, "thanks to you."

He stared at her agape.

"What are you talking about?" Roy Robinson said. "Get a grip on yourself, child. Your sister had some serious problems that led to her accident. You know that."

She took a step towards him. "What I know is that you wouldn't lift a finger to help her with her problems. Wouldn't even talk to her when she needed her father to stand by her. You'd rather swallow the gossip whole than extend to your own daughter some fatherly understanding, some Christian charity and forgiveness. Furthermore, it was no accident, you self-righteous old fool. She killed herself and your grandchild along with her."

"Grandchild?"

Her mother reached out to her. "Oh, Helen... Please, Helen..."

"I'll send you the autopsy report if you don't believe me. Yes, she was drunk. And also four months pregnant. But she couldn't tell you. She couldn't ask you for guidance or comfort or even just your prayers because you shunned her just like all the other good Christians. Why do you think she stopped coming to church? You don't have to be

God almighty to see into the hearts of these folk…" She gestured, swinging her arm in an arc. "…These hypocrites."

The handful of congregants who had remained in the churchyard visiting had quieted. Now they looked away and slunk off.

The nippy air hung still and quiet except for the distinctive call of a chickadee. Her mother had tears in her eyes. Her father's ears burned red. He stood stiff, as if at attention, grinding teeth.

"I think you've said enough, Helen."

She took a deep breath, stared at the ground, and nodded. "Exactly. I've got nothing more to say to you."

She turned and marched down the street.

Back in the car she told Raymond, "Let's go home."

He looked at her. "I thought we were going out to brunch with your folks."

She took Raymond's hand then turned and reached over the seat to grasp A.J.'s as well. "You two guys are my folks. My family. That's who I want to be with today."

The only family she now had left, her thoughts drifting back to Hazel in her grave. She prayed to God to understand and forgive her sister after all he had put her through, to embrace her now, finally.

# 31 | MUTUALLY BENEFICIAL BUSINESS

Madison County, Illinois, December 22, 1962

Few customers for a Saturday night—A.J. counted twenty-five, including himself, as he took a seat at The Blue Note's bar. It was the holidays. People should be celebrating. Maybe they were saving it for Christmas. The small bandstand stood dark. Two older couples danced to Ray Charles's "I Can't Stop Loving You" floating from a jukebox against the wall to his right. He asked the bald bartender for a beer.

"You of age, son?"

"Yes, sir."

He pulled his wallet from his jacket and handed across his military I.D.

The bartender took his time studying it, glancing up twice to A.J. before sliding it back to him on the chrome-topped bar. He pulled a bottle from a cooler behind him and a short beer glass from the back bar and set them before him. "Name's Karl if you need anything else."

"Thanks, Karl."

Elvis Presley followed Ray Charles: "Can't Help Falling in Love." One of the couples left the dance floor.

Richard Dupuis, who had been chatting with Karl at the far end of the bar, approached.

"You remember me don't you, A.J.?"

"I remember you."

Dupuis extended his hand. "Wouldn't have known you. You really filled out."

A.J. took his hand, gold pinky ring and all. He tried not to think of Dupuis's hands vis-à-vis his mother—ancient history. Probably still in his fifties, he looked older. Years sitting inside dark, smoky venues drinking hard liquor and sucking on coffin nails had seemingly taken their toll. Hair and mustache half gray, bags under his eyes, sallow skin as if he had liver problems. A paunch grew over his belt. Dupuis wore a plaid Kuppenheimer sport coat that had lost its shape, a white shirt whose cuffs were frayed, and a stained silk tie. As always, generous with the cologne.

The Blue Note also looked threadbare. A.J. remembered it from a decade earlier when he came with Uncle Raymond one afternoon after duck hunting at Horseshoe Lake. It had seemed magical with its starry ceiling and chrome bar, its padded blue banquettes and barstools. Now it needed paint and polish. Business seemed not so hot. Times change. People sometimes don't.

"Been a while," said Dupuis. "I still think about your mother. Such a terrible accident. She was good people."

A.J. doubted Dupuis's ability to recognize or respect goodness. "Maybe too good."

Dupuis nodded and shrugged as if he got A.J.'s meaning: Too good for the likes of you.

"Looks like you're doing okay. Saw your picture in the *Press-Record*, home on leave. So I sent the note."

"'Mutually beneficial business?'"

Dupuis lifted a cordovan wingtip onto the chrome foot rail, lit a Marlboro, and blew smoke from his nostrils.

"So you're twenty-one now. Still own the house on the lake? Nice place. I knew the mug who sold it to your father. Another bootlegger. In fact, I know a lot about those days. Things you might be interested in. Things about your father."

"Can't imagine what you might know that I'd care about."

Another shrug. "Something that happened thirty years ago during Prohibition. A tale of ill-gotten gains and mayhem that the Feds would still be interested in even if you're not."

Dupuis had a sneer on the right side of his face that A.J. remembered well. As a kid he wanted to wipe it off with his fists.

"I'll bite."

"A little pogrom in north St. Louis. A teenage Polish bootlegger knocking off a Jew and stealing a hundred gees worth of illegal Canadian whiskey he had stashed."

Now it was A.J.'s turn to shrug. "Everyone involved is dead and gone."

"Not everyone. Such as yours truly, though as an innocent bystander. And the money isn't, is it, junior?"

"Seems a stretch."

"Not if the right people are willing to talk. Like the trigger man, who's doing life in Stateville for another hit."

"What's his incentive? Not like he needs money."

"Maybe he wants to clear a guilty conscience. Maybe wants to cut a deal for more privileges. And maybe because he owes me for helping take care of his wife and kids over the years."

"Your specialty, Dupuis, comforting abandoned women and widows?"

The sneer again. "Be a wise guy if you want. See what it costs you. Now that you've turned twenty-one, son, and seen all that's at stake. Maybe time to take out a little insurance to safeguard it."

A.J. lifted his chin. "Insurance is it? And the premium?"

"A mere ten gees. Chump change for the likes of you."

Surreal. A.J. felt like he was in a dream. No, a nightmare. One that had been lying dormant inside him for a decade. He'd gone to The Blue Note out of curiosity, wondering if he still longed to slit Dupuis's throat, as he had when he was eleven. Now he had his answer.

"Lot of money for a fairy tale."

"I'll give you a week to think about it. I leave for Miami New Year's Day. If I don't hear from you by then, I go elsewhere with it. Which could cost you a lot more."

A.J. worked to keep his breathing slow and his hands relaxed. To show nothing of what was roiling inside him—an urge to grab the motherfucker by the scruff and bang his forehead against the chrome bar a few times. Instead he drained off his beer and tossed a buck on the bar.

"Don't hold your breath, old man."

## 32 | A.J. SEEKS COUNSEL

St. Louis, Missouri, December 23, 1962

Next day after church and Sunday dinner A.J. drove the rented Chevy Malibu up onto the bridge spanning the dark Mississippi, headlights reflecting off gleaming streetcar tracks running down its center. Only half past five. The sun had been down for an hour already.

Lana, home for the holidays from Champaign, had been disappointed when he called to tell her he had to see his godfather tonight. They'd planned to go dancing at a Belleville club then get a motel room. Their chemical attraction still pulsed, their paths still diverged. She was applying at med schools, hoping to follow in her parents' footsteps, and he had just re-upped for another four years. What an ironic couple they would make: she trained to save lives, he to take them.

He parked at the curb before Bogdan's redbrick flat, stepped out into brittle night air smelling of coal smoke, and shivered. His blood had thinned after a six-month deployment in the Caribbean. Which made him think of Dupuis heading for Florida the next week. He'd been thinking about it all day.

Three steps up the worn marble stoop to pound on the door, which soon opened. Bogdan pulled him into his living room with a bear hug, took his jacket, and felt his biceps. He patted his bronzed cheek.

"You look leaner and meaner than last year."

"Right on both counts."

Bogdan led him into the kitchen and fetched two beers and a bottle of bourbon from the fridge. At the kitchen table they toasted, downed shots, and chased them with Falstaff. His godfather had grown a bit grayer and a bit heavier though still physically intimidating—even to someone skilled in martial arts—thanks in part to his menacing mien.

Bogdan wanted to know what he'd been up to in the Caribbean. A.J. told him what he could. Next he asked: "You been winning at poker?"

"Not so much lately. Guys won't play me once they realize I always walk away winners. You taught me too well."

"Not well enough. I need to show you how and when to lose so people think you're vulnerable and get lured in. You don't kill the goose until it's good and fat."

Preliminaries out of the way, both men fell silent for a moment.

"What's up, A.J.? I know your people were listening when you called. I got the drift something more than just catching up."

A.J. nodded. "A ghost from Christmas past appeared yesterday, Richard Dupuis. I need your help figuring how best to exorcise him."

"Tell me what happened."

"Tried to blackmail me."

A.J. told Bogdan about the note Dupuis had sent and meeting him at The Blue Note despite loathing the man.

# THE BOOTLEGGER'S BRIDE

"I always hated the bastard. I saw from the beginning, when she first got involved with Dupuis, how it accelerated her downward drift. More late nights, more booze, more men. Then the stories he fed her about my father. So I went to The Blue Note thinking maybe I'd slap him around a bit if the occasion arose, just for old times' sake."

A.J. recounted the details of Dupuis's blackmail attempt. When he'd finished, Bogdan stroked his moustache and goatee then poured them each another shot.

"This is bullshit, A.J., pure bullshit. Could be making the whole thing up—maybe he knows nothing about it. But even if his story's true, how do we know the triggerman is still alive and eager to play, for whatever reason? How could Dupuis get the Feds interested without putting his own tits in the wringer? He's a loser with weak cards hoping you'll fold."

A.J. nodded. "What I figured."

"And if you paid him ten gees he'd feel he had a live one on the line and maybe come back for more. How'd you leave it?"

"I didn't tell him to shove it like I wanted to. Just not to hold his breath. He's leaving for Miami after New Year's Eve. That's the deadline. Probably reckoned he could scare me, like I was a new kid on the block."

Bogdan nodded. "Agree. Whole thing's ridiculous. Like a Prohibition gangster movie. A scheme he just pulled out of his ass. I think you can ignore it or tell him go fuck himself if it makes you feel better."

A.J. sat staring at Bogdan, thinking. He slid his shot glass toward him. Bogdan poured him another and one for himself.

"Agreed. But something else about this bothers me, Godfather. Why I needed to see you. An intuition. It came to me his morning. Something that would make it a different case and demand a cleaner resolution. Some closure."

"What's that, A.J.?"

"I'm wondering whether Dupuis offered my mother a similar deal ten years ago."

Bogdan frowned and tapped his fingers on the table like he was calling for another card. A.J. went on: "A vulnerable woman, a depressed alcoholic who wasn't always thinking straight. And naïve about underworld ways. A sitting duck for a man like Dupuis, who'd already poisoned her against my father. If he was also trying to blackmail her, maybe that's why she killed herself. To end the perceived threat. To guard me and my future. To protect my legacy and my father's name. The more I think about it, the more likely it seems."

Bogdan again stroked his mustache. "Possible. Particularly for a snake like Dupuis."

A.J. shook his head. "All these years, Bogdan, ever since I read her autopsy report when I was twelve and figured she had abandoned me on purpose, I tried to understand why. How could a mother love her son and do that? Yeah, she wanted to shield me from shame. Birthing a bastard in Tank Town, where people have nothing to do but talk, would have been rough on all of us. But maybe there was more. If she was also under a blackmail threat maybe she made the ultimate sacrifice to protect my future. A great unselfish act. Something a loving mother might do."

# THE BOOTLEGGER'S BRIDE

Bogdan pursed his lips, gazed into his whiskey glass, and nodded. "If Dupuis pressing her contributed to your mother's death, yes, that would make it a different case."

"Which means I need to kill him."

Bogdan looked up from his drink to A.J., who sat jaw clenched, nostrils flaring with each breath.

"Don't joke."

"Dead serious."

"Hold on, A.J. You don't know that's the case."

"I've been holding for ten years."

"No, son. Don't think like that. It won't change nothing."

"It'll change everything. At least for me. Justice means something. There won't be any for my mom or me unless I deliver it."

He lifted his chin toward his shot glass. His godfather poured more Old Fitzgerald. A.J. went on:

"Always hated him and what he did to my mom. And to me. Slapped me for mouthing off to him. And more. When I was eleven I was gonna slash the bastard's throat. Not sure I could have done it, but I pictured it time and again, taking my father's hunting knife to him.

"Last night I went to The Blue Note wondering if that anger still lingered, whether I still had murder in my heart. Then to help me answer my question the fucker tries to blackmail me."

Bogdan studied A.J., his thoughts drifting back to Czeslaw Oswiecki's cellar speakeasy on a hot summer night in 1929. There, too, he sat drinking boilermakers alongside another young man with a Roman profile and murder on his mind.

"Thirty years ago, I suggested to your father how to make his troubles disappear. Advice, for better or worse, he took to heart. Now I need to advise you as well, though with benefit of hindsight. I understand your anger even if I can't experience it. And that you want payback for your mom. Maybe vengeance for your father too, in a way. And I know you're trained Special Ops who could pull it off quietly."

"Damn straight."

"Doesn't mean you can get away with it."

"No one will know. Not even you. Fingers will point toward East Side gangsters."

Bogdan shook his head. "Since you met with him in public there's already a trail leading back to you. Not to mention some history. I don't like the odds."

A.J.'s eyes strayed to a church calendar hanging on the refrigerator, the outline of a fish imprinted on each Friday. Bogdan continued.

"I loved your father like a brother. He was a good man though not a good role model in all things. This is one of them. Dupuis ain't worth it. Not worth sticking your neck out for something whose only payoff is abstract."

A.J. now focused on his shot glass, turning it on the mahogany tabletop. "It would make me feel lots better. That's concrete."

"Okay. I get it. But let it cool down, A.J. This just cropped up yesterday. Give it time. Let's figure a way to fuck him up and get some payback without you having to bet the ranch. I'm sure we can."

A.J. kept studying the twirling shot glass. "Yeah, maybe," he said. "But this isn't the sort of thing I can forget or forgive."

# 33 | THE TWO DEATHS LINKED

Edwardsville, Illinois, February 18, 1963

Madison County Sheriff's Department Detective Kenneth LaRose sat with his feet up on his desk, hands clasped behind his head, squinting at the tin ceiling, thinking. Patrolman Bean sat across from him sipping coffee from a stained mug. On the wall behind LaRose hung a framed photograph of Governor Otto Kerner, Jr. that he'd received in the mail from Springfield two years earlier when Kerner took office. Doris had retrieved it from the trash and hung it there.

LaRose had been doing a lot of thinking over the past week—voluntarily and involuntarily—ever since they pulled Richard Dupuis from Long Lake.

"Doesn't make sense dumping the body there. Been bothering me all weekend," he said. "Only a few feet deep. He was gonna be found. Why not slip him into the Mississippi where he could have floated down to Natchez or New Orleans and never been identified or even found? No corpse, no crime."

"Amateurs. Or someone wanting to send a message. But why now? Might have expected some wise guy to whack Dupuis back when he was running with the Sheltons."

"Prohibition and Depression days. Before my time, thank God."

Though the burgeoning East Side gangland mayhem back then might have been more interesting from a professional point of view. Nowadays LaRose had few homicides to deal with. The ones he did work were hardly mysteries: a drunken domestic dispute, a bar-fight knifing, a farmstead mercy killing and suicide. He didn't wish for more homicides thereabouts that might challenge his detective skills. Still...

"If the killer wanted the body to be found why not just roll it into a ditch?" said LaRose. "Why take the trouble transporting it to the lake?"

"Maybe that's where he was killed."

"Who knows? Dupuis had been on ice or under it for weeks. No one had seen him since New Year's."

The iron radiator behind Bean clanked and hissed. LaRose frowned at it. "Goddamn Monday mornings. Friday it was like a hothouse in here. Today it's a meat locker."

"At least we didn't have to chop Dupuis out of the ice like we did that woman who drowned. When was that?"

"Nineteen-fifty-three. I'd just gotten back from Korea. What was her name?"

"One of the Robinson girls. War widow. Worse part it was her boy who found her."

LaRose pursed his lips. "I remember. Been on my mind… We still have that file?"

"If the mice haven't eaten it." Bean rose. "I'll check downstairs."

# THE BOOTLEGGER'S BRIDE

§

LaRose rifled through the moldy-smelling file. Interview notes, most written in his own hand. Photographs of the corpse. Lovely woman, seemingly, even after drowning in the lake, freezing, and thawing. The autopsy report indicated no trauma that couldn't have been caused by falling through thin ice. A whopping amount of alcohol in her. And a sixteen-week-old fetus. Husband long dead.

LaRose had been doubtful about the coroner's ruling of accidental death. Hazel Robinson Nowak had lived on the lake since 1941. An avid ice skater, according to her sister, so she likely knew where the underground springs and thin ice lay. Yes, it was dark, and she was drunk. Still, she would have known the danger if not her exact whereabouts on the ice.

He took a magnifying glass from his desk drawer and lifted one of the morgue shots, focusing on her hands, as he had ten years earlier. If someone had stumbled drunk out onto the ice and fallen through, that person likely would have been clawing to get out from under the ice. But Hazel Nowak's fingernails looked like she'd just come from the manicurist.

He set down the morgue photo and lifted one taken on Long Lake before they chopped away the ice to free her. LaRose again scrutinized her last breath, caught in the frozen lake: small, regular bubbles rising from her lips. As if from someone peacefully falling asleep, not from someone gasping and fighting for her life.

In 1953 the recent Marine MP and eager rookie detective Kenneth LaRose had told Doctor Birkemeyer that the evidence pointed toward suicide, not accidental death. The coroner in turn informed the detective that a suicide ruling would mean her twelve-year-old son would not collect on the life insurance. Worse, he would forever live with the knowledge that his mother had purposely abandoned and orphaned him, throwing him out into the world alone without a care whether *he* would sink or swim. LaRose had responded that, yeah, maybe it was an accident after all.

Next he studied the notes he made when interviewing family members and neighbors back then, which detailed the former schoolteacher's decline after her husband's death in the D-Day invasion. From the stack of scribbled pages three words jumped out at him—words that had been lurking in his subconscious all weekend, trying to break through and float to the surface: "The Blue Note."

This from his interview with the deceased's sister, Helen Robinson Lomax. She said that Hazel often drank till closing hour at The Blue Note, the nightclub owned and managed by Richard Dupuis. LaRose scoured other interview notes and found a neighbor claiming Dupuis had frequently visited Hazel Nowak. And now he had been found in the frozen lake as well. Also, not an accidental death. What if Dupuis had been the father of Hazel Nowak's 16-week-old fetus? Where might that lead?

LaRose again leaned back in the roller chair, lifted his feet onto his desk, and clasped his hands behind his head. He would let it all sink in and set loose his imagination, hoping things would begin to link up and make sense. It was like being a playwright or novelist: piecing together a plausible story, arranging plot dominoes to fall in logical order, orchestrating a beginning, a middle, and an ending—though he doubted this script would have a happy one.

# 34 | A DETECTIVE CALLS

Madison County, Illinois, February 22, 1963

Friday morning Raymond Lomax had the front door of his home on sawhorses in the backyard where he was cutting out the rot, screwing and gluing on fresh wood, and reattaching hinges that had pulled out of the door. A temporary fix at best if it worked at all.

It was always something. Rotten doors, stuck windows, busted screens, electrical shorts, a leaky roof, a leaky pipe, a leaky boat. At least these days he had time to tend to it all. And today wasn't a bad day to work outside. Some sunshine and no wind to speak of. Temperatures above freezing and blue jays squawking.

The sound of tires on the gravel drive made him look up from his work. A county sheriff's department black-and-white with red bubble-gum machine atop the roof edged up toward the garage and stopped. An officer in dark blue tunic and peaked cap rose from the Ford cruiser and strode toward him. He figured he'd been getting a visit sooner or later. Good to get it over with. Good that it came with Helen at work.

"I know you," Raymond said, as they shook hands. "You were here before. When Hazel died."

The cop nodded. "Detective Kenneth LaRose. I was

# THE BOOTLEGGER'S BRIDE

hoping to catch you and your wife home what with the holiday."

"Helen's at the hospital."

"I'm sorry. She okay?"

Lomax laughed. "She's a nurse. Works part-time. Especially on weekends and holidays, when others want to be home with their kids."

"You still at the steel mill?"

"That's history. Got laid off. Between things right now."

"Ever consider police work?"

He shook his head. "Never thought about it. No military training. I was at the mill during the war. Though I'm not a bad shot when it comes to ducks. Besides, it's a little late in the game. But I guess you're not here on a recruitment drive."

"I wanted to talk to you about the body they found in the lake. Richard Dupuis."

"Yeah. So I read in the *Press-Record*."

Lomax led LaRose inside and brought him coffee as he sat at the kitchen table and placed his uniform cap on it. Raymond leaned against the sink, coffee cup in hand.

"Not much I can tell you. Couple of the neighbor kids who were off school that day found it. When I heard the siren and the commotion I went down and talked with the two patrolmen. I'll tell you what I told them: I never saw or heard anything odd going on over there."

"Yeah, I read Patrolman Shands's notes."

"Just because he was found there doesn't mean he was dumped there. Lots of springs moving the water around."

"Were you acquainted with the victim?"

"Knew who he was. And that he had run with Wortman and that crowd. I went in his club a few times over the years to have a beer after my shift. Never talked to him that I recall."

Raymond saw the detective's eyes shift behind him, to the window over the sink, and turned. On the sill sat a framed photograph of A.J. in his Marine dress uniform.

"That the boy?"

"Yep. Hazel's kid. A.J. Ours too now."

"How's he doing?"

"Good. Just re-upped. He's somewhere in the Caribbean. Some sort of special operations group."

LaRose nodded at that. In World War II they were called Raiders, experts in amphibious light infantry assault, landing in rubber boats, operating behind enemy lines.

"When was the last time you saw him?"

Raymond Lomax perceived a shift in tone. He thought for a moment, thinking it best to tell the truth, particularly as it was in the newspaper.

"Christmas. He came home on leave for a couple weeks."

"Glad to hear he's doing well. He had a tough road. I wonder if you'd let him know I'd like to see him next time he comes home."

"What for?"

LaRose pursed his lips and studied the badge on his uniform cap, searching for the right words.

"Just to have a chat. I'll be frank, Lomax. There's some coincidence in the two cases, Hazel Nowak's death and Richard Dupuis's. Some connections."

"Like what? What connections? Why are you dredging that up? It happened ten years ago. It's done. Leave the boy alone."

"I know. I'm not on a fishing expedition here. Just trying to solve a murder case. We know that Hazel was pregnant when she died. Your wife and others told us about her drinking problem after she lost her husband and apparently lost her way. About her being with other men. One of whom neighbors said was Richard Dupuis. Meaning he could have been the father of her unborn child. Now, ten years apart, both are found dead in Long Lake in February. And it was the boy who found his mother." Also, it was the boy, now the man, Special Ops Marine A.J. Nowak, who met with Dupuis at The Blue Note a week before Dupuis disappeared—something LaRose thought it best not to mention just now.

Lomax had crossed his arms over his chest, jaw clamped tight, breathing hard through his nostrils. LaRose said, "I'm not focused on A.J. except to learn what he knows. I'm sure a lot of people hereabouts were aggrieved by Hazel Nowak's demise and death. And a lot who had no love lost for Richard Dupuis. There may be no connection. But it's all I got right now."

Lomax walked him out to his patrol car. When LaRose opened the door, Raymond said: "I never thanked you for what you did for us with Hazel. The accidental death ruling."

"That was the coroner, Dr. Birkemeyer's finding."

"Maybe. I figured you both did the right thing. I trust you to do the same now."

LaRose stared at Lomax. Finally, he said, "Duly

noted." Then he got into his patrol car and backed it down the drive. LaRose felt like he was backing himself into a corner, into a place he didn't belong and certainly didn't want to go. A.J. Nowak a murderer? Or Raymond Lomax? He hoped the hell not.

§

When Helen came home from the hospital that evening Raymond told her about the visit from Detective LaRose. She stared at him across the dinner table and said: "I wonder how much A.J. knew. Did he know she was pregnant? Maybe he overheard us talking about what Hazel told me, how Dupuis took her to bed that first time when she was passed out."

"He knew enough. I'll never forget that day we took him in. When we found him hiding under the kitchen sink clutching Jan's hunting knife to his chest. Lord knows what was in his heart. Doesn't show much. In ten years never seen him cry."

Helen twisted her dinner napkin in her lap, shaking her head. "I can't believe our boy would do anything like that. I hate the thought of it."

"Dupuis needed to die, Helen. I would have done it myself if I knew I could get away with it."

She reached across and took his hand. "Maybe that's what A.J. thought."

"We don't know anything for sure about what happened. Just what they wrote in the newspaper, which wasn't much and maybe not all true."

"I need to write A.J."

"And tell him what? That the cops want to talk to him about Dupuis's murder?"

"No, just how much I love him. How he is the son I never had. Even though he never called me Mom. How my love is unconditional and eternal. That's all I'm going to tell him."

Raymond sat silent looking at his wife then to A.J.'s photo on the windowsill before the dark sky outside.

"Tell him I feel the same."

# 35 | AN INTERROGATION

Edwardsville, Illinois, March 31, 1964

Detective LaRose studied the Dupuis murder file opened before him on his desk. Patrolman Danny Shands sat across from him, silhouetted by morning sun pouring through the tall window on the east wall. LaRose had raised the window a few inches even though the temperature outside still hung below fifty. It had been a hard winter now leaching into spring.

With Bean retired and relocated to the Florida Keys for the year-round fishing, LaRose was grooming Shands as his sounding board. Though eager and diligent (reminding LaRose of himself a decade earlier), it would take him a few more years to develop a grounding cynicism and skepticism to rival Bean's.

"How much do you weigh, Danny?"

"One-sixty, detective."

"Yeah, dripping wet and fully loaded. Autopsy report says the deceased was six-foot-three and weighed two-thirty-five. For argument's sake let's say he went under his own power to the lakeshore where you strangled him. You'd have to know what you were doing to overpower a guy that big."

"Or have the drop on him. Or dope him."

"Autopsy showed a fair amount of alcohol, nothing else. Then how would you get his fat corpus out into the middle of the lake?"

Shands shrugged. "Slide it out over the ice."

"And if the lake hadn't yet froze?"

Another shrug. "Drag him up on a dock and push him off? Or use a rowboat."

"How would you get a guy that big into a rowboat and then into the lake without capsizing?"

"Reckon you and me could do it."

"A two-man job? Possibly. If so, maybe killed elsewhere and transported."

"If not, how do you lure somebody there to be bushwhacked. What was Dupuis expecting?"

"Good question, Danny. What's the inducement?"

"The usual: love or money?"

"I'd bet on the latter. Or maybe he was kidnapped."

"Yeah, pulled a gun on him somewhere else and drove him there."

"Then what happened to Dupuis's car? It never showed up anywhere."

"In the river?"

"Then why wasn't Dupuis in it too?"

LaRose had been mulling the case off and on for a year now, asking himself the same questions time and again. He'd developed some possible scenarios. But without evidence or witnesses, no answers.

A knock came at the frosted-glass door, where LaRose saw Doris's silhouette. The door opened a foot and she stuck her head through.

"A.J. Nowak here to see you."

"Send him in." He looked to Shands. "Thanks, Danny."

As Nowak stepped through the doorway Shands passed behind him looking him up and down. A.J. wasn't that much taller than the patrolman. However, he looked like a different species of primate: broad-shouldered, muscular, lithe, and gaunt. Dark tan, short dark hair brushed forward, penetrating eyes almost black. He wore new Levi's and a white t-shirt under a brown suede jacket. They shook hands and LaRose gestured toward the wooden armchair that Shands had vacated.

"Thanks for driving up. Hope you had a good Easter."

"Holidays stateside are always good."

"I spent Christmas '52 in Seoul with the 7th Marine Regiment. A white Christmas though not very merry."

"I suspect not. Good you made it back."

"I was an M.P. Only fighting I did was with drunken G.I.s." LaRose paused and cleared his throat. "When I interviewed your uncle, he said you were in the Caribbean."

"That was last year. Just returned from Vietnam."

"I read that's heating up."

"Afraid so."

"Understand you're Special Ops."

Nowak nodded. He sat with his feet flat on the floor, elbows on the armrests, hands folded at his waist. LaRose thought of a compressed spring, straining for release. As if to confirm the metaphor's aptness A.J. said: "Can we get down to business? My uncle told me about his interview with you last year and your concern about 'coincidences' between my mother's death and Richard Dupuis's. One obvious one: Both found in Long Lake. Anything else?"

# THE BOOTLEGGER'S BRIDE

The detective shuffled some papers on his desk. "Let's say some tangents, like your mother's relationship with the deceased. I'm trying to solve this murder without much physical evidence to go on and no witnesses. Hoping it was a gangland hit related to the nefarious activities and people Dupuis had been involved with over the years. I'd like to discover something to focus my attention in that direction. Nonetheless I have to do my job, my due diligence."

"Understood."

"Last thing I want is for you or yours to somehow be involved in this directly or indirectly."

With that LaRose lifted a typed sheet from his desktop and frowned at it. "The bartender at The Blue Note said that you had an extended conversation there with Dupuis just days before he was last seen alive."

"I know nothing about when he was last seen alive. And I'd call it a brief chat."

"Can you tell me what you talked about?"

"Old times. He was a friend of my mother and came by the house on occasion. I did not seek him out. I was home on leave and stopped in for a drink for the first time since I was finally legal age. Didn't know he was still running the place. The bartender carded me then tipped off Dupuis as to who I was, as he hadn't seen me since I was ten or eleven. He came over to say hello and pay belated condolences."

"No apology?"

"For what?"

"For contributing to your mother's decline and ultimate suicide."

A.J. nodded once. "Okay. Now after ten years you're calling it a suicide, not an accidental death."

"Maybe someone did you a favor ten years ago. In a couple ways."

A.J. sat staring at LaRose. No comment. But he did tilt his head a millimeter to the left as if to acknowledge that favor. The detective went on.

"Back to Dupuis. You realize he was likely the father of the child your mother was carrying when she died."

The marine sergeant leaned back in his chair frowning. "Child?"

LaRose retrieved the autopsy report from the Nowak file and slid it across the desk. A.J. now bent forward and read, shaking his head.

"You didn't know?" the detective asked.

"No one ever told me."

"Really? Your aunt and uncle never said anything?"

"Not exactly something you'd comfort an orphaned twelve-year-old with, is it?"

LaRose reached for the second file folder on his desk, the Dupuis file, drew it to him, and again cleared his throat.

"Then a few days later, New Year's Eve to be exact—the last time Dupuis was in fact seen alive—another new customer came into The Blue Note to talk to him. This man…"

From a manila envelope he withdrew a composite sketch of a dark-bearded man that he slid across to A.J., who leaned forward to study it, his expression blank.

"Looks like an interesting guy."

"Do you know him?"

Nowak shook his head.

"What about a Dan Boggs? Name mean anything?"

Again the head shake. LaRose put the sketch back in the envelope.

"Did you have any business dealings with Dupuis?"

A.J. smiled briefly. "I don't do business. I'm a grunt. I do soldiering."

"Dupuis left the bartender Karl Maulhardt to close up New Year's Eve. He was not seen again until we pulled him from the lake six weeks later. He didn't drown. He was garroted. The staff figured he'd gone to Miami to play the ponies like he did every winter, but he never made it. And his car was never found."

"Odd."

LaRose leaned his forearms on the desk and locked his eyes on Nowak's. "Do you know what I think is odd, A.J.? That *you* wouldn't want to kill Richard Dupuis with your own hands. Here's how I see it: A young widowed mother learns she's pregnant by a man under whose control she has fallen. A man who took advantage of a damaged and vulnerable woman. Wanting to escape the humiliation her pregnancy would engender and to prevent her shame from attaching to and burdening her only child, this desperate woman decides to take her own life. In despair and drunk she takes a walk on thin ice to bring it all to a halt. Then her only child discovers her body in the frozen lake—an event that surely traumatized him.

"Then later that orphaned son, a dutiful son and trained killer with knowledge and skills that would enable him to clandestinely dispatch most anyone, does not feel obligated to exact vengeance on his dead mother's behalf.

He doesn't see or feel the divine justice in that? Now *that* seems odd to me."

Nowak sat immobile, showing no emotion yet clearly thinking, eyes moving left and right. At last, he spoke.

"You're correct, detective. Had I known the full circumstances it would have been my duty. Given that scenario, I failed. Failed us all—my mother, my father, and myself. I would certainly feel badly about it if that were the case, real bad."

LaRose leaned back in his chair. He pursed his lips and nodded. Maybe now this guy was finally telling the truth.

## 36 | THE PAYOFF

Madison County, Illinois, December 31, 1962

Bogdan Zawadski slid onto a barstool in his wool topcoat. It was a bit below freezing outside and a bit above inside, The Blue Note management saving on the heating bill. Laughing couples sitting coatless on either side of him had likely been consuming antifreeze all night.

Not an overflow crowd for New Year's Eve, yet most tables were taken. Folks drinking, dancing, and enjoying themselves. On the small bandstand a four-piece combo banged out a rockabilly tune with the singer doing a fair job of sounding like Elvis. Though the club had already seen its best days, the sparkling lights and chrome gave it a festive air. He'd been in worse dives.

Bogdan got a gin from the bald, lizard-lipped bartender and spied a tall man in a black blazer and red silk tie lurking at the far end of the bar drink in hand, puffing on a fag. Richard Dupuis. He had seen him but once thirty years earlier at Jellyroll Hogan's bar on Cass Avenue. Even though Dupuis hadn't aged well, Bogdan easily recognized him. The eyes don't change. Pimp eyes. Always leering, evaluating, looking for a weakness to exploit.

Bogdan had always hated shakedown artists. Otherwise honest cops who might take a few bucks to look the other way were okay or corruptible housing inspectors and such. Not people like, say, Leo Gold, who try to bend someone when they've got power over them. Or a snake like Richard Dupuis, always trying to make money off a woman or take advantage.

Seeing him again he knew that, like A.J., he'd have few qualms about killing him. Unlike A.J., whether he had the guts and know-how was another question. He had killed men in the war but always miles distant with five-inch guns or twenty fathoms below with depth charges. Never face-to-face with his own hands. Not that he doubted having the strength to do it. He still lifted weights at the Polish Falcon Nest on St. Louis Avenue. And Dupuis looked old and flabby. Nonetheless, Bogdan lacked his godson's Special Ops expertise in such matters.

The band played "Are You Lonesome Tonight?" The two sets of couples at the bar moved to join others on the dance floor. As the singer crooned the refrain he gestured to the man in topcoat and black turtleneck sweater sitting solo at the bar. In return Bogdan blew him a kiss, which brought a smile.

Bogdan signaled the barkeep for a refill. When it came, he said, "Please tell Mr. Dupuis I'd like a word with him."

The bartender tilted his head. "And who are you?"

"My name won't mean anything to him."

Lizard Lips stared at him. "Didn't hear you."

"Dan Boggs."

"What's it about?"

"An offer on the table with a friend."

Bogdan turned his back to him to watch the dancers. The bartender moved off.

Three songs later and still no direct response from Dupuis. Nonetheless he was communicating by his inaction: slow playing it. Which to the professional gambler often indicated a cover for eagerness.

When the band took a break he spied Dupuis moving down the bar in his direction, shaking hands, slapping people on the back, touching cheeks with a bottle blonde. His Happy New Year wishes floated over the soft jukebox music, general conversation, and jingling of ice and glass. At last he worked his way down to Bogdan and shook hands.

"Happy New Year, Dan. Glad you could make it."

"I'm enjoying the music."

Dupuis laid a hand on Bogdan's shoulder. "Maybe we should step into the back room for a minute where it's a little easier to talk." As if Dan Boggs might have ten thousand smackers in his coat pocket that he was itching to hand over in private.

He followed Dupuis past the jukebox right of the bar and through a door labeled "Private." On the other side of it sat a small, windowless, and dimly lit room with a gray Army-surplus desk, lone wooden chair, sticky floor, and beery smell. Cases of bottled suds—Stag, Falstaff, Schlitz, Budweiser—stacked to the ceiling and covering three walls.

Dupuis sat on the desk and lit a cigarette, all cool and relaxed like Humphrey Bogart in the movies. Except somehow he came off more like a kid sneaking a smoke in the boys' room.

"I have a message from my young friend," Bogdan said and paused. He could see the anxiety in the club owner's eyes, hoping for the big payoff but fearing the message might well be "Fuck off!" He let Dupuis twist for a moment before giving him the good news.

"All he can get his hands on is five gees." (A greedy glimmer in those serpent eyes despite the frown.) "You can have it tonight on condition he never hears from you again."

Dupuis shook his head. "That wasn't the deal."

"This is the new deal."

Dupuis pursed his lips and scratched his cheek as if making up his mind. Clearly he already had. He let out a phony sigh.

"Okay, five thousand now and the rest when he can pull it together."

"No, he wants to finish this now and not have it hanging over him. He's going overseas next week. So, it's five large tonight or nothing. You chose."

Dupuis acted like he was thinking it over then raised his palms in defeat. "Okay, let me see it."

"I'm not the bagman, just Western Union. He wants to meet you at his home on the lake at two a.m."

Dupuis tilted his head. "Uh, why there? And why two in the morning?"

"He figured that's a safe place you both know. Right now he's across the river at a party with his fiancée."

Dupuis shrugged. "I don't get why he just didn't give you the dough to make the handoff. Cleaner and easier."

Zawadski returned the shrug. "He's a weird kid, even now. I think he trusts you in some stupid way. Don't ask me

# THE BOOTLEGGER'S BRIDE

why. He wants to look you in the eye when you promise this is the end of it and shake hands on it."

Dupuis sneered. "A real Boy Scout, huh? Tell him to come alone."

"Ditto for you, boss."

Bogdan made as if to leave. Then with his hand on the doorknob he turned back.

"The house is closed up. He's got a lantern in the boathouse so you can count the cash. He'll meet you on the dock."

§

From a desk drawer in The Blue Note office-cum-storeroom Richard Dupuis took a Smith & Wesson Model 10 snub-nose revolver and checked the chambers. He didn't plan to use it and never had to, but always carried it when transporting cash. He slid it into his overcoat pocket, smiling at the irony: It was the same gun he carried the summer day he met A.J. Nowak's fucking Polack father on the St. Louis wharf back in '29. Took only thirty years to get a fair cut on that deal. The five gees tonight would square it nicely.

Out front Karl Maulhardt was locking the door behind the last customers.

"You know the drill, Karl. Call me if anything important crops up."

"When was the last time that happened? Won't bother you unless I have to. You have a good trip, boss. And a Happy New Year." The two men shook hands. The bartender locked the door behind Dupuis as the latter stepped out into the cold, starry night, just a sliver of moon hanging over him like a scythe.

The leather seats of his '55 Cadillac Series 62 convertible felt like ice. The V-8's starter ground and the engine fired. Dupuis turned the heater to high, pulled on his gloves, and sat in the cold car anticipating the drive south the following day. He always put the top down after crossing the Georgia-Florida line.

It took a few minutes for the heater to warm the ragtop. Probably time for a new model. He'd look around when he hit Miami. A '63 listed for five grand. This one still worth a couple gees, so he'd have some extra cash in his pocket to play the ponies and pay the ladies.

Warm air began blowing from the heater ducts. He pulled out the headlight switch, illuminating the dashboard. The clock there read a quarter to two.

He turned on the radio and tuned it to KATZ, the St. Louis Negro station that played old jazz and blues tunes after midnight. He sat listening to Blind Lemon Jefferson, James Johnson, and Fats Waller. The music put him in a nostalgic mood, taking him back to the 1920s and '30s when he was a young man about town.

As the clock ticked near two he put the automatic into reverse, backed out over the gravel lot, and moved onto the deserted road leading toward the lake.

At the lake road he turned right. After a minute he slowed and eased the Cadillac onto the gravel drive where the wooden sign reading "Lazy Lane" still hung from a post. She'd always worn nice, sexy stuff—silk stockings, garter belts, lacy bustiers, and such. Pity she bought it so young. He could still be tapping it from time to time.

# THE BOOTLEGGER'S BRIDE

Ahead he spied a new Chevy with Missouri plates and a Hertz bumper sticker—a rental that A.J. likely picked up at Lambert Field when he flew in. Dupuis pulled to a stop behind it and killed the Caddy's headlights. He removed his driving gloves, rose from the car, and slipped his right hand into his coat pocket where it grasped the Smith & Wesson.

In dim moonlight Dupuis picked his way through the dark toward the lake bank. He paused at the thick-trunked maple tree where the steep plank stairway led down to the dock. There light seeped beneath the boathouse door. Then a black-gloved hand passed before his eyes. A wire tightened round his neck, pulling him back and away from the stairs.

Gagging, eyes bulging, he grabbed at the wire, the snub-nose revolver tumbling from his grasp to the ground and bouncing down the stairs to the lake. He pulled on the wire. It cut into his hands, though he hardly noticed. But the more he tugged on it, stretching it way from his throat, the deeper it cut into his windpipe somehow.

Dupuis kicked and gurgled. A dark cloud approached from behind, consciousness slipping away. Then he felt warm breath in his ear and heard a voice rasp, "This is for Hazel Nowak. This, you pimp bastard, is for Magdalena Sheehan."

# 37 | AN AVENGING ANGEL

St. Louis, Missouri, April 1, 1964

He spied Bogdan sitting on the front steps of the Central Library along with dozens of workers on lunch break enjoying the warmer weather, face directed up to a noon sun that had just parted puffy clouds. Dressed in sweatshirt, gym shorts, and basketball sneakers, A.J. approached, perched beside him on the marble steps, and shook his hand.

Bogdan said, "Thought you might stand me up. Good April Fools joke."

"Sorry. Up the street at the Y working out and lost track of time. Rushed out without a shower."

Bogdan studied two miniskirted young women passing on the sidewalk.

"Just like your father. Always at the Falcon Nest flying around on the rings and horse. Me, I was more down to earth, working the weights and wrestling. If he wasn't there he was here," he said, tilting his head over his shoulder at the white marble structure behind them, "nose in the books. Guess the fruit don't fall far from the tree."

A.J. looked across Olive Street to the park and the World War I Memorial set amid leafing oak trees. The pink-granite City Hall loomed in the background.

"Wish I'd known him better. Wish he was still around. How different things might have been." Even after all these years working to stay in the moment and not dwell on the past and punish himself in that way, A.J. still pictured it. A fairy tale that would never come true.

"Life is suffering and loss, A.J., and you've had a good share. Best you can do is offer it up to God in redemption. He has plans for you, I am sure."

"I have my own plans. Just hope He doesn't interfere too much. Come, Godfather," said A.J., glancing at others sitting nearby, "let's stretch our legs."

They crossed into the park where they passed downtown office workers out for a stroll. Construction workers from a nearby project lounged on park benches. Transients from the Salvation Army Harbor Light and other downtown flophouses stretched out on the grass. All drinking in the warm, sunny day in their own manner.

As a man in a business suit walked past, A.J. said, "How simple life could be if I was normal. Get a job, go to work, go home to your family. Safe, secure, nurturing. Not God's plan for me. Nor for these guys," he said lifting his chin at those dozing on the grass.

"The workaday world takes a special sort of fortitude," said Bogdan, "that neither one of us has demonstrated."

They strolled on toward 12th Street. After covering a half block A.J. said:

"Visited the Sheriff's Department in Edwardsville yesterday. Detective LaRose wanted to chat about the murder of Richard Dupuis."

Bogdan stopped and turned to him, frowning. A.J. went on. "Showed me a sketch of a man, a customer at

The Blue Note on New Year's Eve 1962 seen talking with Dupuis. Who in turn was not seen alive again after that night. The customer—who went by the name Dan Boggs—resembled you somewhat, Bogdan."

The older man lowered himself onto a park bench and stared up at A.J. as a nearby mockingbird improvised a medley. "Come. Sit." He patted the bench.

A.J. sat beside Bogdan, who studied the trees, cocking his head as if listening to the birdsong.

"I was supposed to look after you if anything happened to Janusz. Didn't do a very good job at godfather for years. When he and I were kids I looked out for him. Later he took care of me. Bankrolled me more than once when I was tapped out. Which kept me afloat and stopped me from sticking my neck out. I owed him for that. Felt I could square things if I could keep you from a risky act that could threaten your future."

He fixed his gaze on A.J. "I've done with my life what I had to. Followed my heart and my instincts, for better or worse. You still have your life ahead of you. You had more to lose.

"That night when you talked about taking him out, I thought it was the heat of the moment. Thought it would go away. But I didn't know for sure. How do we know what's in someone's heart? How do we know what they're capable of? People have surprised me. I didn't want to be surprised by you and see you in trouble. So, I decided to tie up loose ends. You were right. Dupuis needed to die."

A.J. nodded. "I guessed something like that. When my uncle sent me the newspaper clipping about Dupuis's murder just two months after I told you I had to kill him, I figured it wasn't just happy coincidence."

"Sorry that it has the coppers sniffing around you."

"Everything's okay. The detective admitted having nothing much to go on and hoping I had nothing to do with it. Which I think he now believes."

Bogdan reached into his pants pocket and withdrew a key with a gold medallion attached by a chain. He held it out to A.J. "For you."

"What's that?"

Bogdan dropped it into his palm. "Key to a safe-deposit box at Cass Avenue Bank & Trust. If they ever come after you hard and I'm not available for some reason—like I'm dead or left town or something—you'll find your insurance policy there."

"What insurance policy?"

"A deposition. My confession to Dupuis's murder with details only the killer would know. Gives the coppers my motive—that has nothing to do with you—and clears you or anyone else of involvement. All signed, witnessed, and notarized."

"Many thanks, Godfather. For everything. But I doubt it will ever come to that."

"Just in case."

"Still, I'm curious what the deposition might say. Can you give me a summary?"

Bogdan laid a hand on A.J.'s shoulder.

"I can do that. Remember though that I'm just an amateur at these things, not trained Special Ops. It didn't go exactly as planned. Promise you won't judge my methods too harshly."

A.J. raised his palm. "I do."

Bogdan stared off through the trees toward the white marble library with its arched windows. His eyes stayed focused there as he began to spin his tale. He told of going to The Blue Note on New Year's Eve, meeting Dupuis, and conducting their negotiations in his storage room/office. When he mentioned the deal he'd put before Dupuis, A.J. turned to him.

"You offered him only five thousand? Why jew him down if you were planning to fix him anyway?"

Bogdan tapped his temple with his forefinger. "Psychology. A wager can pull people in or scare them off. I could see the desperation on this mug, getting old, down on his luck. But he'd been around the block and wasn't no sucker. If I agreed too easily to the whole ten gees he might smell a rat. But when I lowballed him he's thinking about if he should take it or make a counteroffer rather than whether he's being set up. And as soon as I dangled the promise of a fast five gees in front of him I could see he was already wiggling.

"I read him like a book. Knew he was bluffing about the whole deal, about being able to feed Jan to the cops for the Leo Gold hit and having the Feds come after your money. The pissant had nothing to sell. And five thousand bucks for nothing is pretty good return on investment."

Bogdan went on to detail the setup and his instructions luring Dupuis to the lakeshore. He explained how he baited him with the rental car in the driveway and hid behind the old maple tree atop the lake bank where he waited for his mark.

"Damn cold night though not much wind. But I wasn't thinking about the weather. I never had to kill nobody before, not up close like that with my hands. Only with munitions. I felt shaky. Took a nip or two from a half pint while I waited. Courage in a bottle.

"He drove up in his Caddy—I heard the motor before I saw the headlights. Parked in the drive, walked to the lake bank, and looked down to the dock and the lighted boathouse. That's when I stepped out and lassoed him from behind."

Bogdan paused, rubbing his hands together and staring at the ground, as if reliving the moment. Again he looked to A.J.

"Used a double-loop garrote—Spanish invention— that a Filipino shipmate showed me. If he tries to free himself by tugging on one of the coils, he only pulls the other one tighter. So Dupuis was actually strangling himself though he didn't know it. He was choking, getting weak, ready to breathe his last breath. So, I told him why he was dying. On whose behalf."

A.J. patted his godfather's knee. "That took guts."

Bogdan shrugged. "Guess I could have shot him. Had a .32 in my pocket just in case. No one gets jumpy about a gunshot on New Year's Eve when everyone's firing away. But it was two in the morning, not midnight. Could draw attention. Seemed risky. So, I figured it would be safer and more enjoyable to kill the bastard with my own two hands."

Bogdan scratched his beard. "Now here is where I screwed the pooch. He took his last gasp, shuddered, and kicked out. Went tumbling down the bank to the lakeshore and almost took me with him. Not what I planned. I was gonna back his Cadillac to the maple tree and lever him up into the trunk somehow. Then put the Caddy in the Chain of Rocks Canal. Czeslaw was on standby to pick me up after I done the deed and telephoned him. And eventually Dupuis would have been just another missing person. Not to be.

"I tried but no way I could drag two-hundred-fifty pounds of dead meat up the steep bank on icy stairs. So, I slid him out onto the thin ice that stretched from the shore. Got on the dock with an oar and pushed him out till he broke through and went under.

"Next I put the rental car in your garage and drove Dupuis's Caddy back to St. Louis. Tossed his gun off the bridge on the way. When I got home I moved my DeSoto from my garage to the street, drove in the Cadillac, and removed the plates. Next morning Czeslaw drove me back across the river to fetch the rental.

"Following day, the cold front moved in, and Dupuis got trapped under the ice for a month and a half. Dumb luck. Gave me time to cover my tracks. I know a guy who deals in untitled cars. The Caddy went out of state somewhere. So, I made a few bucks on it. End of story."

A.J. sat thinking, looking down at his gym shoes. "Hell of a story. You took considerable risks on my behalf."

"Only thing worried me was if Dupuis told the bartender or someone about going to meet you at the lake. But no one ever says, 'Hey, I gotta go pick up some blackmail money. See you later.' Anyway, that's why I bought tickets for you and your girl to the New Year's Eve

Party at the Chase Hotel. To make sure you were twenty miles away and alibied up."

"It was a good party. Thanks."

"One more thing I need to tell you about. My motive. Wasn't something I had to make up. Though all I said about being indebted to your father and feeling duty toward my godson is true, there's more to it. Self-interest. Personal vengeance. Always tastier when served up good and cold. After telling Dupuis he was dying to avenge your mother, I muttered a second name: Magdalena Sheehan. My sister."

A.J. turned to Bogdan. From behind came the sound of traffic moving up Market Street past City Hall. After a moment his godfather went on.

"The Great Depression was, well, depressing. Particularly compared to what came before. Life was good in the twenties. We'd just fought and won The War to End All Wars. America dominated world finance. The stock market boomed. People prospered. Jazz, flappers, movies, and money. Ordinary folks got radios, telephones, and automobiles. Grand while it lasted.

"Magda married Tom Sheehan in '28 when all was going gangbusters. Nice enough fellow. A lawyer seduced by all the progress—though he wasn't alone in that. His belief in a rosy future cost him big time. Lost everything in the stock market crash and then some—a rich man one day, a bankrupt the next. And people he had taken down with him were gunning for him.

"Tom had come from a powerful political family. Never missed a meal. Not one to stand in breadlines or take his wife to dinner at the soup kitchen. He shot himself in the head, saving others the trouble. But didn't do such a great job of it. Took him three days to die.

"Magda still had their big house in Kerry Patch and some jewelry. That was it. One day a sexy flapper going to jazz clubs and speakeasies with her handsome husband, next day a penniless widow.

"She sold off the jewelry bit by bit. The money didn't last long. There was no work for her other than as a domestic or emptying bedpans at the hospital, which she could never stoop to. I offered to help, but she was too proud and independent for charity, even from family. Then after a while I hear she's getting around again and doing just fine—new clothes, new jewelry, the works.

"Not sure how Dupuis hooked up with her. Probably seen her around town with Tom. Maybe had his eye on her for years and now saw a chance, realizing what a valuable commodity she was—beautiful young widow with political connections. Soon he had her working as a companion for senators, congressmen, police chiefs, and others connected to the Shelton brothers' bootlegging operation. In other words, Richard Dupuis turned my sister into a whore.

"When I learned about it I talked to Father Marek at St. Stanislaus Kostka, who was still hearing her confession, figuring him to be sympathetic. Which he was—particularly after I agreed to secretly bankroll a bookkeeper job for her at the church. An off-the-books donation.

"My timing was good. She was on the sidelines, gotten sick from one of her johns. Jumped at the opportunity. Eventually she remarried but couldn't have kids after that."

Bogdan stroked his salt-and-pepper mustache and beard. "I don't blame her so much as the times. Lots of folks suffering and had to make tough choices. Maybe I don't fault Dupuis that much either, just running to form. If it hadn't been him it would've been some other pimp or pol. Guys who have their way with women by hook or crook. But everyone's responsible for their choices and in the end must answer to God. Or, in Dupuis's case, to His earthly emissary in the role of Avenging Angel.

"Magda's always been a good Catholic. Maybe she believed that her syphilis and barrenness was divine justice that she rightly earned for her sins. Now I've gotten some extra-celestial justice for her as well. Though I would never tell her."

"It might do her good to know."

"I think she already conned onto it. Thanks to Dupuis's gangland ties and the way he died, the newspapers ran front-page stories on it. Suggesting it was a gangland hit and rehashing the antics of his pals Buster Wortman and the Sheltons. Then next time I see Magda she asks out of the blue, 'Long Lake—isn't that where Jan Nowak moved, and you guys went fishing?' 'Yes, it is. What makes you ask?' She shrugged. 'I don't know. It just came up.' But she said it with a smile. Never was a good liar."

A.J. sat staring off, eyes unfocused. "In my heart—or at least in my dreams—I really wanted to kill Dupuis. Nonetheless, Godfather, I'm grateful you stepped in. I likely would have done something stupid and incriminating like scalp the bastard with my dad's hunting knife."

Bogdan laughed then turned serious. "You're passionate for good reason. I can't imagine how losing both mother and father might affect a boy. Maybe exorcising Dupuis can let you return home to recoup the good memories. I know there were lots before your father died. I was there for some of them."

A.J. nodded. "I'm also haunted by recollections of my mother's decline and demise there. But I'm working on it."

He raised his eyebrows and shook his head. "I still dream about finding her. But sometimes it's me trapped under the ice, struggling to breathe, trying to crack through and free myself. I pray someday I will."

## 38 | INDEPENDENCE DAY

Madison County, Illinois, July 4, 1967

He sat on the dock of his lake house sipping a beer and staring out over the blue moss-edged water. The weather had turned cool that week though warmer today, approaching eighty at noon. The still air held scents of the lime-green moss, the sandy shore, and the lake, where dragonflies—"snake doctors," kids called them—buzzed the surface. Atop the far shore before towering cottonwood trees sat a line of yellow-flowered Jerusalem artichokes bending west toward the sun.

The day lay placid, but A.J. was not. Moving into new territory. More foreign in a way than Nam. Though he had a plan. To show her the house for the first time. Then to tell her about his journey thus far and into the future—as well as he knew. And how he wanted her to join him on it. Finally, he would repeat to Lana the first six words he had uttered to her a decade earlier. Still, he had no clear idea how she might respond. A lot can happen when you're apart. Feelings can evolve. Your situation can alter. Things can turn on a dime.

That thought drew him back to another fateful Independence Day, the hot afternoon twenty-three years earlier when he learned of his father's death. Then the frigid February morning he found his mother's body captured in lake ice, his eyes now moving involuntarily to the spot beyond the dock where the underwater spring poured forth. The two defining events of his young life forever linked by their suddenness, locale, and emotional freight.

His early childhood paradise loomed in hazy memory, like a fading dream. His parents ice skating hand-in-hand across the frozen lake. In summer, Father fly-fishing from the bow of the rowboat. Mother astern paddling them over the hushed lake at sundown, A.J. sitting on the slats at her feet. Playing checkers with his father in front of the glowing, good-smelling fireplace as his mother, legs bent beneath her on the sofa, read from a thick book, soft music floating from the radio. Bogdan and others arriving for a Labor Day barbecue, the women in flowered dresses, the men in linen shirts, the conversation at times lapsing into his father's incomprehensible mother tongue. Kneeling beside his mother and father in the garden atop the lakeshore pressing seeds into moist, sandy earth. Those memories framed a longing for the Eden from which he, along with his mother, had been banished. Yet now he hoped to recapture it with Lana.

A.J. heard tires scrunching on the gravel drive above the lake bank. He rose and climbed the stairs to the backyard. He spied her rising from a lime-colored Pontiac GTO. She wore jeans, sandals, and a white silk blouse opened at the neck, her dark brown hair just touching her shoulders. He approached and they brushed cheeks, her familiar scent invading him. They embraced—not passionately but tentatively, like brittle old women.

She laid a hand on his chest. "How long has it been, A.J.?"

"Nearly a year."

"Seems longer."

"Yeah, it does."

With A.J. then home on leave and Lana doing her residency at a St. Louis med school, they had managed to spend most every night together. Their lovemaking still transcendent. They lived in the moment, avoiding any talk about the future, where life might take them professionally, geographically, or emotionally. Or what danger A.J. might face wherever he might next be deployed. Uncertainty in the air. Neither knew whether their paths would one day forever dovetail or diverge.

He turned to admire her car. "Nice ride."

"When I finally got a real job I thought it time to ditch the Rambler, metaphorically speaking."

"Never figured you for a muscle car."

"You know I've always liked muscle."

"I noticed. Come on in. I'll get you a beer and show you around."

He led her through the back door into the den. Her eyes moved from the white baby grand to the fireplace to the bookshelves.

"Lovely. What a great room."

"For some families life centers around the kitchen or TV room. This was our bivouac."

She moved to the books that lined the western wall, standing on tiptoe to examine the top shelves. A.J. studied her sharp Greek profile and the way she moved, as lithe as a teenage cheerleader. And still with a curiosity for all things. It reminded him of his parents, always delving into something new.

"Wharton, Twain, Fitzgerald, Tolstoy, Chekov, Dostoyevsky, Bobby Burns, and Walt Whitman. Nice stuff."

"Mom's books. Dad's are down here. Fiction, too, but also history, philosophy, psychology."

She followed him into the kitchen where he pulled two brown beer bottles from the Frigidaire. Then to the front room. It lay cool and dark thanks to the tall maples, willows, and sycamores in the front yard shading the home from the early afternoon sun. She sat on the curved turquoise divan.

"Given that it was abandoned for ten years, the place looks great."

"Fifteen. Supposed to be a temporary thing. My aunt and uncle asked whether I wanted to sell it or rent it and put the money aside for college, but I couldn't swallow the idea of anyone else living here. So, I told them to wait until I was ready to come back and collect stuff I wanted to keep. Which took only a decade and a half. Now I want to keep the house and everything in it."

"What changed your mind?"

After a beat he said: "Well, some things got settled."

He avoided her gaze. How much might she have heard or surmised about Richard Dupuis's unsolved murder? Lonnie Sullivan told him that when The Blue Note subsequently closed, local Baptists looked upon Dupuis's strangling as a community service, with some gossip crediting A.J. as the likely perp. If Lana had heard those rumors, how might it have affected her regard for him? But she merely pursed her lips and said nothing. He went on.

"Over the years Aunt Helen checked on the place and kept it clean. Raymond winterized it, fixed whatever needed fixing, and cut the grass. Year after year it stood vacant, like a mausoleum, or a museum of a family that had ceased to exist. I came only once to get some books and ventured no further than the den."

He sat next to Lana and lifted from the coffee table there a black leather-bound journal. "Aunt Helen left this here for me—Mom's diary. Begins on the day she met my father and ends the day she learned he'd been killed."

He leafed through it, running fingers over the pages as if caressing the words penned there. "Their first kiss, first date, first time they made love." From it he pulled a black-and-white photo. "A snapshot from the day they met." He turned it over and read, "'Fairmount Park, Collinsville, Illinois, August 5th, 1939.'" He handed it to Lana, who studied it.

"What a handsome couple. Heartbreaking to see them so happy knowing how things turned out."

"Here's her entry from July fourth, 1943, a year before Mom learned he'd been killed:

*I sit abed writing by candlelight flickering in humid night air that carries the fresh green scent of the sleeping cornfield across the road and the creamy fragrance of the gardenias I planted beneath our bedroom window. Jan lies asleep beside me, breathing softly. At sunset, after friends and family had gone, we sat arm-in-arm on the front steps watching A.J., barefooted and bare-chested, swing from weeping willow branches pretending he was Tarzan. Then he chased fireflies, golden eyes winking at us in the dark, signaling all was right with the world—at least the small sphere where we happily reside… Now the cicadas have begun to serenade me. Sleep steals up.*

He folded the cover closed. "According to her journal they had five years of sublime happiness. A mandate to grab and savor whatever life hands you while you can. It's been hard to grasp why she gave up on herself. Why she had to die. But she's still alive and vital in these pages. So is he, as little as I remember of him. His scent—I recall that, a tobacco and man smell. Most always smiling. Strong arms tossing me in the air and catching me. I figured he'd always be here to do that. Can you love someone you never really knew?"

"Likely easier than someone you know only too well."

"Then I'll continue being enigmatic," he said, bringing a smile from Lana but nothing more.

They moved back outside and down to the dock, now in the shade of the tall lake bank, and sat on the Adirondack chairs there. He asked about her new job.

"It's perfect. A South St. Louis pediatric clinic co-owned by one of my professors. And more money than I'd hoped for. A dream come true, to be able to work with kids and stay close to family and friends."

"Good for you. I admit I know nothing about children except for my inner child, always in need of correction."

"What about him, A.J.? More adventuring?"

He shook his head. "I'm hanging it up. One more deployment, six months, and finished. For a while it was okay. But my recent gig training ARVN Special Ops recruits got me thinking. Bad enough dying like my father in a good cause—if there's ever is such a thing in war, but…" He bit his bottom lip. "I read in yesterday's paper that we just flew a hundred and fifty bomb missions, blowing the hell out of whatever and whoever was below. Poor fucking Vietnamese. Good for the St. Louis economy though, churning out napalm, ammo, and fighter jets."

"War. The way of the world. What drove my parents here. So, what next for you?"

"I've been in touch with an archeology professor who's running some digs nearby. A chance to lend a hand and learn a bit."

"A career path?"

"Possibly. Or maybe I should study psychology, given that I'm such a head case." He lifted his chin toward the lake. "I took a swim here yesterday. First time since I found Mom."

Lana shook her head. "Of course. Never occurred to me."

"Over the years I've learned bits and pieces about what led to her death and my father's. More connections than the obvious ones. It's taken a long time for me to accept and embrace that history. Part of who I am. The trick is not to let those two events define the rest of my life. At last, I've been able to come home. Now again it signals peace and happiness, not death and decline."

Lana patted his hand. "That's why I fell for you: You were the most determined boy I'd ever met. The strongest and most independent."

A.J. shrugged. "Didn't have much choice. I saw that no one else was going to do it for me. Me against the world and me versus myself. Despite Aunt Helen and Uncle Raymond giving me a good home, I was still an orphan at heart, cut off from the continuity my parents would have provided. But then you came along and humanized me. Made me feel like I was part of things, like I belonged. I was always afraid of losing you—an orphan's lament, the fear of abandonment. I understand that now."

She took a deep breath. Now was the time before he got in over his head.

"You'll never lose my friendship, A.J."

He turned to her. She held his gaze. They always could communicate with few if any words.

"Nor you mine," he said. He looked away and took a deep breath. "Who's the lucky guy?"

She stared off at the cottonwoods on the far bank. "A colleague. We've not set a date yet."

The professor, his intuition told him. But it made no difference.

"I hope, Lana, this doesn't sound too shallow or hedonistic or whatever. My anger didn't start to peel away until we lay naked together. For me it was a communion with nature and humanity. I felt part of it all for the first time. Felt that I belonged in the cosmic scheme."

"We all need to feel we belong somewhere. Even if it's just a family of one, being comfortable in your own skin."

Silence—except for the buzz of insects, a frog's croak, and birdsong—held for a minute. A family of one. That nails it, doesn't it?

"You remember the first words I ever said to you? When you asked after the game what you could do to make me smile?"

She nodded. "I'll never forget: 'Marry me and have my baby.' Always thought it would be the other way around, baby first."

A.J. smiled. "I worried about that too." He looked off at the far lakeshore. "Felt sure I'd repeat those words to you someday."

She laid her hand on his and gripped it tight as tears came. "You've always been a dreamer, A.J. Don't chastise yourself. We all want love and certainty. You've lived through chaos."

"Life does dish up disorder, doesn't it? You kick it aside, keep in the moment, and focus on what's within your power." He made it sound easy.

"I'm sorry, A.J."

"Thanks for coming to tell me face-to-face and not just sending a postcard. I know that would have been easier."

"We were lovers and best friends for ten years. We've always been square with each other. No reason to stop."

"Right. No reason."

He walked her to her car. A final embrace—this one more emphatic—that left them both speechless. He watched her drive off. He stood stock-still, staring at the sycamores that lined the driveway.

Another door closing behind him, Lana on the other side. And he was on his own again. The Buddha had it right: Desire leads to suffering. But how much of it was destined love thwarted, how much jealousy, how much ego, how much lust? He couldn't imagine that she had the same visceral feeling with the old professor. But then there are other things for a woman. For a man, too. Which, for himself, he still needed to figure out.

§

He drove up the lake to his aunt and uncle's place for supper. Whenever possible they spent the Fourth together, as they had twenty-three years earlier on the day Western Union came calling.

A somber and thoughtful occasion as usual. Raymond had grilled lake fish and Aunt Helen had set the table on the screened porch, what had been A.J.'s room. She said grace, thanking God for His bounty and praying for the soldiers once again at war. A.J. stared at the purple gladiolas he had brought, now in a green glass vase on the table, flowers his father and he had planted one Mother's Day near Lazy Lane's vegetable garden.

After dinner Raymond carried a pail of iced beer to the dock, A.J. following. The two men sat in sling chairs as the lake darkened, flat and unmoving, like black glass. The still air hung warm and fragrant, smelling of the wheat fields across the lake. The cicadas started in droning. When they momentarily quieted A.J. said:

"Saw Lana earlier. She came by to see the house for the first time. And the last."

"How's that? What happened?"

"She's marrying one of her professors or colleagues. Funny. After all those years together today was the day I was gonna ask her to marry me."

"Oh, hell. Sorry A.J."

"Yep. A sorry situation. She sensed what I was up to and steered me straight before I drove off the cliff." He drank from his bottle. "A smart move for her, partnering up with someone who could advance her career and guide her. Someone who would share and understand her work. She has to deal with sick and dying kids. You need someone who appreciates the toll that takes."

"Guess that figured into it."

But more than that likely figured in, Raymond thought. A.J. came from steelworker families on both sides, Lana the daughter of educated doctors, Europeans. She wasn't going to live her life in a coarse working-class community like Tank Town. He had seen it before with young bourgeois women and men alike. The sex could be great, but for them it's just basic training before they go back to their own people. You think they're taking you seriously but they're not really, not in their heart and soul. Now, however, was not the time to get into that, the invisible walls. Some people never really see them. But they're still there.

"I never seem to make the smart move," said A.J. "Always doing the impulsive thing, the risky thing."

"Maybe for you that is the smart thing."

"Perhaps you're right. I was just telling Lana that I planned to go to college and study archeology or the like, something with fieldwork that would get me out of the classroom and library. But maybe that was just to please her, not me. Much as I like reading and ancient history I can't see myself as a professor angling for research grants and sifting dirt for trinkets."

"Safe and peaceful. Not what you're used to."

"Not sure I could stand it. I need movement. Maybe I need danger and adrenaline too. I know I need the camaraderie and teamwork."

"Being an archeologist sounds like lonely work. Maybe with colleagues who might be more competitors than teammates. But what does a factory worker know about it?"

"I don't know much about it either." A.J. took a pull on his beer. "Thought I could live a peaceful life here on the lake with Lana and kids and a dog. Not sure I'd want to do it alone."

Raymond sipped his beer and again held his tongue. A.J. felt raw tonight but would get over it and find someone else. Or they would find him. Raymond imagined what it might be like for a chiseled twenty-seven-year-old with dark hair and a trust fund. He loved Helen but wouldn't mind changing places with his nephew for a bit.

"I'll get us some more beer," said Raymond.

He went back up to the house and filled Helen in on what had occurred. Raymond added more beer to the bucket and grabbed the bourbon bottle from the pantry.

"Don't wait up for us. And fix his bed."

She nodded, tears in her eyes. "Tell him he's still my boy. Always."

## 39 | REQUIEM FOR A GAMBLER

St. Louis, Missouri, August 3, 1967

He had expected his next flight out of Camp Pendleton would be a C-130 military transport carrying him west back to Vietnam. Instead, it was a TWA 707 flying east back to St. Louis.

Other expectations proved wrong as well. A.J. had anticipated an ill-lit and funereal Slavic sanctuary with dark, grisly murals and iconography like he had seen in Guatemalan churches when deployed there. The décor warning parishioners of the wages of sin and the pains of eternal damnation. However, the spacious Saint Stanislaus Kostka Polish Catholic Church interior signaled the opposite: a bright and heavenly optimism.

Large stained-glass windows allowed multi-colored sunshine to stream into the sanctuary, illuminating shining marble pillars, light pink walls, and a gleaming gold-and-white altar, above which sat a mural of Calvary with a sky blue, rose, and lavender palette. Even Bogdan Zawadski's casket, a gleaming silver, worked to deter dark thoughts.

The lengthy Requiem Mass—conducted at turns in Latin, Polish, and English—allowed A.J. periods of incomprehension when he might reminisce. So, he sought to summon the high times and camaraderie they had shared, pushing aside darker remembrances.

Those happy memories, however, worked only to exacerbate his sense of loss. His godfather, mentor, protector, and best friend all rolled into one man now forever gone. Bogdan's passing signaled to A.J. the end of an era, closing the vault door on a bank of knowledge and know-how from the past he could never again access. It felt a bit like being orphaned once more.

Afterward, outside on marble steps lying in the shade of the massive redbrick structure and its twin six-story steeples, he approached an older woman dressed in black who had been seated in the front pew and who now received condolences from attendees. Perhaps seventy years old, she stood tall and elegant, with the same strong features and dark eyes of Bogdan.

"I take it that you are Bogdan's sister, Magdalena."

"Yes, I am."

"I am Bogdan's godson, A.J. Nowak."

She gasped and embraced him, tears springing to her eyes. Such emotional outbursts not uncommon among the Zawadski clan.

"My dear Janusz's son! Bogdan was so proud of you."

"He was a good and true godfather to me," A.J. told her. "A guide and friend. He took care of me just as he did my father."

"My brother cared for and protected us all, even when we didn't realize it. Such a crafty and secretive soul."

Exactly, thought A.J. Good traits for a gambler. "And a good soul, with a big heart."

Speechless, she bit her lips and cried more, nodding.

A.J. went on. "I saw him just a month ago. He came to visit me at Long Lake when I was home on leave and talked about being best man at my parents' wedding in 1940 and crying throughout the ceremony." A memory keyed in part by A.J. telling him of his plan to marry Lana and asking Bogdan to be *his* best man. Never to happen on a couple scores now.

Magdalena smiled through her tears. "Sentimentalists one and all. It runs in the family."

"He was in high spirits that day. Full of life."

"As always. He died at the racetrack, sitting on a bench at the finish line with the Daily Racing Form on his lap and winning tickets in his pocket."

A.J. pictured it and nodded approval. "Going out winners. I couldn't imagine a better finish.

§

A.J. drove the rental car the few blocks from the church to the Cass Avenue Bank & Trust building at 13th Street and Cass Avenue. There he was shown into a vault and left alone with the safe-deposit box to which Bogdan had given him a key years earlier.

It held but few items. An envelope containing his signed confession to Richard Dupuis's murder. Four gold double eagle coins wrapped in cheesecloth, along with a note reading, "For the new Nowak generation." And Bogdan's U.S. Navy dog tags.

A. J. slipped the envelope and the coins into his suitcoat pocket and grasped the dog tags in his fist.

# 40 | A.J. RETHINKS SOLDIERING

Sihanouk Trail, Cambodia, September 24, 1967

He sat on wet earth, leaning against a towering conifer, warm rain dripping from the forest canopy and collecting in the overturned helmet beside him, concealed in a half-ass manner by surrounding shrubs and stunted palms. Rainwater also dripped onto his bare head and down his neck into his sodden, sweat-stained fatigues.

As the sun lowered, A.J. studied a gecko eyeing ants that marched around and over his canvas boots. The occasional earthworm or snake slithered by; at times an errant partridge would perch in a nearby laurel tree. Yet despite the welcome cloud cover, ample water supply, and summery temperatures, his situation was, in military parlance, FUBAR: Fucked Up Beyond All Repair. Nonetheless, he had no choice but to repair it. Either that or likely die.

Here was a real-life opportunity to put to good use his extensive exfiltration training, that is, his tactical know-how on removing an intelligence agent (in this case, Marine Special Operations Sergeant A.J. Nowak) from the enemy's midst.

He wondered how he got there. Not in the logistical sense. That he knew quite well. With the collusion of

Cambodian ruler Prince Norodom Sihanouk (at the behest of the People's Republic of China), the Viet Cong and the People's Army of Vietnam (PAVN) were moving men and materiel through eastern Cambodia to oppose South Vietnamese forces across the border. To discover the extent, U.S. President Lyndon Johnson had endorsed covert cross-border reconnaissance operations by the Secret Studies and Observation Group, with whom A.J. had been deployed. Then in the dark of night (and the fog of war) he had been cut off from his team and left behind in the claustrophobic, hilly rainforest, surrounded by scores of PAVN troops. Fortunately, they were unaware of his presence. Unfortunately, they seemed in no hurry to move on. This would be his second night sleeping with the enemy.

However, he did wonder what psychological and sociological forces—what demons in his nature and what misguided directives in his nurture—had compelled him to become a solider who went blithely off trotting about the globe abetting dubious cross-national ventures about which he did not really give a damn.

Up to now his work as a Marine had been playing soldier. Just as he and the Sullivan boys, all five of them along with their tomboy sister, had done at Long Lake during the Korean War, when Inchon, Pusan, and the 38th Parallel dominated the news. More recently he had trained Cuban exiles in amphibious landing tactics, worked with Guatemalan Special Forces on anticipating and neutralizing guerrilla actions, played Caribbean war games with the British Commando Brigade, and taught ARVN Special Forces recruits hand-to-hand combat techniques (while they in turn schooled him in Mahayana Buddhism). None of which involved actual enemy combatants who might actually kill you. This, however, was different.

Though not per se a combatant attempting to harry the PAVN and Viet Cong, he was in fact a spy gathering critical information on their efforts to resupply forces fighting in South Vietnam. In other words, someone destined for enhanced interrogation and summary execution if captured—something that never ever happened in allied war games.

Further, he was on his own. It being a covert operation violating various U.S. and international laws, he could expect no forthcoming Hollywood cavalry charge to rescue him. He would somehow have to exfiltrate his own sorry ass, personally.

As a longtime loner and maverick, he had some experience relying on his own resources to solve his problems. Nonetheless this was a new breed of solitude and a new, exalted level of problem-solving difficulty. He had pondered his dilemma at length without finding a plausible solution. Further, despite passing endless hours studying the rainforest flora and fauna and picturing the placid wheat fields of his youth, all in hopes that by forgoing a direct intellectual assault on his predicament an answer might arise from his subconscious mind, none did. He was stumped. As a result, he could not hold down the taste of fear in his throat, bile rising as if he were eating his own liver, as the phrase went. There you go, Nowak. Just what you'd bargained for: danger and adrenaline.

# THE BOOTLEGGER'S BRIDE

A.J. tried his damnedest to stay in the moment as the Buddha counseled and not think about what the Cong might do to him with bamboo wedges if captured. "There is no fear for one whose mind is not filled with desire." Easy for old Gautama to say, sitting peacefully in his lotus position munching jackfruit. A.J.'s mind, however, overflowed with desire—the desire to stay alive somehow and return home someday soon. Sooner than he might have desired just a few days earlier.

No way could he allow himself to be captured, face torture, and become a PAVN propaganda poster boy. His well-meaning (though some would argue self-interested) handlers had provided him a painless encapsulated way to end it all and thus avoid such agony and ignominy. So perhaps it would in fact end here, halfway around the globe in an alien land never on his must-see list, for no good purpose as far as he could in fact see. This was what he was born for? This was his destiny, a self-inflicted cyanide exit in Southeast Asia hinterlands? A sad and fruitless farewell indeed, Mother Earth.

Which led him off on reminiscences of his youth on Long Lake. Among them, of course, the day Western Union came calling with news of his father's death, and the morning he discovered his beautiful mother frozen rigid in the Long Lake ice. But those two days were anomalies, human failure (of one sort or another), overridden by countless enriching days embedded in him by the steady hand of nature. Endless hours running the fields with the Sullivans in search of rabbit or quail or imaginary villains as children had done for eons. Passing hot summer afternoons lying on the cool, fresh-smelling grass under towering sycamores as marshmallow clouds floated in from the Southwest, eyeing them for lurking monsters or cream-colored puppies running aloft. Then fashioning a necklace of white clover flowers for his mother. And the games with the other lake children—Indian Ball, Mother May I, Hide-and-Seek, Statues, Marbles, Red Rover, and Tag. Cops and Robbers, GI's and Nazis, and Cowboys and Indians, whose presence vibrated from the earth and the burial mounds lining the lake. But always drawn to the lake, as were his mound-building predecessors. In winter skating and chaotic hockey, with tree branches in lieu of actual hockey sticks and a tin-can puck. In warm months urging fish and crawdads from the lake and rowing over its shimmering surface at a summer sunset, the air alive with the chirp of insects and the scents of the mossy water and fertile fields. And longing for that freedom and the sustenance of nature on rainy days (or school days) spent inside. Those days often lived in the guise of make-believe personas vanquishing tyrants and rescuing maidens, just like in the movies. Or with pencil and paper sketching battles scenes or Sioux camps. And later with books on Americana—the explorers, frontiersmen, soldiers, statesmen, and tribesmen—biographies he would devour at one sitting. But how was all that preparation for this? Or did it all argue against it?

But back to the Buddha and his corollary admonition to employ Right Thinking. Get your head straight, Nowak, or you will be dead meat for sure. DO NOT become a fuckup at this crucial juncture and pave an autobahn to your own oblivion. Now was the time to kick it into FOM: Full Orphan Mode. And if not to morph into

Tarzan or Superman, at least somehow to now become the hero of your own life and not die pointlessly in this Godforsaken land for a botched reconnaissance mission of dubious provenance, to say the least.

Thoughts of Superman flying over Metropolis and Tarzan swinging from vine to vine made him look aloft at the green rainforest canopy. *That's* where he belonged, where he might see a way out, instead of trembling here on the ground like a worm, waiting for someone to step on him. Yes, he needed to rise above it all.

## 41 | AN ANSWER

Madison County, Illinois, April 10, 1971

He strolled on Long Lake's sandy shore, the evening sky darkening, the air now quickly chilling, songbirds quieting. As he passed beneath a leafing willow a cardinal hidden there offered up a solo, a short "chip…chip…chip." Along the mossy shore frogs commenced croaking.

As much as A.J. might once have relished his globe-hopping days it was always good to be home. He never tired—at least not yet—of the lake and the fields that had long sustained and fortified him. However, this would be a new test though one he welcomed: whether he could stay home.

At his boat dock he climbed the wooden stairs to the backyard. Smoke rose from the chimney, the homey, welcoming fragrance of a log fire wafting to him. A.J. moved past the sprouting vegetable garden to his left and pushed through the back door into the den.

Hadley lay dozing on the couch before the fire, her long blonde hair curling on a dark green pillow. Finally, it seemed, she had found something that completely wore her out. "Indefatigable," he had thought when he first encountered her in the martial arts class he taught at the university. She since had proved him correct in that first impression.

Next he moved to the white bassinet nearby and gazed down upon their daughter. She boasted her mother's blue eyes and blonde hair, at least for now. He leaned close. "Welcome home," he whispered to her. "Welcome home, love."

He hadn't expected a girl. No Nowak daughters that he knew of. But just as well. Less likely to be a wandering warrior like her father. Or cannon fodder like her grandfather, who was A.J.'s age when he died, and with so much to live for. Now A.J. would strive to live for them both, to make up for lost time in a way if that were ever possible.

At the credenza beside the piano A.J. poured himself a brandy—a day to celebrate and commemorate, surely. Homecoming. From his mother's library shelves he retrieved a black leather-bound tome, her journal, and settled into an armchair by the fire. He paged through it and found the entry he sought, October 18, 1940.

*Home today from DePaul Hospital with Alexander Jan Nowak in my arms. He favors me, not his father. Another generation. Another step in the long march of Mankind, wherever we may be headed. A journey couched in mystery and promise. Always promise, ever hope. And today, for me, happiness, unbound happiness beyond compare.*

*Arthur Miller once wrote that all literature seeks to answer the question, 'How does a man make for himself a home?' I feel I have found an answer, at least for myself. As of today, with my dear husband*

*Janusz and our wide-eyed boy A.J., we are a family, and I am home. No matter wherever that may be. For now, it is our apartment on Forest Park, overlooking the Grand Basin, where Jan and I ice-skate. Yet who knows what joys the future may hold and where we might land.*

*I had always thought "Home is where the heart is" a hackneyed and sentimental saying repeated by old ladies and sermonizers who lacked originality. Now, however, I see that it speaks to the essence of our existence. While we live in the objective physical world, the core of our being is subjective, internal. We reside, I see, in our own hearts.*

*And when we are lucky—really, really lucky, as I was the day I first met Jan at the racetrack and continue to be—we come to inhabit that sweet gingerbread cottage in the woods that can never be foreclosed. For it is of our own creation and construction and located where no one else can find it: in our hearts. Its foundation stronger than any stone. A home impervious to flood, fire, or windstorm. And we hold the only key.*

*This is why one fights with all one's might and soul to guard and protect it. With all one's heart. Its maintenance and care transcend all other concerns one might have. For once you have such a home, you have fulfilled your foremost desire. Your life takes wing, even though you may sit quietly by the hearth as I do this evening, warmed by the fire and comforted by the nearness of husband and child. Whatever prayers I have ever said or left unsaid, all longings conscious or unconscious, have now been answered. I have made for myself a home.*

A.J. took in a deep, halting breath. A sizzling log popped, sending a glowing ember to the bricks at his feet.

§ THE END §

# ACKNOWLEDGMENTS

The messy, years-long process of invention involved in writing and publishing a novel is both pleasurable and painful at turns. To lessen the latter and augment the former it helps to have knowledgeable and frank friends, colleagues, and fellow writers willing to lend a hand. In this case early readers included Michael Mewshaw, Terry Baker Mulligan, Jayne Navarre, Rick Boettger, Gard Shelley, the late Jeff Dunlap, Sid Goldman, and Ethan Allen. Also, Magdalena Hope corrected and honed the Polish-language copy. Finally, Amphorae Publishing's Lisa Miller aided with editing and helpful suggestions.

I should also acknowledge my parents' contributions. Their stories from Prohibition days helped enrich the novel, including their youthful involvement in family bootlegging activities and their witnessing deadly gangland violence as Eagan's Rats and the Hogan Gang fought for control of liquor, gambling, and prostitution in St. Louis. Also their remembrances of The Great Depression, the nation's largest Hooverville on the St. Louis riverfront, and the sudden impact of World War II also informed this book.

I also relied on the *St. Louis Post-Dispatch* archive and other online sources to get the daily weather, war news, economics, food, fashion, architecture, sports, movies, and other historical data right. Any errors are likely mine.

# ABOUT THE AUTHOR

Rick Skwiot is the author of four previous novels: the Hemingway First Novel Award winner *Death in Mexico*, the Willa Cather Fiction Prize finalist *Sleeping With Pancho Villa*, *Key West Story*, and *Fail: A Carlo Gabriel Mystery*. He has also penned two memoirs, the highly praised *Christmas at Long Lake: A Childhood Memory* and *San Miguel de Allende, Mexico: Memoir of a Sensual Quest for Spiritual Healing*.

He has taught creative writing at Washington University in St. Louis and served as the 2004 Distinguished Visiting Writer at the University of Missouri-St. Louis. A veteran journalist, he also works as an editor, writing coach, and feature writer.